Love Scars

Love Scars

T. Friday

www.urbanbooks.net

Urban Books, LLC
300 Farmingdale Road, N.Y.-Route 109
Farmingdale, NY 11735

ISBN 13: 978-1-64556-748-6
EBOOK ISBN: 978-1-64556-749-3

First Trade Paperback Printing February 2026
Printed in the United States of America

10 9 8 7 6 5 4 3 2 1

Distributed by Kensington Publishing Corp.
Submit Orders to:
Customer Service
400 Hahn Road
Westminster, MD 21157-4627
Phone: 1-800-733-3000
Fax: 1-800-659-2436

The authorized representative in the EU for product safety and compliance
Is eucomply OU, Parnu mnt 139b-14, Apt 123
Tallinn, Berlin 11317, hello@eucompliancepartner.com

Love Scars

by

T. Friday

Dedication

This book is dedicated to the most important five people in my life, my brat pack: Jordin, Jacob, Jacory, Jakayla, and Jalisa. Please understand that everything I do and every struggle I overcome is so that you guys don't have to worry about a thing. I love you guys and don't ever forget it.

Acknowledgment

To my Blunt, you have been in my corner and stood by me for the last fourteen and a half years. Although I've been getting on your nerves, you never switched up on me. Our bond is unbreakable.

To my wonderful readers and supporters, I'm nothing without you guys. For the last three and a half years and twenty-four books later, you guys have read and reviewed all my books, and I appreciate every one of you guys. I really want to say thank you from the bottom of my heart. It touches my heart when I hear some of you say that I have become one of your favorite authors. You all make me keep going stronger.

To my baby sister, Amanda Jordin Hollis, I love and miss you so much. I swear, fifteen years wasn't long enough to have you here with us.

To my mom, Lisa, and dad, David, I wish you guys were here to see that I'm finally doing something that I love. I love and miss you guys so much. Please continue to watch over the family.

* * * *Trigger Warning* * * *

This book touches on a few sensitive topics that are pushed under the rug, especially in the Black community, such as mental health issues, abuse, and a broken bond between a mother and daughter.

Overall, you will love the book.

Chapter 1

"Aye, man, I swear I wasn't trying to step on nobody toes. I was just trying to make a couple of dollars to feed my family," Trevor cried out with his hands up in the air.

Trevor had only been in the city of Detroit for a few weeks, and because he already had two strikes against him, finding a legal job was more complicated than he thought. Not knowing any better or doing any research, he fucked up by thinking it would be smart to set up shop on the corner of his block. Although he was only nickel-and-diming it at the moment, never did he picture having a gun pointed in his face over a few bags of weed.

"Shut that crying shit up, nigga. Do you know who corner this belongs to?" KC yelled, ready to blow Trevor's head off if he made a sudden move or said something stupid.

Trevor was scared, and it showed all over his face. "I-I just moved here; my bad. I wasn't trying to fuck up what y'all got going on around here," Trevor said, stuttering over his words.

Just as KC was about to say something, Monsta's truck pulled up. He parked in the middle of the street before jumping out.

"What the fuck y'all niggas over here doing? It's the middle of the day, and you got this nigga about to piss in his pants," Monsta said, laughing.

KC tried to explain himself. "This the nigga that been over here shitting on us and stealing our clients. You know we don't play that shit."

Although KC was dead serious, Monsta laughed at the situation. "Be easy, my nigga. Put that gun away."

"What the fuck you mean? That nigga been making money on our block," KC damn near yelled.

Thinking Monsta was on his side, Trevor spoke up for himself. "I didn't mean no harm. I was only making a few bucks each day, nothing serious. Just enough to put food on the table."

"Shut the fuck up!" KC barked.

Monsta looked over at Trevor, then back to his home-boy, KC. "Let that nigga go on about his business."

"What?" KC asked, confused.

Trevor slowly put down his hands. He wasn't sure what was going on between the friends, but he knew he was about to get the fuck on.

"Go ahead and be on your way. It's like you said, it was only a few dollars that you were taking from my pocket. No biggie, right?" Monsta calmly said.

As soon as KC dropped his gun, Trevor took off running up the street, praying he made it home to his family. Being new to Detroit, Trevor never got the story behind why they called the guy who he thought spared his life . . . Monsta. But before Trevor could make it far, Monsta stopped him with a shot right through the head.

Pow!

Then Monsta calmly walked back to his truck as if nothing had happened.

"Bring your stupid ass on," he barked out the window to KC.

Not wanting to be around when the pigs showed up, KC did as he was told and jumped into the passenger side of Monsta's truck.

"Aye, nigga, you know you fucked up back there, right?" Monsta asked.

"What you talkin' about, Monsta?" KC nervously asked. He had no idea what he meant.

Monsta turned down KC's block.

"You did too much talking to that nigga, and I tell you niggas all the time to be about that action."

"My bad, Boss Man. I was just trying to scare the nigga," KC tried to explain.

Monsta parked in front of KC's mother's house. "In this line of business, you gotta stop talking so much and just handle your business."

KC opened the car door. "You right, Boss Man. Next time, I'll know better."

Monsta watched as KC got out of his truck, but before he could walk off, he called him back to his vehicle.

KC stuck his head in the window. "What's up?"

Monsta quickly put a bullet through his head. *Pow!* Before KC's body could hit the ground, Monsta was already turning the block with an evil smirk on his face.

Monsta not only ran his crew to be in the streets pushing work on the blocks, but he also taught them never to take shit from nobody. In his eyes, every mistake they made was a slap in his face, and that's precisely why KC had to go. The only way a nigga could come and set up shop on another nigga's block is when the owner wasn't around to work. KC must've been bullshitting around and said, "Fuck the money." So, he had to pay back them few dollars that Trevor was able to make with his life.

"What you want, Sunshine? Monsta not here right now," Ms. Caldwell said through the screen door.

"Hey, Ma. I just texted him. He said he would be home in a few and to wait for him," Sunshine responded.

Ms. Caldwell rolled her eyes as she unlocked and opened the door for the young girl. For the most part, she got along with Sunshine, but only because she learned how to keep her mouth closed. Since it was Monsta's street dealings that bought the house and paid all the bills, she learned to sit back and just enjoy the free ride.

Sunshine walked straight past the living room and dining room to get to Monsta's room. She really didn't like sitting in his mama's face because she learned early on that she played sides, and she couldn't get with all that fake shit. After pacing the floor, Sunshine finally took a seat on Monsta's bed. Getting impatient, she was ready for him to hurry and get to her. She had already texted him twice and didn't see what the holdup was, especially when she told him it was an emergency.

Nineteen-year-old Jasmine "Sunshine" Mathews had just confirmed she was indeed two and a half months pregnant with Monsta's first child. In a way, she was happy because she knew deep down inside they were in love. On the other hand, she was scared to tell her mom. Her mom never cared for Monsta, and she knew that having his baby wouldn't make things any better.

Sunshine kicked off her shoes and got comfortable in bed. She was dead tired and could use a nap before he got there. She hated how his five minutes always meant half an hour or more.

Forty-five minutes later, 23-year-old Montez "Monsta" Caldwell walked into the house looking crazy as always.

"Where your truck?"

"Damn, Ma, mind your own business. Is Sunshine back there?"

Ms. Caldwell nodded. "Yeah, her ass back there and been here for a minute now. You trust that girl to be in your room by herself?" she asked, trying to stir up some mess.

"Fuck you talkin' about, Ma? The real question is, should I trust *your* ass? Why the fuck you even down

here, huh? Didn't I buy yo' ass a TV for your room?" he
yelled.

"Calm your crazy ass down, punk. Didn't you tell me to
wait for Henry to stop by and deliver your package? Next
time, keep your stupid ass in the house and wait yourself,"
she yelled, getting up from the couch. As she walked
past her son, she mumbled about him being crazy and
disrespectful, just like his daddy.

Standing in the doorway of his bedroom, Monsta
watched as Sunshine slept so peacefully.

"Who the fuck you dreamin' about, nigga?" Monsta
yelled as he jumped into bed, waking Sunshine from her
sleep.

"Damn, bae, you play too fucking much," she yelled.

Monsta grabbed her by the neck before pulling her in
for a kiss. "Who the fuck you talkin' to like that?"

Sunshine gave him another kiss. "Nobody, baby."

Monsta let her go. "That's what the fuck I thought with
your sexy ass."

Sunshine couldn't even stay mad at him for long. The
way he stared into her brown eyes always made her heart
smile. When she first met him a little over a year ago, her
friends warned her that he had a bad reputation and was
known for being a wild nigga in the streets. Sunshine
tried to stay away, but it was like he always ended up
wherever she was. Over time, they ended up spending
that whole summer together. As crazy as it sounds, she
fell in love with him in a matter of months. Her best
friend, Keisha, told her she was crazy, but what she didn't
know was the sweet side to Monsta. When they were
together, he was a totally different guy.

Sunshine closed her eyes, hoping she'd be able to go
back to sleep again.

"Get your ass up. You rushed me to get here, so now I'm
here. What's up, muthafucka?"

"Monsta, come on now. Chill out, baby."

He watched as she climbed out of bed and walked over to the dresser. Sunshine pulled out paperwork from her bag. Her worried expression alerted him.

Sitting up in bed, he decided to be serious. "What's up, Sunshine?"

Taking a seat on the bed, she handed him the papers. "Monsta, I'm pregnant."

Monsta looked at her, then back at the papers in his hand. "Damn, you sure is. Fuck you tellin' me for?"

"What?" Sunshine asked, fighting back the tears that threatened to roll out of her eyes.

Before she could jump up and run out of the room, Monsta grabbed her.

"Damn, sit your sensitive ass down. I know that's my fuckin' baby."

As he held her in his arms, Sunshine cried. "Why you gotta fuck with me all the time?"

Monsta lifted her head. "You know I love your ass, girl. I just be playing with you."

"I told you I don't be liking all that shit, all the time."

Monsta kissed her. "All right, baby. I'm gon' chill out, all right?"

"OK."

While sharing a kiss, Monsta started pulling at her shirt. "Why the hell you laid up in here with all this shit on?"

"This is exactly why I'm pregnant now. Your ass stays horny," she giggled.

Lifting her shirt over her head, he smirked. "Just be grateful I only be horny for your ass 'cause these bitches do be out here wanting a nigga."

"You better tell those hoes to go play in traffic because they'll have a better chance of surviving."

By now, Sunshine was stepping out of her pants, and just like any other time, Monsta was brick hard, waiting for her. It wasn't long before she was sitting on the edge of the bed with his dick disappearing down her throat.

Monsta climbed out of bed, careful not to wake Sunshine.

"I know you bought this house and all, but you and your li'l girlfriend could at least have enough respect for me not to be so loud when y'all in there fucking."

Monsta shook his head. "You weird as fuck for sitting down here listening and shit. I thought yo' ass was going to yo' room. Fuck happened?"

Ms. Caldwell got up to get a package off the dining room table. "Here go your fucking package you've been waiting on."

Monsta smiled. "Thanks, Ma."

"Yeah, whatever, boy," Ms. Caldwell said, taking a seat and turning her attention back to the movie she was watching.

Monsta went into his room, then returned to the dining room table with a scale so he could go over the package that Henry dropped off. Ms. Caldwell pretended to be into the TV as she tried to eyeball what her son was up to. She dealt with so much of his bullshit, but mainly because he did look out for her. Whenever she wanted or needed anything, he was there. Now, he might have talked shit, but he never left her on hold.

"Ma, what I tell you about minding my business? You sittin' in there but got antennas up all in here."

"Montez Caldwell, stop playing with me. How much all that shit worth?"

"Damn, Ma, stop asking me questions like that. Yo' ass better learn how to eyeball the shit like I used to," he jokingly said.

"You know what? I can't stand your black ass."

"Damn, Ma. I got something for you, one of the best gifts in the world. I guess you don't want it then?"

Ms. Caldwell was all smiles now. She jumped up from the couch and walked into the dining room. "What you got for me?" she asked, standing over her baby boy.

"Sunshine's pregnant. We givin' you a grandbaby."

"I know you fucking lying," she said in a serious tone with a straight face.

Monsta was excited about his girl carrying his baby, and his smile showed it. "I'm dead-ass serious. She went to the doctor and everything."

Ms. Caldwell shook her head. The last thing the city of Detroit needed was another Monsta running around, not giving a fuck about shit.

"Boy, are you crazy? Nah, scratch that. You *are* bat-shit crazy. What happened to you wearing protection with these li'l hoes? The last thing you needed was a fucking baby."

"Sunshine not a ho, so that rule ain't work on her. I use protection on the *real* hoes."

"Lord Jesus. What the fuck I'm gon' do with you? I'm so disappointed right now."

"Damn, Ma. This moment really ain't about you and how you feel. Matter of fact, why don't you take your disappointed ass in the kitchen and make something to eat? My baby gon' be hungry when she wakes up."

Ms. Caldwell learned years ago that Monsta's screws weren't too tight, and he had different personalities. On one side, she could sit up and talk shit with him all day, and that was the one who was staring at her that very moment. She knew his temper was bad, and at any moment, he could snap and hurt her. Being afraid, she walked into the kitchen to fix dinner.

Standing in the kitchen, chain-smoking her Newports, Ms. Caldwell waited for Monsta to calm down before she walked back into the living room. She hated that he was his father's son in so many ways. She actually felt bad for Sunshine. She was a sweet girl overall, and now, she was really about to be stuck with his crazy ass for life. She probably thought carrying his baby was about to be everything from glitter to gold, but she really needed to be running to the closest abortion clinic. Monsta was going to give this girl hell.

Monsta sat at the dining room table, packing up the product Henry had just delivered to the house. He couldn't help but grin as he thought about bringing his first seed into the world. As soon as Sunshine told him she was pregnant, he prayed for a baby boy. He couldn't wait to teach his son how to run these streets just like his pops taught him. "No talkin', be about that action" was their family motto.

"Ma," Monsta called out.

Ms. Caldwell snapped out of her thoughts. "What is it, Monsta?"

Instead of responding, he got up to walk into the kitchen. "Ma, I'm sorry for trippin'."

Turning to check on the food, she simply said, "Yeah, OK."

As Monsta walked back into the dining room, Sunshine walked in.

"Hey, baby, how was your nap?"

She took a seat across from him at the table. "It was all right."

Monsta's face was puzzled. "Why you ain't sit closer to me?"

"You know I don't want to be around that shit. Once you done and clean up, I'll move over there," she explained.

Monsta nodded his head in agreement. "Yeah, you right. I'm just about finished anyway. Aye, my mama in there cooking for the baby. She real happy to finally be a grandma," he said, eyeballing his mama.

Ms. Caldwell put on a fake smile before walking toward Sunshine. "I'm happy for you two. Can't wait to spoil the baby."

Sunshine smiled. "Thank you."

"So, how did your mama take the news about the baby?" she asked Sunshine.

Sunshine lowered her head. "I haven't told her yet."

"Oh wow. Don't you think you need to tell her?" Ms. Caldwell asked.

"I'm going to once I go home. I left after my doctor's appointment and came straight here to talk to Monsta about it."

Ms. Caldwell shook her head before walking back into the kitchen. She already knew her mom was going to flip the hell out. They had spoken before, and from the brief conversation, her mom didn't want her daughter even living in the same state as Monsta. He was the type of guy that only a mother could love, and sometimes, it was hard for her to do even that.

"Baby, you gon' spend the night with me?"

Monsta and Sunshine had just eaten dinner. They were both full and tired. Just like any other night that she visited, Monsta tried talking her into spending the night with him.

"You know my mama gon' trip if I don't bring my ass home. Maybe another night."

Monsta wasn't trying to hear all that shit. He knew her mom didn't care for him, but he didn't give a fuck. "You ain't really got no choice but to stay. I got into some shit earlier, and I don't have my truck."

"Are you fucking serious?" she questioned.

"Hell yeah. What you think took me so long to get here earlier?" he asked.

Sunshine sat up. "I'm gon' have to catch an Uber or something, Monsta. I don't wanna hear her mouth. On top of that, I'm already scared to tell her I'm pregnant."

"What the fuck you scared of? You know what? Don't trip. I'll take you home in the morning when my truck gets here, and we can tell her together."

Sunshine shook her head. "Fuck no. You know she gon' flip out just seeing you walk in the door. I gotta do this on my own."

Monsta sat up so he could look into her eyes. "You know, no matter what, I love you, and you'll always be mine."

Sunshine blushed. "I love you too, Monsta."

Although he was against her leaving him that night, Sunshine left anyway. Knowing her mom was going to flip out about the baby, she didn't wanna add to the problem by not coming home.

"Girl, where you been?" Sunshine's older sister, Zoey, asked.

Sunshine walked right past her, then went straight to her room. She hated how her sister was always in her business, acting like she was the mother. Zoey followed Sunshine upstairs to her room.

"You know Mama been asking about you."

"Oh, OK. Well, I'm here now. I don't know why she didn't just call my phone."

Zoey rolled her eyes. "I'm just gonna keep it real with you, Sunshine. We know you were with Monsta. That boy ain't shit but trouble, and you crazy for fucking with him."

Sunshine was so tired of everyone trying to tell her who she should love. She knew Monsta had a temper and sometimes acted out in the streets, but when he was around her, he never showed her that side everyone feared. Yeah, sometimes he played a little too much, but he showed her love.

"If you done talking your shit, step outta my room. You don't see me talking about the bum niggas you be fucking with. At least my nigga got money. Maybe you should ask him if he's hiring, so you and Darryl can get a house for y'all and those three kids."

"Bitch, fuck you. With all the shit your nigga be in, trust me, he'll be locked up or even dead soon. That crazy nigga ain't gon be running the streets for long," Zoey yelled.

Just the thought of Monsta locked up or even dead caused Sunshine to jump in her feelings quickly. Truthfully, she couldn't see life without him, especially now, since she was pregnant with his child. Sunshine hung her head low thinking about what her sister said. At the same time, she wanted to cry.

"That's what the fuck I thought. You ain't got shit to say now. Look at your young, stupid ass. You think you know everything, but don't know shit."

Sunshine stood up from her bed. "Bitch, get the fuck outta my room before your kids see you get stomped out. Save that energy for helping that bum find a job and getting the fuck outta Mama basement."

Zoey shook her head. It never fails. Every time she and Sunshine got into it, the first thing that came out of her mouth was how Darryl didn't have a job. In her eyes, Sunshine was a weak-ass little girl, and that argument just proved her point.

"Yeah, bitch, you funny as hell. I'm not gon' beat your ass 'cause the road you goin' down, life gon' fuck you up."

Before Sunshine could respond, Zoey was walking out the door. Then Sunshine slammed the door shut. She hated being in that house. If it wasn't her sister, it was her mama with the shits and getting on her nerves.

After a hot shower, Sunshine lay across her bed thinking about how different her life was about to be. She couldn't believe she was about to have a baby. At the same time, Monsta refused to wear condoms when they were together, so it was bound to happen. He always said he fucked with a lot of bitches before he met her and didn't have any kids, so he couldn't have any. Sunshine knew she was foolish to believe that, but she wanted him so badly that he could have said anything, and she would have gone along with it.

"What the hell going on between you and Zoey?" Ms. Mathews asked, walking into Sunshine's room.

Sunshine sat up. "She came into my room messing with me and running her mouth. I don't even understand why she just don't stay in the basement where she lives."

"First of all, Sunshine, she is your big sister, and all that bullshit got to come to an end. You need to show her some respect and stop talking down on her and Darryl. They're trying so hard to get back on their feet since he lost his last job."

"You always taking her side. She followed me up here, starting with me."

Ms. Mathews wasn't trying to hear all that. She had already made up her mind that Sunshine was the problem. "You can't be walking in this house any time you want to because you out having your head buried in that boy's ass."

Sunshine was pissed now. In that household, it was never about what was actually happening. It always boiled down to Monsta. He was to blame for everything. If it rained, it was because of him. Too hot or too cold? Monsta was to blame.

"So, Zoey can say whatever to me because I'm with Monsta?" Sunshine questioned.

Ms. Mathews wasn't in the mood for Sunshine's bullshit. Without saying shit else, she walked away. She harbored so much hatred for Monsta that her head started to ache whenever his name was mentioned. She loved her daughter and only wanted the best for her.

Sunshine got up to shut the door behind her mama. She knew that no matter what went on in that house, it was always Monsta's fault.

The next morning, Sunshine jumped up to run to the bathroom. Ms. Mathews was getting ready for work while still in her room when she heard Sunshine throwing up in the bathroom.

"I know you fucking lying," she yelled before charging toward the bathroom.

Snatching open the door, she walked in just in time to see Sunshine getting up from the floor.

"I know you fucking lying. I know like hell you ain't let that crazy nigga get you pregnant. How could you be so stupid?"

Sunshine pretended not to hear her as she grabbed her toothbrush. Ms. Mathew stood there watching her daughter brush her teeth, then wash her face. She was trying not to knock her head off in the tub somewhere.

"So, you really let that boy get you pregnant?" she asked again.

Sunshine wiped her mouth. "Ma, can we talk about this when I'm feeling better?"

"No, the fuck we can't. We gon' talk about this shit right *now*. Are you pregnant?"

Sunshine hung her head low. "Yeah, Ma," she mumbled.

Without giving it a second thought, Ms. Mathews slapped her daughter. Sunshine instantly grabbed her face, crying. Instead of trying to fight back or even saying anything, she tried to push her way out of the bathroom.

"Where the fuck you think you going?" Ms. Mathews yelled, pushing Sunshine back toward the toilet.

Sunshine lost her balance right before she tumbled back into the wall. "What the fuck is wrong with you?" she yelled, not realizing she was cussing at her mama.

"Oh, so you all the way grown now? That boy got you losing your fucking mind," she yelled before attacking her daughter.

Sunshine never wanted to be that type of girl, but she couldn't just stand there and let her mama hit on her. Without even thinking it all the way out, she swung back.

All the noise already had Zoey peeking in the bathroom, but when she saw Sunshine swing back, she rushed in. She wasn't trying to break up shit, but instead, to finally fight her sister.

"Hold up, bitch. You wanna fight my mama?" Zoey yelled, jumping in and swinging wildly.

Sunshine tried her best to fight both of them, but she ended up on the bathroom floor, balled up, crying, and begging them to stop. Once the fight was over, Zoey walked out of the bathroom smiling and feeling so proud of what she did. Although Sunshine did have too much mouth at times, it was the dirty looks and crying coming from her oldest daughter, who was standing in the hallway watching, that made her mama feel a little bad.

"Go sit down somewhere," she yelled at Zoey.

Ms. Mathews walked out of the bathroom, upset at herself. She too had been a young mother and remembered how much she had hated it when her family started to treat her differently. She never really wanted to hurt her daughter, but while trying to talk to her, all she could see was Monsta's evil, dazed-out smirk in her head. She honestly felt like he got her pregnant on purpose, and that thought alone drove her crazy.

Sunshine waited until she heard her mama's bedroom shut before getting up off the floor. She broke down in tears looking at herself in the mirror. Since she was so light in color, every bruise or bump appeared, making things look worse than they were. As she limped out of the bathroom, she could hear her mom on the phone telling her boss there was a family emergency and she couldn't come in. She quickly went into her room. As Sunshine sat on the bed, she texted Monsta.

Sunshine: Baby, can you come get me?

Monsta: I can't right now. I'm still waiting on these niggas to get done getting my shit together.

Sunshine popped her lips. After everything she went through this morning, he was really irritating her.

Sunshine: I'm about to set up an Uber to come over.

Monsta: What the fuck you trying to get over here so bad for? Didn't I just give you some dick?

Sunshine: I'm not in a joking mood, Monsta. Some shit popped off at the house, and I don't wanna be here anymore.

Monsta: All right, do what you gon' do.

Sunshine set her phone on the bed so she could pack her spend-the-night bag. With all the bullshit going on, she wished she had just stayed at Monsta's house like he begged her to. Just as she was looking through her closet for something to wear, her mama walked in.

"Look, Sunshine, I'm sorry about what happened earlier. You being pregnant, especially by that boy, really pissed me off. I can't believe you allowed this shit to happen, especially after I told you how I felt about him."

Sunshine turned around to face her mama. "It's not about how you feel; it's about what *I* want. I love Monsta, and I know for a fact that he loves me."

"How can you be so foolish to think a nigga named Monsta really loves you? That boy is nothing but trouble.

If you stay in his life and have this baby, you'll learn the hard way."

"You and your daughter jumped me, and now you back in my face talking about Monsta. He has never touched me in a way that would hurt me. You never gave him a chance just because of the crap your friends had to say about him."

"Girl, bye. Don't sit in my face and act like you don't know how he is in these streets. That boy sells drugs, and he's quick to kill whoever ain't scared of his crazy ass. I remember his daddy was the same way back in the day when I was growing up. I can't believe you throwing your life away for that fool."

Sunshine was never the disrespectful type, but she was still pissed at her mama. It didn't matter if she apologized; she was still pissed. "You talkin' down on him, but when I told him about the baby, he was happy. When you told my daddy about me, that fool went ghost. I'm grown now, and he only saw me like twice."

"This not about me and your stupid-ass daddy. This is about you having that crazy-ass boy's baby. Why the fuck do you think everyone calls that nigga 'Monsta'? That boy's gonna bring you down, and I know your ass gon' run back this way when he does. Just watch and see. How are y'all even planning on taking care of this baby? Let me guess . . . off his dope money?"

"Yeah, and I'm gonna find a job."

"Oh really, Sunshine? You spent all that time getting your license to do hair and ain't done shit yet. It's like you put your life on hold to sit up under him."

Sunshine walked to her bed so she could answer her ringing phone.

"Hey, baby," she sang into the phone, prompting her mom to walk away.

After hearing what Monsta had to say, she hung up with a smile on her face. He let her know that as soon as they got done texting, his boy dropped off his truck, so he was on his way to get her. She quickly tossed some clothes and personal things into her bag. She planned on being gone for a few days.

As she walked downstairs, she could hear Zoey at the door, asking Monsta what he wanted.

"Maybe he wanted to see if your bum-ass baby daddy was ready to pay him back for that vial he gave him the other day," Sunshine snapped.

Monsta's laughter really upset Zoey. Her baby daddy wasn't on that shit, but it was funny to him.

Zoey turned around to confront her sister. "Didn't you just get your ass beat?"

"That's only because y'all weak asses jumped me in the bathroom. You could never beat me one-on-one, and we both know that."

Monsta stood there listening, but since he didn't like what he was hearing, he pulled out his favorite girl (his gun).

"You letting muthafuckas put their hands on you? Drop that bag and beat that bitch ass right now. I can't fuck with no weak bitch."

Sunshine dropped her bag as she was told and attacked Zoey. Just as she said before, Zoey couldn't fuck with her on that fighting shit.

Ms. Mathews ran down the stairs. "Break up this shit," she yelled, trying to pull Sunshine off Zoey.

Once the girls were separated, Zoey rushed back downstairs in embarrassment. She couldn't believe that after all these years, her little sister was still tagging her ass.

"Boy, get your ass outta my house," Ms. Mathews yelled.

Monsta knew she didn't like him, but that only made him fuck with her even more.

"Damn, ma. I'm givin' yo' ass a grandbaby, and this how you wanna treat me?" he jokingly asked.

Sunshine shook her head at Monsta. Sometimes he played way too much.

"Get the fuck outta my house before I call the police on your stupid ass."

"Ma," Sunshine yelled.

Ms. Mathews turned toward her naïve daughter. "If you're leaving with this fool, please do so now. I don't like him and wish you would just go get an abortion so you can have a chance to live your life without that fool."

Monsta took a step toward her. "What the fuck you say?"

Sunshine hurried to grab him. "Come on, baby, let's go."

"Fuck that shit. She really talkin' about you fuckin' my baby?" he said as Sunshine pulled him out of the house.

As they got into the truck, Monsta wasn't too quick to drive off. Sunshine tried to rub his arm to calm him down.

"Calm down, baby. You know she always talking shit."

"Let me ask your ass a question," he said, turning her way.

"What is it, Monsta?" she questioned.

"It ever crossed your mind to abort my baby?" he asked.

It didn't take her a second to think about her answer. "No," Sunshine quickly blurted out.

"Call your mama right now and tell her that when my baby gets here, I don't want her around it," he demanded.

"Monsta, it ain't that fucking serious. You know people say shit when they mad."

Monsta hated how she wasn't listening to him. "Man, fuck her. Call her ass now before I really get pissed and shoot up that fucking house," he yelled, slapping the steering wheel.

"Monsta, that's my mama," she whined.

"I don't give a fuck. If a muthafucka don't like me, they will hurt whoever is closest to me. I'm not about to let no bitch be in my baby's face pinching him and shit."

Sunshine sat there with tears in her eyes. As much as she loved him, she hated how demanding he could be at times.

In his eyes, she wasn't moving fast enough. "What the fuck you over there crying for? Matter of fact, don't even answer that. Just get the fuck outta my shit. Take your ass back in there so they can jump on your stupid ass again."

Sunshine knew she had to choose between him and her family, and since all that bullshit jumped off, she knew it had to be him. Pulling out her phone, she dialed her mama's number.

"Put that shit on speakerphone," he ordered.

"What is it, Sunshine?" Ms. Mathews snapped when answering the phone.

"Ma, I just wanted to tell you that when I have this baby, I don't want you or Zoey in my child's life. If y'all don't like my baby's father, then y'all don't deserve to be in its life."

To their surprise, Ms. Mathews took the news better than expected. "Girl, fuck you and that boy. I know he made you call my phone with his punk ass. Tell that muthafucka I'm not scared of his ass, and I'm the right bitch to fuck with. He ain't the only muthafucka out here that need meds."

"Hang up on that bitch," Monsta ordered.

"Sunshine, if you hang up, don't bring your stupid ass back to this house, and I mean that shit."

The look Monsta gave told her everything she needed to know. It wasn't often that she saw that crazy look in his eyes, but when she did, it scared her. Sunshine quickly hung up before tossing the phone back into her purse.

"You wanna get something to eat?" he asked, as if she hadn't just made a life-changing decision.

"Yeah, I guess," she mumbled.

Since her face was a little swollen, Sunshine spoke briefly to Ms. Caldwell before rushing to Monsta's bedroom.

"What the hell you do to that girl's face?"

"I beat her ass. Ain't that what it looks like?"

Since he had a straight face, his mom was easily fooled. "Boy, have you lost your fucking mind? Didn't you just tell me she was pregnant? Why the fuck are you putting your damn hands on her?"

Monsta laughed. "Damn, Ma, I was just playing with your ass. Her sister and mama jumped on her this morning."

"Damn, boy, you got to stop playing so fucking much. That type of shit ain't funny," she yelled.

"Ma, on some real shit, that's my baby. I don't be doing shit like that to her. She too fuckin' loyal to a nigga to be fuckin' over her like that. I know I might have smacked or even backhanded a few bitches, but not her," he explained.

She didn't say anything as she shook her head. It puzzled her sometimes how comfortable he was saying certain shit.

Monsta walked into the room to give Sunshine her food.

"Get your ass up and feed my baby."

Sunshine sat up. "I wasn't asleep."

As she ate, he kicked off his shoes, then climbed into bed with her.

"You know if something bad would've happened to my baby, I probably would've killed one of those muthafuckas."

"We good, baby. Don't even speak on that shit," she said, getting irritated about the whole situation all over again.

"I'm just sayin' . . . I'm sittin' here feeling like a bitch for letting that shit slide."

"Bae, you did the right thing by walking away from the bullshit. You know she would have called the police in a heartbeat. My mom never liked you and would do whatever to see us apart."

"Do you love me?" he questioned.

"Yeah. Why are you even asking me that?"

Monsta stole one of her fries. "That's all that fuckin' matter then. Fuck her."

Not wanting to argue, Sunshine didn't bother to say anything else.

Chapter 2

"Why the hell that girl act like she scared to be outside that room? You must have told her she couldn't come out or something, huh?"

"I ain't tell her shit. She probably just don't wanna be around your ass," Monsta said, laughing.

"Whatever. She needs to go home to her people if she got a problem. Shit, whenever she do come out, she got a fucking attitude. What's wrong with her? I'm starting to think she retarded or something."

Monsta was no longer laughing. "Chill out, Ma. She just be pissed at me all the time. My baby got her trippin'."

"I'm just saying, she been here for a damn month and still be acting funny. Like she's mad at the world. She needs to take that shit to her mama's house."

Monsta stood up from the couch. "Didn't I just say chill the fuck out on her? You always got something to say. That's probably why she don't be wanting to be around your ass," he barked.

Monsta got up to check on Sunshine. She had been sitting around the crib unhappy, and he wasn't feeling that shit.

"What's up with you? Why the hell you sittin' in here looking stupid?"

Sunshine rolled her eyes. "You know exactly why I'm mad. You stayed out all night, then came home and jumped in the shower. Now you say you about to leave again. When you gon' have time for me?"

"Before you stayed here, I told you I had to be in the streets to make money. Gettin' money is what the fuck I do, and sitting up under your yellow ass ain't making me shit. I gotta be out here in these streets making moves and shit."

"Whatever, Monsta. I feel like a fucking prisoner in here. Your ass stays gone all the time, just leaving me here. While you talkin', when I was at my mama's house, you always came to get me and made time for me."

Monsta sat there thinking about what she said, and truth be told, he did get her almost every day back then. The reason behind that was just to irritate her mama since she called herself not liking him. Monsta chuckled just thinking about it.

"Ain't shit funny, boy," Sunshine yelled.

He tried not to snap on her ass, but she was pissing him off. With that last eye roll, he snapped. "Take your ass home then. I'm trying to be a good nigga, but you don't appreciate a boss like me. Get the fuck out with yo' funky-acting ass." Out of anger, he pulled her up from the bed by her hair. "Take your stupid ass home," he ordered, pushing her toward the room door.

"Let me go, Monsta," Sunshine yelled as she struggled to get away from him.

Seeing she was trying to get away from him, Monsta tightened his grip on her hair and tossed her down on the bed. No matter how crazy he acted and told her to leave, he wasn't gonna let her leave him for real.

"Leave her the fuck alone, boy," Ms. Caldwell yelled, walking into her son's room. She usually didn't get in his business, but she wasn't about to let him put his hands on Sunshine, especially while she was pregnant.

"Get the fuck outta my room, Ma. This ain't got shit to do with your ass. This bitch in here trippin'."

"Boy, bring your stupid ass out here and let me talk to you before you end up hurting her and that baby."

Monsta looked down at a crying Sunshine before letting her go. He mushed her head before walking out of the room.

As soon as he walked out, Sunshine started grabbing her clothes and stuffing them in her bag. She knew he was crazy, but he had never acted out on her like that before. For the most part, he only yelled at her. Honestly, she was afraid. Just the thought of him actually hitting her scared her to death.

"I let you do and say a lot of crazy shit around here, but what you *not* gon' do is start hitting on that girl. You took her away from her family and moved her in here. I'll be damned if you start that shit. If you don't want her here, then let her go, but don't play with her and that baby's life."

"You right, Ma," he said, feeling bad for tripping on the only girl who really loved him.

"Go sit your ass on the porch somewhere so you can calm down, then go talk to her," she advised her son.

Monsta nodded his head as if he understood his mom. For the first time in a long time, he didn't try to talk shit back and stepped outside to calm his nerves. He knew he needed to get his act in order, or he'd lose Sunshine for good. After a few seconds, he walked back into the room, thinking he could apologize to Sunshine and everything would be normal. But upon entering the room, he could hear her on the phone while packing her clothes.

"Yeah, please just come get me. I'll tell you what happened when you get here," she cried in the phone before hanging up.

"Where the fuck you goin'?" he asked, getting upset again.

Sunshine jumped before turning around to see Monsta standing there. "You want me gone so bad, so I'm leaving. You can go back to doing you and playing boss in the streets since that's what's important to you."

Monsta snatched the clothes from her hand. "You sound stupid as fuck. Yo' ass ain't goin' nowhere."

"Yes, I am. Keisha's on her way to get me now. I don't have time for your shit, Monsta. *I'm* your girl, *not* these niggas in the street. You trying to handle me like I'm them and not carrying your baby." She continued to cry.

Sunshine had always been his weakness. As crazy as he acted toward anyone else, she was the only one who really gave a fuck about him besides his mama, even though sometimes she made him spazz on her ass too. As he looked at Sunshine, he could tell she was really upset with him, and a simple kiss or hug wouldn't make things all right between the two. Even when he tried to pull her in for a hug, she shot him down.

"I'm not falling for that shit this time, Monsta. We need some space before one of us end up hurt."

He wasn't trying to hear that shit. "What the fuck is space? You think your ass slick? Yo' ass 'bout to leave me, so you can go be a ho with Keisha's nasty ass? You gon' go over there and run your mouth to her, and she ain't gon' do shit but wear your clothes and talk bad on my name."

Sunshine continued packing her stuff, which only pissed him off all over again.

"Did that bitch ever tell you how we had her in the spot sucking us up? That's why she never wanted you with me."

Sunshine zipped up her bag. "Boy, move outta my way. I wasn't a ho before I met you, and I'm for damn sure not about to become one now. And just to let you know, I don't care about that other shit. You just saying shit to get me to stay here with you."

"You damn right, 'cause you ain't going nowhere. You doin' all this extra shit, makin' yourself tired and stressin' out my baby. Go put them clothes back up."

With her bag in hand, Sunshine walked right past Monsta, not caring if he was mad or not. He followed her to the living room.

"You know if you walk outta that door, we gon' have some problems," he said, trying to scare her into staying.

"*Really,* Monsta? What you gon' do, shoot me like you do everyone else who goes against you?"

"Stop testing me, muthafucka."

Sunshine stopped at the front door to say something else. "You just don't get it. You trying to manhandle me and shit is a problem. I told you I don't like that shit. I'm not those niggas you boss around in the streets."

"I know who the fuck you is, and I know you mine. You better not leave this fuckin' house, or we gon' have a problem, and I'm gon' fuck you up to solve it."

Sunshine pulled her phone out of her front pants pocket to read the text message that had just come through.

"My ride is pulling up. Call me when you grow up."

Monsta tried to stop her from walking away from him. "Look, you makin' me do too much talkin', and I don't like that shit. Tell that bitch to get the fuck outta my driveway before I shoot up her car."

Sunshine knew Monsta was crazy, but at the same time, he was all talk when it came to her. So, instead of giving in, she walked out the door. As Monsta tried to grab her again, Ms. Caldwell stopped him.

"Boy, let her go. She needs some space."

Monsta watched as Sunshine jumped into the car with her girl, Keisha. What pissed him off more than her leaving was Keisha's ho ass sticking up her middle finger at him. When the right time came, he planned on doing her dirty.

"Fuck that bitch and that baby. I'm done with that ho."

Ms. Caldwell shook her head as she watched as her son walked back into his room. She knew he was hurt, but he could only be mad at himself. He needed to calm down and realize Sunshine just needed to be loved right. At that moment, she needed a little space. Although she didn't like it, she knew Sunshine would be back because she really loved Monsta's crazy ass. Thinking back on her own life, she could remember going through the same shit with his daddy, Big Monsta.

"Girl, you finally free from that muthafucka, and you laying around my shit all depressed and shit. Bitch, you act like you can't live without that nigga," Keisha said as she sat beside Sunshine on the couch.

"I can't help it. I miss him so much. I've been here for three days, and he hasn't even called or texted me yet. I wonder if he misses me."

"Whatever, girl. That nigga out doing him, and I'm willing to bet any amount of money on that."

"Oh my gawd, don't say that," Sunshine whined.

Keisha grew irritated. As long as they'd been friends, she admired how smart Sunshine was. But for some reason, she was a big dummy for Monsta. When they first started talking, Keisha stayed in her girl's ear, telling her that Monsta wasn't the one for her. Over time, she eased up because Sunshine got a feel of that dick he was carrying around and was stuck. For her own selfish reasons, she wished she had never stopped telling her girl to stay away from him. Over time, Keisha saw that Monsta really loved Sunshine and sometimes, he refused even to let Keisha smell the dick.

"I got an idea, bitch. We gettin' out of the house tonight."

"I'm not getting off this couch. Besides, I know you about to be on some bullshit, and I'm not about to get caught up in shit fuckin' wit' yo' ass," Sunshine explained.

Keisha popped her lips. "Bitch, you boring as hell. You single and wanna spend all your time lying on the fucking couch."

"Bitch, did you forget I'm pregnant? Besides, Monsta will flip the fuck out if he even found out I was sharing the same air as some of these niggas out here."

"Girl, bye. Like I said, you single as hell, so fuck his ass. I bet he already out fucking other bitches."

One thing's for sure. Sunshine hated to even picture him with another bitch. Just the thought made her eyes water up. As badly as she wanted to be strong, she started crying.

"Girl, you need to stop it. He a street nigga and not just a regular one. That nigga is a boss, and I'm sorry to say it, but these bitches do be on him. He a heavy name in these streets. He could fuck a bitch, her sister, and the mama all in the same night, and they wouldn't see shit wrong with it because he is who he is."

"I'm carrying his baby and still love him. Do it look like I wanna hear that shit? When I got with him, I knew he had a past, but he not like that anymore," Sunshine cried.

"Girl, bye. You crazy as hell if you think he was ever faithful. He always gon' be a doggish-ass nigga," Keisha warned.

She wasn't letting up and soon put in her friend's mind that she needed to get out of the house. Maybe other scenery could take her mind off reality.

"So, where's the party at?"

Keisha turned to face her friend. "*That's* what the fuck I'm talkin' about. Bitch, get ready," she said, jumping up from the couch full of excitement.

After a shower and fixing her hair, Sunshine was ready to go out and see what the night would bring. Keisha walked into her room with a towel wrapped around her.

"I see you looking cute tonight. You need to let me get something to wear. I know Monsta ain't buy you shit but the best."

Sunshine agreed to let her borrow an outfit, but in the back of her mind, she couldn't help but think about what Monsta said about Keisha. She had been there just a few days, and all she heard was how much of a dog Monsta was. And now, just like he said, she was borrowing clothes.

Keisha pulled up to the building where the party was being held.

"Hey, before we go in here, let's get some rules laid out," Sunshine suggested.

Keisha smacked her lips. "Bitch, I'm grown. I don't play by nobody rules but mine."

"Fuck all that *I'm grown* shit. When we out together, we need some rules. First, we came together, so we for damn sure leaving together. Second, don't get too drunk 'cause I'll be pissed if I have to carry your ass to the car, and I'm not cleaning up no fucking vomit."

Keisha opened the car door. "OK, Grandma. You ready to go in?"

"Yeah, bitch, and you better behave yourself," she said, laughing.

When they walked in, Sunshine found a table toward the front to chill at. She didn't plan on being there long or even enjoying herself. She also didn't plan on walking around, trying to be friendly.

"OK, look. When I'm at parties, I like to dance and have a good time. I understand your rules and shit, but I'm not about to sit here and watch everyone else have fun. I'm about to grab a drink and dance on one of these niggas."

"Keisha!"

"I'll bring you a water or something, but I'm not about to sit here like a fuckin' nun or something."

Sunshine watched as her friend walked off. She was starting to hate that she even came out. Getting off the couch was beginning to look like a bad idea all over again.

"Aye, cutie, you want a drink or something?"

Sunshine looked up to see some random-ass guy standing over her.

"Nah, I'm good," she replied.

Although she wasn't interested, the guy took a seat across from her. "Look around. Everyone's having a good time, and your sexy ass sitting here looking bored. If I can't bring you anything, can I at least keep you company?"

"Nah, I'm good," she replied again, this time a little more aggressively.

The guy started laughing. "Yeah, my niggas told me you were gonna turn me down 'cause you Monsta's property. You too pretty to be letting a nigga that's in the back room getting his dick sucked control you like that."

Laughing, he got up and walked over to his boys. Soon, Sunshine saw his boys all laughing with him about her. She shook her head before getting up. She prayed she wasn't that stupid to let Monsta play her ass like that. Storming toward the back, something in her wanted to see him in action for herself. Although she knew it would kill her to see him with another bitch, she needed to know if he really gave a fuck about her.

Sunshine had dated a guy before Monsta, but things didn't work out between them. When Monsta first approached her, she was scared of another failed relationship, but his being so real with her made her fall for him quicker than she wanted to. Monsta had gained her heart within three months, and with all the bullshit that was going on, you would have thought he was losing it just as fast.

She stormed toward the back, where the rooms were. She turned her face up, not believing people really came to a party to get fucked. Seeing two of Monsta's workers, she stopped to ask if they had seen him.

"Hey, have y'all seen Monsta here tonight?"

They both told her no before getting back to their conversation. Sunshine stormed off. To her, them niggas were high and too busy looking for some ass for the night even to pay her any real attention.

Cracking each door open just enough to see if Monsta was really in one of the rooms getting his dick sucked, Sunshine said a silent prayer that the guy lied to her. Each room held a random couple fucking each other's brains out, or was empty. When she got to the last room, her heart raced. She was scared to death about what she would find, but she needed to know the truth. If he was in that room with a bitch, she promised to be done with his ass for good. Sunshine was able to breathe again, seeing that the room was empty. Turning around with a smile on her face and feeling foolish, she returned to the party.

"Damn, girl, where were you at?" Keisha asked as Sunshine returned to the table.

Not wanting to prove to Keisha just how stupid she was when it came to Monsta, she lied. "I went to the restroom."

For some reason, Keisha wasn't as excited about the party anymore. "You ready to go, or you wanna sit around some more?"

"I been ready. Remember, I only came out because you wanted me to," Sunshine reminded her.

As they headed for the door, the guy who gave Sunshine the warning grabbed her hand. "You need to pay more attention. Muthafuckas doing shit in your face."

Sunshine snatched her hand back. "Boy, fuck you."

Keisha grabbed her hand. "Come on, boo, let's go," she said, giving him the evil eye.

He stood there shaking his head. He hated how naïve and stupid females could be at times.

As they got in the car, Keisha decided to pick her brain. "What the hell was that guy talking about?"

"Shit, I don't know. I don't even know that nigga."

Keisha shook her head. "Girl, I thought you were trying to find my godbaby a new daddy."

Sunshine popped her lip. "Girl, stop that shit. My baby got a fucking daddy and don't need nobody else but him."

"Damn, bitch, you ain't got to be all like that. I was only playing. Anyway . . . I thought with him putting his hands on you that y'all were done."

Sunshine was irritated. "Girl, just drop it. I don't wanna talk about Monsta tonight."

Keisha didn't say shit else as she drove them back to her place. If she had known Monsta was gonna show up, she wouldn't have forced Sunshine to go out with her that night. She drove home pissed that she didn't even get a chance to catch that big nut Monsta promised to give her. She was also irritated that muthafuckas stayed running they mouth, trying to start shit. Keisha could see she was pissing her friend off even more, so instead of continuing the conversation, she turned up the radio, hoping to arrive home soon.

After a hot shower, Sunshine lay on the couch with a lot on her mind. Between Keisha and Monsta, she was stressed out. As Sunshine drifted off, her mind went back to the good times she and Monsta shared. Although it had only been a few days since she left him, she couldn't help but cry out and miss him in every way.

   Monsta's Plan A didn't go as intended that night because Keisha's stupid ass brought Sunshine, and her wild ass got up to look for him. So he decided to put Plan B in motion.

   Earlier that day, he had lost a rack in a dice game. He wanted to murk the nigga that won his money, but to call it even, he decided to fuck his baby mama instead. It really wasn't about the money he lost. It was really because the nigga laughed in his face. For that reason alone, Monsta wanted to bust in his baby mama's face. He felt like he was growing a little because he realized killing wasn't always the answer.

   Seeing her at the store earlier that day only made things easier for him. He was actually surprised that he didn't have to go looking for her rat ass. He played it off good and got the bitch's number. Before walking off, he let it be known he was gon' hit her up later that night.

   Dominque was so drunk when she showed up at 3:00 a.m. that she bumped into the chair in Monsta's room.

   "Damn, bitch, you drunk as fuck. Maybe you need to take your ass home and sleep off that shit."

   Dominque wasn't about to pass on the chance to finally fuck Monsta. She had been trying to pull him in for the longest, but he always passed her to one of his workers because he had a girl. Now he was talking that single shit, and she was ready to replace the bitch quicker than a heartbeat.

   Her words slurred out, "Nah, baby, I'll never be too drunk to take that dick. I've been waiting so long to swallow that muthafucka whole."

Monsta shook his head. Being around thirsty bitches like her made him miss Sunshine even more. His baby was never a groupie like the rest of these hoes. Hating that Dominque's baby daddy made him look stupid in that dice game is the only reason why he wasn't so quick to put out her ass. Besides, he hoped fucking someone else would take his mind off Sunshine, even if it were only for a moment, since she still hadn't brung her ass home yet. He even thought about putting his pride aside and calling her first. He was gonna make her bring her ass back, but after listening to his mama, he gave her the space she needed. So, now, he was stuck trying to act like he was entertained by the drunk bitch Dominque.

Dominque quickly dropped to her knees so she could get a taste of his dick before he beat up the pussy.

"Hold the fuck up, bitch," he rudely said before pulling out a condom from the shoe box under his bed.

"What we need that for?"

Monsta gave her a strange look. "You serious? Girl, let's be real. You got more than a few bodies, and most of them niggas bums. You got me doin' too much talking. Either get wit' it or bounce."

Dominique snatched the rubber from his hand. She was so desperate to tell her girls that she finally fucked him that she pushed aside his rudeness. Rolling her eyes, she placed the rubber on his long, thick dick before making it disappear in her mouth. Monsta stood there looking down at Dominque. He wasn't a bit impressed by her head game.

"Damn, girl, just get the fuck up. That shit felt like I was rubbing my dick across sandpaper. Yo' ass need to drink more water."

"What?"

"Get yo' ass in the bed. I hope your pussy get wetter than that desert throat you got."

Dominque popped her lips. "You trippin', boy. I came over here to please you and help you bust a nut since I heard your bitch left you. Now, if you gon' be an asshole about the shit, I'll leave."

Monsta couldn't believe she really thought he was pressed about her bringing her ass over there to fuck. "Bitch, fuck you. Matter of fact, get the fuck outta my house."

Before she could react or respond, Monsta was snatching her clothes up from the floor and rushing out of the room. With his dick out and all, he opened the front door to toss her clothes out on the grass. Dominique was embarrassed, but grateful it was three in the morning and not daytime when everyone would be out. She quickly grabbed her clothes before running off toward her car.

"Tell that bum-ass nigga of yours that I'm on his head, bitch," Monsta yelled before she drove off.

Walking back into the house and returning to his room, Monsta snatched the condom off, then tossed it in the trash. "Stupid, dry-mouthed ho," he mumbled as he climbed back in bed.

Dominique couldn't turn him on for shit like the head doctor he hooked up with earlier at that party. But at the end of the night, couldn't no ho compare to his Sunshine. The thing with Monsta was, he never gave other bitches his all. Whenever he did cheat, them other bitches only got drunk, sloppy dick, and he was okay with that.

Feeling a hand rub up her legs, damn near touching her pussy, Sunshine jumped up to an older, dread-headed guy standing over her.

"What the fuck?" she yelled as she pulled her shirt back down to cover herself up.

"My bad, beautiful. I was just trying to see if you wanted to hit this blunt," the guy said, trying to pass her the blunt.

"First of all, you shouldn't be touching on me because I don't know you. Second, no, I don't wanna smoke that garbage. And last but not least, get the fuck outta my face," Sunshine snapped.

"Damn, you feisty. Your girl said you would be, but I like that," the dread said.

Sunshine grabbed some items from her bag before storming into the bathroom. She never thought staying at Keisha's house was a good idea because she was a ho, as Monsta said, and what happened that morning was the other reason why. How the fuck did she think sending a nigga she brought home to seduce her would be all right? That was the bullshit Monsta stayed trying to warn her about.

After dropping Sunshine off at the house the night before, Keisha left again. Sunshine heard her come into the house around 4:00 a.m. Based on the noise coming from her room, she knew her girl had come home with company.

As Sunshine walked out of the bathroom, she saw the guy had gone back into the room with Keisha. She took that moment to put on her shoes and get the fuck on. Before walking out the door, she made sure to grab all her shit. If Monsta was all right with her coming back, she promised herself not to fuck with Keisha's ho ass anymore. She knew from what that guy said that Keisha sent him her way, and that's why he was in her face trying to get some of her attention. She didn't know what would make Keisha even think she fucked with her on that level. She never even gave her the impression that she liked bitches 'cause she didn't. The only mouth that was gon' be sucking on her pussy belonged to Monsta.

Sunshine made it up a few blocks before stopping at McDonald's to grab her and Monsta a breakfast sandwich. After getting their food, she patiently waited outside for her Uber. Being pregnant and always tired made her wanna hurry and get a car.

Sunshine missed Monsta and prayed he missed her even more. In her head, she would walk in the house, and he'd greet her with open arms. However, as they got closer to his house, Sunshine started to feel funny. Just thinking about him not accepting her with open arms made her ill. Something in her wished she'd never left in the first place.

"Who is it?" Ms. Caldwell yelled as she walked to the front door.

She never had company, so she knew it had to be for Monsta. Never did she think it would be Sunshine this soon. It hadn't even been a whole week before she returned. She secretly prayed she'd stay away so she and that baby could have a better life. She loved her son, but he wasn't in the right mindset to have a baby.

"What you want, girl?"

"Is Monsta here?" Sunshine asked, praying she said yeah.

Ms. Caldwell opened the screen door for her, but the look of disappointment was all over her face.

"How you doin', Ma?" Sunshine asked, trying to break the awkward silence between them.

"I'm all right. How you been?"

"I'm OK," Sunshine mumbled.

Ms. Caldwell shook her head. "Something must be wrong with your ass. Why would you come back to this nigga and you were free?"

Sunshine wasn't sure what she meant by that, but she didn't like it. Without saying shit else, she walked away. Dealing with his mama, she learned just to walk away before she gave her the energy to argue with her.

Opening up Monsta's room door, the first thing she saw was him lying across the bed, knocked out asleep. She smiled at the sight of him, but that quickly changed. The gold condom wrapper on the floor caught her attention next. Picking up a shoe from the floor, she threw it right at his head. That caused him to jump up.

"What the fuck?"

"Really, Monsta? You just out here doing what you wanna do?"

"What the fuck you talkin' about? I ain't been doin' shit," he yelled, jumping up from the bed.

Sunshine was scared, so she quickly grabbed the other shoe to bust him in the head if he tried to hit her. Monsta looked down at the floor, trying to see what she kept eyeballing. He shook his head. He couldn't believe he was caught up in some bullshit and didn't even get no pussy from Dominque.

"Before you go off, let me explain some shit," he pleaded.

Sunshine turned around to leave. From what she thought she knew, he had been fucking someone else and no longer needed or wanted her. Monsta grabbed her arm to stop her.

"Let me go, Monsta. Go grab on whatever bitch you had over here. I've been nothing but loyal to you, and your ass out here fucking all these hoes. I bet the bitch was a fucking thot box. I guess you think the shit cool 'cause y'all used a fucking condom, and I'm the only dummy walking around carrying your baby—"

Monsta cut her off. "Damn, if you gon' be mad at me and try to accuse me of fuckin' on a ho, at least make sure you know what the fuck you talkin' about. I swear I ain't been fuckin' on nobody."

Sunshine wanted to slap him, but instead, she threw the bag of food at him. "That's fraud, nigga. Ain't no way there's an empty condom wrapper on your floor, and you ain't fuck nobody. Stop playing in my fucking face."

"Ain't nobody lying about shit," he yelled, trying to get his point across.

Sunshine pushed him. "Get outta my way, boy. I'm so done with you and this bullshit. I don't even know why I came back in the first place."

Usually, when they got into it, there would be just a lot of yelling between them. But hearing her say shit was over between them did something to his mind. Before she could get out the door, he was snatching her back in the room by the back of her neck.

"Get the fuck off me, Monsta!" Sunshine screamed as he tossed her down on the bed.

He was now on top of her, yelling. "Shut the fuck up before I hurt your stupid ass. I was telling you the fuckin' truth."

Although he had his hand wrapped around her neck, trying to get her to shut up and make her listen to him, Sunshine still tried to fight and get him off her. "Get off me!" she screamed again.

This time, his mama ran into the room. She couldn't just sit back and listen to that bullshit any longer. "Monsta, get off that girl before you hurt her and that damn baby."

Evil face and all, Monsta jumped up, snatching his gun off the dresser. He didn't point it at her, but she got the picture. "Get the fuck outta my business!"

If she didn't know before, Ms. Caldwell knew then that her son had lost his fucking mind. She looked at Sunshine before walking out. She hated leaving that girl in the room crying like that, but she couldn't do much at this time.

"Monsta, don't you hurt that girl. I'm gon' call your uncle over here to deal with your ass," she yelled from the other side of the door.

Monsta was crazy, but not kill-his-own-mama crazy. He picked up the shoe that was still resting on his bed and threw it at the door. The loud thump made Ms. Caldwell jump and run upstairs to her room. She couldn't do shit but hope and pray he didn't hurt Sunshine. As she sat there, she picked up the phone to call her brother. He knew how to get Monsta to calm down.

While Monsta's attention was on his mama, Sunshine thought about making a run for it. However, with him holding a tight grip on his gun, she was too scared to move.

Monsta turned with the gun pointed her way. "Now, are you ready to listen to me, or do I gotta use this muthafucka for real?"

"Baby, you're scaring me. Please put that gun down," she cried as she scooted farther on the bed as if the distance really mattered.

Seeing that he still held the power to scare her, he kept it pointed her way. "You gon' listen to me now?"

"I'm listening. I swear I'm listening to you. Just please, Monsta, don't hurt me." She continued to cry.

Monsta set the gun down on the dresser before sitting on the bed as if nothing was wrong. Looking over at Sunshine, he took the time to wipe away her tears.

"What I was trying to tell your ass is that this bitch did come over here last night. I invited her over to get some head and pussy, but not because I liked her or anything. Her nigga beat me in a dice game the other day, and I was just trying to piss him off. I couldn't even fuck. Her mouth was dry, and I was missing your ass."

Sunshine didn't say anything. She was too scared to, but her silence only pissed him off.

"Is you fuckin' listening to me?"

"Yes, baby, I hear you."

"Do you believe me? I can pull the rubber out of the garbage over there if you need to see it."

Sunshine shook her head. "Baby, I believe you. There's no need for all that."

Monsta lay his head on her belly like he'd done almost every day since he found out she was carrying his baby. "Your stomach growing a little, but you still small as hell. Was you feeding my baby when you were with that bitch Keisha?"

"Yes, Monsta, we ate daily," she dryly said.

"You hungry?" he then asked.

Mentioning food, Sunshine tried to sit up, thinking about the food she got from McDonald's. "Damn, I did bring some food, but that shit gotta be cold now."

Monsta got up to get the bag. He laughed as he pulled out the sandwiches. "You really were gon' come in here and McMuffin and sausage biscuit your way back into my heart?"

Sunshine couldn't help but laugh. "Why you so fucking silly?"

"'Cause, man, I hate having to act up when it come to you. I swear I do love you. Sometimes I feel like I gotta constantly prove that shit to you because I know muthafuckas be in your ear trying to tell you I ain't shit."

"I love you too, Monsta. You just gotta calm down and handle me with care. I'm not used to all this shit," she explained.

"I don't like trippin' on you like this, I really don't. I just need you to understand I'm not about to lose you or let you go be with any other nigga. When you say crazy shit like you done with me, I be ready to fuck up shit."

What should have been a red flag went way over Sunshine's head. Hearing those words only turned her on. She jumped out of bed and walked over to him. He stared down into her eyes as she looked into his. Some couldn't see what she saw and loved about him, but it was there.

Within a quick movement, Monsta and Sunshine locked lips as he picked her up, carrying her back to the bed. The way his hands touched her body at that moment was precisely what she had always wanted to feel. They were in love and couldn't nobody tell them different.

After a while, Ms. Caldwell returned downstairs, but only to make sure Sunshine was all right. It wasn't until she got down there and heard the loud moans coming from his room that she realized there was nothing wrong with her. As she went upstairs, she shook her head at the whole situation. She had once been that foolish girl who chased behind a crazy fool. She wanted so much more for Sunshine. She called her brother again to tell him everything was all right for the moment, and there was no need for him to pull up.

Monsta climbed out of bed, pissed he'd slept most of the day away but happy to have his girl back. If staying home and being laid up was all he had to do to keep Sunshine, that's what he was gonna do. He was surprised his mama wasn't downstairs, all in the TV. Then he thought back to how he acted earlier when he had a meltdown and put it together that she was probably still pissed at him. Walking to the bottom of the stairs, he called her down.

"Ma."

She wasn't in the mood for his shit, but she decided to answer him anyway. "What you want, boy?"

"Can you come down here? I need to talk to you."

Ms. Caldwell walked out of her room and yelled down the stairs, "You don't have that gun on you, do you?"

Monsta laughed. "No. Can you come here? I'm sorry about that," he asked again, getting somewhat irritated.

Ms. Caldwell walked downstairs with a metal bat in her hand.

"Fuck you doin' with that?" Monsta asked with a grin on his face.

"You know I'll kill you if I have to," she said with a straight face.

Monsta laughed as he walked back toward the living room. "You always calling me crazy and shit, but I got that shit from you and my pops."

"You got that shit from your daddy," she said, defending her name.

"Yo' ass be with the shits too," he added on, laughing.

Ms. Caldwell lit her cigarette. "Nah, nigga. I just learned how to play my role. Being with your daddy for so many years before he got killed taught me a thing or two."

Monsta put down his head. Whenever his daddy was brought up, he always got in his feelings. The happy memories of having him around were always overpowered by the day Big Monsta was taken from him and his mama. Monsta could remember the horrible day as if it were just yesterday.

Monsta rode along with his pops just like any other day when it was time to handle business. His pops didn't trust too many, but when it came down to his son, he had no problem putting his life in his hands. Big Monsta wanted him to learn the ins and outs of running the streets; failure was not an option in his eyes.

"Now, Monsta, I want you to be on your shit while we out here handling this business. I don't trust these niggas, and I got a feeling I might have to pop one of these sons of bitches if they don't have my fuckin' money."

Monsta looked up from his phone, then reached under his seat. "You know I got you, Pops."

His pops let out a little laugh. "That's my boy."

Big Monsta and Li'l Monsta were known to laugh even when something serious was going on. Their enemies and friends never knew what was going on in their twisted minds.

At the age of 13, Monsta had never killed anyone, but his father had already schooled him on the street life. He was constantly reminded to shoot first if a nigga playing in his face or be a dead nigga. His mind always rapped Tupac's lyrics to his song "Hail Mary" when he had his gun around him. "I ain't a killa, but don't push me."

Monsta admired his pops and loved how niggas feared him. Knowing he was next in line to run the streets of Detroit made him proud to be who he was. Just knowing niggas feared who he was gonna become also boosted his ego.

As they rode in silence to the spot, Monsta stayed on his phone texting a li'l shorty from the hood.

"What the hell you over there smiling about, boy?"

"Nothing, Pops. Just ready to handle this and get back on the block."

Monsta really wanted to hurry home to hook up with Nicole. She told him he could sneak over to her crib later that day because her mom would be at work. Being 13 and still a virgin got him clowned in his hood, and he was ready to change all that shit around.

Big Monsta kept driving as his son looked back at his phone. He was no dummy and could tell it must have been a girl involved. Ain't no way his young ass was cheesing over anything else but some pussy.

"Don't be in such a rush that you can't stay focused on what's going on in front of you. You my right hand, and I need you to be focused on business, not pussy. Trust me, that shit gon' come. And when it do, one or two things gon' happen. Either you gon' be a sucka for it, or you gon' learn to get it, then dip. In life, you not gon' love too many, but find you the one that's gon' have your back no matter what. Don't wife up no ho."

Monsta gave his dad a strange look as he wondered how he knew what was going on.

"I'm the man in these streets. I know everything," he answered before being asked.

Monsta shook his head with a grin on his face. "I'm focused, Dad."

"Don't just be focused on these streets, son. Watch these hoes too. And just like I tell you always, your ass better make sure you strap up in these streets and in that pussy," Big Monsta explained.

Pulling up in front of an old, run-down building, Big Monsta looked over at his son. "Hey, boy, put that phone up and get ready to handle this business."

Monsta set his phone down on his lap. "I'm ready, Pops. I just needed to check on something right quick."

Big Monsta got out of the car to talk business with two men that he'd done business with before. Monsta looked up from his phone and saw his father in a heated conversation with the men. He couldn't hear what they were saying, but he saw their hands moving around while they were talking. Getting back to texting Nicole, he never saw what happened next.

The loud gunshot made him jump and drop his phone. Monsta looked up and saw his father holding his chest as his body fell to the ground. Seeing one guy walk to-

ward the car with his gun still in hand alarmed Monsta. Jumping into action, he quickly pulled out the gun from under his seat and started busting out the window. Monsta was able to shoot the guy four times before his body dropped to the ground, and he was out of the car. Looking around to find the other guy was pointless because he had already dipped.

Quickly running to his pop's side, Monsta could see he was barely breathing.

"Pops, get up, man. You gon' be all right."

Big Monsta opened his mouth to say something, but the only thing that came out was blood. Monsta wasn't a crying-ass nigga, but seeing his pops dying in his arms tore him up.

"Come on, Pops, you can't leave me," he cried.

His father reached out to touch him before taking his last breath. Monsta cried and screamed out for his pops to return to him, but it was too late. From that day onward, Monsta became a different man. Someone everyone feared.

Snapping out of his daydream, Monsta wiped away his tears. He had spent many nights crying over his pop's death and blaming himself. Now that he was grown, he promised himself to never cry over the past again, but to make his father proud by keeping their names ringing hell in the streets.

Chapter 3

"Sunshine, why the fuck that ho Keisha keep calling you like that?" Monsta asked, looking at Keisha's name pop up on Sunshine's phone screen.

Sunshine pressed ignore on her phone. "I don't know. I really don't see why she even calling me after I been ignoring her ass since I been back over here with you."

Monsta gave her a strange look. He had to make sure his bullshit wasn't catching up with him. "Why are you ignoring her anyway?"

"'Cause that bitch was on some real bullshit, and I'm tired of it. I need a break from her, or maybe just drop that friendship altogether," Sunshine tried to explain as she brushed her hair.

Monsta nodded his head in agreement. "I been told you to stop fucking with that ho. You know muthafuckas think you freaked out like her."

"What?"

Monsta laughed. "Don't worry, I handled the nigga who said that shit," he said, placing a kiss on her lips.

Sunshine tried to look away. Knowing him, he probably was telling the truth and really did hurt somebody for speaking down on her. With him, sometimes you never knew if he was playing or dead serious.

"Bae, you really need to calm down. You can't be out here doing that shit while you got a baby on the way."

"Niggas gon' know not to cross me or my son. Just how muthafuckas feared my pops, they gon' fear me and my fuckin' son," he said, full of excitement.

"Hold up. Who said anything about it being a boy?"

Monsta stood up from the bed. "Shid, all that fucking work I be puttin' in, I be having your ass run up these fucking walls. It better be a boy," he jokingly said, laughing in her face.

"Whatever, boy," Sunshine said, laughing.

Monsta leaned over to kiss her. "You love this dick, don't you?"

Smiling, Sunshine quickly answered. "Yeah, boy, but more importantly, I love you."

Monsta gave her another kiss. "I love your bighead ass too."

They both laughed as he put on his shoes. That Saturday was his homie Lamar's birthday, and they planned on stopping by for a few. Usually, Sunshine didn't like being around his crowd, but he promised everybody would be on some chill shit and not on that bullshit. According to him, it will be more of a chill session for his friend.

"What you need that for if we just about to go chill?" Sunshine asked as she saw Monsta tuck a gun in his pants.

"Stay outta my business, baby."

Sunshine took a seat on the bed. "I told you I'm not going if all that shit gon' be going on."

Monsta laughed. "You know you full of shit, right? You act like I'm not the same nigga you fell in love with awhile back. I'm the same nigga who had you sneakin' outta the house to get that pussy tore up."

Sunshine giggled. "You so silly, boy. If I go, can you promise me you'll chill out and not hurt nobody today?"

Monsta pulled her up from the bed and wrapped her up in his arms. "I can't really make no promises, but I'ma try."

"I guess that's good enough, baby," she said, rolling her eyes.

As they drove to Lamar's house, Keisha kept blowing up Sunshine's phone.

"What the fuck that bitch want?"

"You see I haven't been answering her calls, so I don't know," Sunshine answered.

"I think you was over there lettin' that bitch eat your pussy or something. Now that you back with me, she calling 'cause she want some more of that sweet, juicy shit."

Although Monsta was laughing his ass off, Sunshine didn't find shit funny. "Don't fucking play with me. You know I'm not into bitches."

"Then why that bitch actin' like that? I know when I first tasted that muthafucka, my ass was hooked and called you like a junkie looking for its next fix. See, that's exactly what that bitch doin'."

Sunshine still wasn't laughing.

"Damn, baby, chill out. I was just playin' with yo' ass."

With a straight face, she responded, "Yeah, OK. Don't play with me like that."

"On some real shit, what the fuck happened?" he asked again.

Sunshine really didn't want to tell him because she knew he was going to nut up. He already spoke freely about not liking her, and he was just looking for a reason to drag her ass.

"Sunshine, I know you hear me talking to your ass."

"All right, dang. When I was over there, she had some nigga over there. When I woke up, he was standing over me, rubbing on me."

Monsta's face turned cold. "Oh, for real?" he asked with a smirk on his face.

"Yeah, but I handled it," she then said.

To her surprise, he took it better than she thought.

"How you handle it?"

"I went off on him."

"What you say to her?" he calmly asked.

"Nothing. Once he told me she sent him out there to get me, I got up to leave. That's why I've been ignoring her ass. She was on some bullshit," she explained.

"So, these two muthafuckas still alive?"

Sunshine shook her head. She knew it was only a matter of time before he went off.

"Yeah, baby."

"Then you didn't handle shit. You know if I see that bitch, I might stomp her head in."

Sunshine didn't say shit. She knew that if he even thought for a moment she wanted to defend Keisha, then he would have probably stomped her head in too. Monsta was a little too quiet for her. As much as she told him to be calm, he was *too* calm, and it scared her.

"Monsta, you all right?"

"Yeah. I'm just thinking about if I'm gon' use my right or left shoe to dent that bitch head in."

Sunshine hated that she even asked.

"Let me ask you a question."

"What's up, baby?"

"If you see the nigga again, would you be able to point his bitch ass out? I swear I got something for his ass too. Matter of fact, I got plans to bury them together."

Monsta didn't even wait for her to answer before he turned up his radio. Knowing that he and Keisha fucked around from time to time made him question what the hell was going through her mind trying to get Sunshine in bed with her and another dude. He was gon' beat that bitch ass real good whenever he saw her.

As they finally arrived at Lamar's house, Sunshine prayed there wouldn't be no shit. A yard full of street niggas was never a good sign. She prayed they all had a bitch on their side to keep them calm.

Monsta grabbed her hand as they walked toward the backyard. He loved to show her off. In his eyes, she was naturally beautiful. Most bitches in the hood didn't spend money on rent, bills, or even they own damn kids. All their money went toward hair weave and lashes. Not with Sunshine. She had a pretty-ass face with nice hair. She wore weave when she wanted to, but had a head full of hair. She was bad and all his, and he was willing to kill to keep shit that way. She often talked about working in a shop to do hair, but he wanted to prove to her that he could and would take care of her and their baby. He felt like she didn't need to do shit but have his baby and help him get his nut out every night.

As they entered the backyard, Monsta could see a few bitches rolling their eyes and turning up their noses. Not because he came, but because he brought Sunshine. He searched the party, giving them all the evil eye, letting them know he would show out if he had to. All who knew him knew he had no problems knocking a bitch out if she tried him.

For the most part, he didn't even have to worry about shit. Most of the bitches he hit wanted to fuck just to say they had their chance to have him. He never fucked outside of his relationship to make another bitch feel special. He didn't even give a fuck if they came or not. As long as he got his, he was good with that.

Monsta went over to speak to his boy Lamar as Sunshine went over to talk to Kyra. Out of all the hoes at the party, she was the coolest.

"Hey, Sunshine, I'm surprised your ass is out of the house. I be asking Monsta where the hell you be at."

Sunshine took a seat. "Girl, this baby be having me fucked up. I be in the house chilling, laid up, and watching TV."

"Oh my gawd, girl, tell me about it. When I was pregnant with my daughter, I stayed irritated and away from everybody. Everybody and they mama got on my damn nerves."

Both girls fell out laughing. Monsta turned around to see who had Sunshine laughing and shit. He was relieved to see she wasn't with a fake bitch, and Kyra's ass was holding her attention. He hated seeing her walk around the house with her face all turned up with attitude.

"What the hell y'all over here talking about?"

"Pregnancy and the different moods it can put you in," Sunshine answered.

Monsta looked Kyrah's way. "Is it something she can take to fix her attitude? Muthafuckas call me wild, but she the one," he jokingly said, pointing at Sunshine.

"Oh, trust me, I know. She fucks with you heavy, so I knew from jump she had to be wild to deal with your ass," Kyrah jokingly said.

Monsta kissed Sunshine on her forehead. "Aye, I'm about to run to the store right quick. You good?"

"Yeah, baby."

"She good," Kyrah added on.

Just that quick, Monsta walked away, not really liking Kyrah's ass anymore. He couldn't put his finger on it, but she was being a little too friendly, like she wanted some dick or something. Bitch was moving funny, so he took note to watch her ass.

Keisha walked in the backyard looking for a nigga she would leave with once the party was over. Although she wasn't really invited, she knew that if she wanted to afford her next shopping trip, it was time to find an easy trick. Looking around, she was surprised to see Sunshine chilling with that bitch Kyrah, kee-keeing and shit, when she had been trying to get ahold of her since she left her crib. She never minded sharing a nigga, but she wasn't the type of bitch to share her bestie.

"Oh, so your ass don't know how to answer your phone, but you can show your face at this bullshit?"

Kyrah and Sunshine both looked up to see Keisha standing there looking crazy.

Rolling her eyes, Kyrah stood up from the table. "Girl, don't be coming to my brother's house with all that."

Keisha rolled her eyes back, giving off major attitude. Kyrah then turned her attention back to Sunshine. "Let me go get another drink and leave you to deal with your little friend."

As Kyrah walked off, Sunshine stood up. There was something about the attitude on Keisha's face and the point that she was standing over her that bothered her the most. Pregnant or not, she would never let a bitch get one in on her.

"What's the problem?" Sunshine asked with just as much attitude.

"I'm just sayin' I know you saw I've been calling you. What shit you on, girl? You actin' fake as hell."

Sunshine shook her head. It was weird how Keisha acted like the bullshit she was on with that bum-ass nigga was normal. "First of all, I don't have to answer my phone for you."

"Girl, that baby must got you fucked up 'cause you trippin', for real, for real," Keisha said, trying to sound as if she were joking and downplaying the situation.

"No, you had me fucked up sending that bum-ass nigga to me as if I wanted to fuck a nigga that your nasty ass fucking on."

"Bitch, little do you know," Keisha said, laughing and walking away.

Sunshine was confused. "What the fuck is that supposed to mean?"

Keisha wanted to bust her bubble and fuck her whole world up by telling her she was one of many bitches fucking Monsta. She was never scared of Sunshine, but fearing Monsta's reaction, she decided to walk it off. Besides, she'd already said too much.

Sunshine started to follow Keisha, but seeing Monsta walking back in the yard made her stop in her tracks.

"Where you goin'?"

"I'm about to go beat this bitch ass," she said, trying to get past Monsta.

Monsta held her hand. "Calm down."

"Nah, fuck that bitch, but I'm sure you already doing that."

This time, when Monsta tried to grab her hand, she pulled away.

"Fuck you talkin' about?"

Sunshine stormed off. As much as she wanted to check his cheating ass, she also wanted to beat Keisha's ass first.

"So, you been fuckin' Monsta?" Sunshine yelled, following behind Keisha.

By now, everyone was walking out of the backyard to see what the hell was going on. Keisha set her purse on her car hood.

"Bitch, ask your man if we been fuckin'. Matter of fact, ask him about most of those hoes in that backyard."

Sunshine had a stupid look on her face.

"That's right, bitch. Your nigga for everybody," Keisha added on just to make sure Sunshine was hurt to the core.

Turning to face Monsta, Sunshine looked him straight in the eyes. "You fuckin' this funky bitch? The same bitch you clown every fuckin' day?"

Monsta played it cool, although he hated being caught up in some bullshit. Without giving Sunshine an answer, he slapped fire out of Keisha.

"Bitch, I told you about runnin' your fucking mouth. You the only bitch that got to be messy."

They didn't realize they had an audience until everyone started laughing at Monsta and calling him crazy.

"Hold up, do you hear what the fuck you saying, Monsta? You really been fucking this dirty bitch?"

Keisha stood back up, holding her face as Monsta and Sunshine started arguing.

"I'm sorry, Sunshine, but I told you from jump he wasn't shit," she cried, still holding her face.

"If he wasn't shit, why the fuck were you fuckin' him behind my back?"

Before Keisha could answer, Sunshine's fist connected with her face. She was tired of muthafuckas running over her and hurting her feelings. Yeah, she knew Keisha was a ho, but she never thought she would be creeping with Monsta, especially since they hated each other so much. At first, Monsta enjoyed watching Sunshine beat Keisha's ass over him, but when it crossed his mind that she was pregnant, he tried to grab Sunshine off Keisha.

"Come on, girl, you can't be out here fighting and shit while you pregnant."

As Monsta was pulling Sunshine off Keisha, Keisha decided to kick Sunshine in the stomach.

"Stupid bitch."

In a hot second and out of anger, Monsta stomped on Keisha's head before his boys pulled him away from her.

"Aye, bro, get off that bitch," Brandon yelled.

No matter what he did to Sunshine, he never wanted nothing bad to happen to his baby. Kyrah was there to help Sunshine get to her car and make sure she was all right.

"Oh my gawd, Sunshine, you can't be out here fighting and shit. You about to be somebody's mother."

Sunshine held her stomach as she cried. "I can't believe this shit. I was always loyal to him and a real friend to that bitch."

"Don't sweat that shit right now. You need to make sure that baby is all right. Fuck both of them."

Sunshine nodded her head in agreement. "You right. It just hurts so bad."

Brandon couldn't control Monsta by himself, so Lamar got up to help calm him down.

"Come on, dog, you can't be jumping on that bitch like that. Your ass gon' fuck around and kill her," Shawn said, trying to pull Monsta back inside the backyard so he could chill out.

Monsta snatched away. "I'll kill that bitch! She better hope and pray ain't shit wrong with my baby."

Monsta saw Kyrah getting in the driver's seat so she could leave with Sunshine. Racing to the car, he held the car door open to stop them from leaving.

"Baby, you good?"

"Are you fucking serious, Monsta? Get the fuck outta my face and go play with that bitch," Sunshine snapped, slamming the car door.

Monsta opened the car door. "Get the fuck outta the car."

"Get away from me, Monsta. I swear, I'm so done with your ass."

Monsta hated how Sunshine stayed trying his gangsta. He never took shit from nobody, but her ass stayed playing him. He knew it was time to start treating her like a regular bitch if she wanted to act like one.

"All right then, bitch. Come get all your shit outta my crib."

Sunshine's mouth dropped.

"What the fuck you looking stupid for? If you ain't with me, bitch, you for the streets like that bitch Keisha."

Sunshine put her head down to cry some more. His words hurt her feelings, but maybe it was time to leave his crazy ass alone. Raising her baby was all she needed to be worried about. Kyrah felt bad for Sunshine and hated how she sat there crying over Monsta's words. Instead of staying there, watching him give Sunshine the death stare, she started her car and drove off.

"Stupid bitch," Monsta yelled out as they drove off.

He tried to act like he didn't give a fuck, but deep down inside, he wanted his baby back. Sunshine was the only bitch he ever loved for real.

"Aye, bro, you good?"

Monsta looked up to see Lamar standing next to him. "My bad for fucking up your party, but you act like you don't know who I am. I keep me a bitch."

Lamar gave him dap, then walked off. No matter what Monsta said, he knew that nigga was butt hurt over Sunshine leaving his ass.

Not in the mood to be around anyone, Monsta jumped in his truck and drove off.

"What you gon' do, Sunshine?" Kyrah asked.

"I didn't want to do this, but I think I need to call my mom and see if I can go home," she mumbled.

Thinking back to the day she left her mama's house, she remembered telling her mom she didn't need her and that she didn't even want her around her baby. Now, she needed her mama's love more than ever.

Kyrah drove around, giving Sunshine time to gather her thoughts and rearrange her life. It was fucked up how Monsta did her, but he'd always been a dog-ass nigga. That's why everyone was shocked when he got with Sunshine awhile back. He was known in the streets for fucking bitches and never wife'ing them up.

Sunshine pulled her phone out of her bag. "I'm not sure how this gon' work out."

"Just put your pride to the side and make that call. At the end of the day, your mom don't wanna see you and that baby on the streets. If you serious about not fucking with Monsta, make that call, but don't get her involved if you gon' get right back with him."

Sunshine took in her advice but was still unsure what she really wanted. She wanted to be free, but she loved that man. Yeah, he played her and made her look like a fool in front of everyone, but she couldn't just turn her heart off that quickly.

"What you thinkin' about? You gon' go back to his ass?" Kyrah questioned.

"I love him, Kyrah, and I'm carrying his baby. I'm so confused about everything."

Kyrah had once been a dummy in love, so she knew the exact feelings Sunshine was going through. Getting over a nigga that you genuinely love is hard, but she did it. She was pretty sure Sunshine was strong enough to live without Monsta.

Sunshine dialed her mom's number, but before she could actually make the call, Monsta FaceTimed her.

"What do you want?"

Monsta was grinning like everything was normal, but he was hurting deep down inside.

"When you coming to get your shit?"

Sunshine thought he was going to apologize and make her feel loved so that she could come back home to him, but he was on some other shit.

"I'm on my way now," she said before hanging up in his face.

Sunshine put her head down, trying to fight her tears. Monsta really hurt her by cheating and pretending she was the one in the wrong for being hurt and in her feelings.

"So, you about to go get your stuff?"

"Yeah. If you drop me off, I'll be good from there."

Kyrah shook her head. "Oh, hell nah. I'm not about to leave you over there with his ass. There's no telling what he gon' do."

"He not gon' hurt me and this baby. I'll be good. I'm gon' have my mama come pick me up once I'm done packing."

Stopping at a stop sign, Kyrah looked at Sunshine. "You sure you gon' be all right?"

"Yeah, I'm sure," Sunshine said even though she wasn't really sure.

The rest of the ride was quiet as each young lady was lost in their thoughts. It didn't take long before Kyrah was pulling up to Monsta's house.

"Now, you sure you good before I leave you here?" Kyrah asked, still concerned.

"Yeah. He might be crazy, but he not like that with me for real," Sunshine assured her.

Monsta stood in the doorway watching Sunshine get out of the car. He'd already told himself that if Kyrah didn't drive off, he was gon' act a fool and make her not want to help Sunshine with anything. He hated how people got in his business, like he wasn't about that life.

"Took you long enough. I was just about to throw all that bullshit away," he said, opening the screen door for her to step in.

Sunshine didn't want to argue with him. After all the bullshit she just went through, she really just wanted to be at peace. Walking into the bedroom, she noticed he had already started throwing her clothes out of the drawers and closet.

"Why would you throw my shit on the floor?" she questioned.

"'Cause you ain't shit," he said, taking a seat on the bed.

Sunshine started picking up her clothes and stuffing them in a bag. She wanted to go off on Monsta, but she knew that was all he wanted. What she didn't understand was why he was acting out when *he* was the one cheating with Keisha.

"How the fuck you gon' play me in front of my people? Do I fuckin' look like one of those goofy-ass niggas you used to fuck with?"

He was trying his hardest to get her to say something so that he could have a reason to act a fool.

"Bitch, you keep actin' like you don't hear me, and I'ma get up and show you the *real* reason they call me Monsta."

Sunshine finally turned to face him. "You cheated and got caught. What the fuck do you want me to say?"

Standing up, Monsta jumped in her face. "You know I'm not gon' let you leave, right?"

"Monsta, get outta my face. If you really loved me like you say you do, then you wouldn't have been fucking my best friend."

"I told you that bitch wasn't your friend from jump. You actin' all extra for nothing," he said, trying to take the blame off himself again.

Sunshine shook her head. "Just get outta my way so I can finish packing my shit," she said, pushing him away.

Monsta stood there for a second just watching her pack her clothes up. He was thinking of what he could say to make her stay with him. "I love you, Sunshine."

With much attitude, she responded, "No, the fuck you don't. You love all these rat-ass hoes that be on your dick just because you known in these streets."

"Fuck all those hoes. I only want you."

Sunshine went back to getting her shit together. She tried so hard not to fall for his shit. Monsta was good at sweet-talking her into forgiving him, but this time, he had really crossed the line.

"I'm dead-ass serious, Sunshine. I only wanna be with your ass," he said, deep in his feelings.

"Fuck you, Monsta."

Monsta snatched her up, then tossed her against the wall. *"Fuck me?* Bitch, I'm sitting here tellin' you how much I love you, and you really gon' say, 'fuck me'?" he yelled, slamming her head back into the wall.

Sunshine had tears in her eyes; she was scared. The look in his eyes told her he was pissed enough to really hurt her.

"Monsta, let me go. You're scaring me," she cried.

Pissed off, he gripped her shirt and pulled her up, just to slam her head back on the wall for the third time. "I'm not about to let you leave me. I fucked up, and I'm sorry about that shit. You know that was just a fuck. Won't no feelings in that shit."

"That don't make it right. You crazy as hell if you think I'm about to stay here with you. You got bitches. Have one of them move in with you."

Sunshine didn't realize how much she was hurting his feelings and ego. Monsta slammed her head against the wall again. This time, harder.

"You need to stop playing with me," he warned her.

He was trying his hardest not to knock her ass out, but she needed to know he was running shit. Monsta started kissing Sunshine's neck before he kissed her lips.

"I love you, and I can't let you go. You gon' be mine forever," he whispered in her ear between kisses.

Tears rolled down her checks as he kissed and touched on her body. She hated being so weak for this man, but he was making her feel so damn good. Monsta continued to work his magic on Sunshine. Her soft moans let him know she wasn't going anywhere.

"I love you, girl."

Sunshine didn't respond. Instead, she pushed him off her. "I can't do this shit no more. I don't wanna be in this toxic shit anymore. It's too toxic and unhealthy for us and the baby."

"You fuckin' somebody else?"

Sunshine was confused. "What the fuck are you talking about?"

"You trying to leave me while you pregnant? That shit makes me feel like that ain't my baby."

"You the one who told me to leave, so that's exactly what the fuck I'm gon' do. You puttin' your hands on me, then telling me you love me ain't gon' work this time."

Monsta let go of her shirt. As he paced the floor, Sunshine grabbed the rest of her clothes. He wasn't sure what to do, but he knew for sure he wasn't about to let her leave.

Now, Sunshine pulled out her phone so she could talk to her mama about coming back home.

"Hey, Ma," she softly said into the phone.

Monsta wasn't sure what her mama was saying, but he knew she better had not pull up to his house.

"Ma, I'm so sorry about everything. I really need to come home," she cried into the phone.

Monsta stopped pacing the floor and stood right in her face.

"OK, Ma. I'll be ready, and thank you so much," she said before putting her phone back in her bag.

Without warning, Monsta slapped her hard across the left side of her face. "I told you yo' ass ain't about to leave me."

Sunshine cried as she held her throbbing face.

"I don't give a fuck about all that crying, bitch. You sayin', 'fuck my feelings.' You trying to leave and just forget about me. I swear to God I'll kill your ass before I let you walk outta my life," he yelled in her face.

Sunshine just stood there crying, too scared to make a move. All she could think about was how her mother told her he wasn't the right one for her. Now she was pregnant with his baby, and he was tripping.

"Monsta, you the one who told me to get out. Do you remember?"

Frustrated, he punched the wall behind her, making her scream and jump.

"You're scaring me," Sunshine yelled out, still crying.

Monsta started grabbing her clothes and throwing them back in the dresser drawer.

"What are you doing?"

"You not leavin' me," was all he said.

Sunshine remembered his mom telling her about his breakdowns, and now she could say she'd seen it for herself. Scared to make a move, she stood there watching him put all her clothes back in place. He was known for being "off," and this right here was all the proof Sunshine needed.

Once Monsta was done, he started walking toward her. She looked in his eyes and could tell he wasn't himself. He was the man everyone feared.

"You not goin' nowhere. I don't give a fuck what I said. I told you before, you gon' be mine forever."

He tried to kiss her, but she turned her head. She wasn't over the fact that he smacked her. Everything about that day was off. Monsta was tired of playing games with her ass. Plus, he hated it when someone played with his feelings, especially someone he loved.

"You got me fucked up," he said, grabbing her face and making sure they kissed this time.

Sunshine tried to push him off her, which only made him even more upset. Tightening the grip on her neck, he tossed her onto the bed.

"You gon' stop playing with me."

He struggled to pull up her dress because she was fighting him. After learning he had been cheating on her, she didn't want his dick nowhere near her.

"Oh, for real? I can't get none?" he asked, standing up from the bed.

Sunshine tried to get up, but Monsta quickly turned around from his dresser, holding his gun.

"Fuck you think you goin'? Lay your bitch ass back down."

Sunshine wiped away her tears as she followed his order. "Monsta, you don't have to do this. Baby, put the gun down before it goes off."

Monsta set the gun down, but only so he could undress. "Take that shit off."

Sunshine was confused about this situation. She couldn't believe the man she loved was actually trying to force her to have sex with him. She didn't want no parts with him, and this was rape.

"Monsta, I don't want you. I told you I was done with you," she cried out.

He picked up his gun again, and Sunshine scooted back on the bed. She was scared, and he knew it. He had her right where he wanted her.

"Baby, I don't want to hurt you. I'm just trying to make love to you. I told you I was sorry about fuckin' with Keisha and any other bitch."

Sunshine cried as he started pulling at her dress, forcing her to help him take it off. She knew this wasn't right. She needed to get away from him before he fucked around and killed her for real.

"Monsta, please. If you really love me, you'd put down the gun."

"Take off them panties," he said with the gun still pointed at her head.

Sunshine was scared out of her mind, but she listened. As she undressed, besides crying, all she could do was pray the gun didn't go off.

Monsta placed the gun down on the bed before placing himself between her legs. Although he was smiling while making love to Sunshine, she lay there, not showing any interest in what was going on. She was hurt and couldn't believe he was enjoying what he was doing to her. She hated him for his actions. If that gun weren't close by, she would have run far away from his ass.

Monsta stopped grinding for a second. "Damn, bae, you that mad? That muthafucka not getting wet for me or nothing."

Before she could respond, he was already working his way down to lick on her pussy. Sunshine hated how weak she was. Not even a whole two minutes, and she was already moaning out and pulling his head closer. Monsta couldn't help but smirk. They were each other's weakness. Whenever she got to talking that bullshit about leaving him, all he had to do was eat and fuck her good.

"I love you, baby," he whispered in her ear as he slowly fucked her.

Wrapping her legs around his waist, Sunshine moaned out, "I love you too, Monsta."

"You know we in this shit together, forever. I can't let no other nigga have you or even get a chance to have a piece of your heart."

Sunshine nodded her head in agreement. "I don't want nobody else but you, Monsta. Just love me right."

"I'm trying, baby. I swear I'm trying so hard. Just give me some more time. I'm gon' get it together. I can't lose you, Sunshine. I'd kill us all in this bitch before I let you walk outta that door."

Sunshine flipped back over on her stomach so she could enjoy the back shots he loved to give her. She was so caught up in the strokes Monsta was giving her that she missed her mama's call. Luckily for her, she called right back, believing her daughter was in trouble.

"Monsta, I gotta answer that. It's my mama."

"Fuck her. We busy anyway, and I'm not about to let her take you away from me."

Sunshine placed a kiss on his lips. "I'm not going nowhere, baby. At least let me tell her everything's OK, and I'm not going nowhere."

Monsta rolled off Sunshine so she could get her phone.

"Hey, Ma," Sunshine said in a shaky voice.

By this time, Ms. Mathews had an attitude because she'd been calling her daughter and hadn't gotten an answer. "Come outside. I'm here. Or do I need to come in?"

Sunshine looked over and could see out of the corner of her eye that Monsta had put on his shorts and now had his gun back in his hands. Even if she wanted to leave for real, he was gon' try to kill her and her mama.

"It's all up to you how this shit ends. I told you already where I stand on the situation," Monsta said, staring straight in her eyes.

Walking back toward the bed, Sunshine placed a kiss on Monsta. "Ma, I'm sorry for even calling you with my mess. I'm not ready to come home."

Monsta snatched the phone, then placed it on speakerphone. Just knowing her mama hated him and talked crazy always excited him.

"Sunshine, I can tell you were crying and upset when you called. I don't care about none of the bullshit that happened before. If you wanna come home, bring your ass outside."

Sunshine tried not to start crying. "Ma, I promise I'm good," she lied.

"Sunshine, I know shit not right in that house. Do I have to come in there to get you my damn self?" Monsta smiled. "Sunshine, do you fucking hear me? Do I need to come in there to get you?" Ms. Mathews yelled into the phone.

Monsta took over the conversation since Sunshine was back on that crying shit. "Nah, ma, she good here with me. You know I'm gon' make sure her and my baby good."

"You stupid muthafucka. Don't fucking play with me. Let my daughter go."

Monsta laughed. "I'm not gon' lie to you. She's free to go if she wants to. Matter of fact, walk in this muthafuckin' house and get her."

Sunshine looked up and watched as he set the phone down on the bed before getting his shotgun out of the closet. Monsta picked up the phone just to hand it back to Sunshine.

"Sunshine, tell yo' mama to come in this bitch."

"No, Ma. Please, just leave," she yelled when she realized he was gonna kill her mama.

"I don't know what bullshit y'all got going on in that damn house, Sunshine, but I'm not about to play games with you or that stupid bastard. Call me when you *really* ready to leave his ass."

With that being said, Ms. Mathews drove off, pissed for even wasting her time. She wanted to be in her daughter's corner whenever she called, but she didn't have time to play with her and Monsta. As she drove off, she had no idea how close she was to seeing just how crazy her daughter's boyfriend could get.

"Monsta, were you really gon' kill my mama?" Sunshine asked, scared to know the truth.

He laughed. "Nah, but if an intruder walked in this bitch, I was gon' be ready for whatever."

"You gotta stop this shit, Monsta. I told you I wasn't leaving. You gotta calm down and put up these guns."

"I'm calm, but don't ever tell a muthafucka to pull up over here. If anything had popped off, it would have been all on you. I told yo' ass I wasn't gon' let nobody come between me, you, and my fuckin' baby. Y'all mine, and this the last time I'm gon' talk about it."

Grabbing the shotgun, Monsta gave Sunshine a kiss before putting it back into the closet. He didn't really want to hurt anybody, but now that she knew he wasn't playing, he didn't have to worry about her trying to leave or having nobody to come get her.

She reached for her phone again, but Monsta snatched it from her. "Fuck you doin'?"

"Nothing, baby. I was about to take a shower. I wanted to hook my phone up to the speaker," she explained.

Monsta slammed the phone down on the floor before stomping on it. "Don't play me, Sunshine."

"Baby, you gotta calm down. If I wanted to leave, I would have left or said fuck my shit and had Kyrah take me straight to my mama's house. You gotta trust me, baby."

Monsta sat on the bed, feeling like he was going crazy. He loved Sunshine with everything in him, and now that she'd shown she was there for him, he didn't know how to act. Sometimes, his thoughts scared even him.

"I trust you, baby. It's these other muthafuckas I don't trust. You got too many muthafuckas in your ear, trying to pull you away from me."

"Let these folks talk, baby. At the end of the day, I'm here with you."

Monsta stood up from the bed. "You right. Now, go run the water so we can get in the shower."

Chapter 4

A good two weeks passed, and the couple was on good terms. Sunshine was happy and could see that Monsta was really trying his best to treat her better. He still went out and handled his business, but he made sure to spend time with her too. Sunshine was fully back in love with him. Monsta loved walking into the house to see his baby waiting for him with a huge smile on her face. Since the last time he cut up and smashed her phone, things had been going well. She didn't have muthafuckas in her ear, and he enjoyed having her to himself.

"You nervous?" Monsta asked.

Today was the day they'd been waiting for. They had an appointment to find out their baby's gender.

"Nah, I'm not. How about you?"

"Fuck I gotta be nervous for? I told you from jump it was a boy. I need somebody to take over once I'm gone," Monsta said confidently.

Sunshine laughed. "Whatever. I can't wait to hold my baby girl."

"Stop playing with me, Sunshine. I swear, if it's a girl, I'm leaving your ass here at this doctor's office until they fix it."

Sunshine was really laughing now, which made him laugh too.

"I'm glad you think shit so funny. Yo' ass gon' be laughing all the way to the bus stop."

Before Sunshine could say anything, the nurse was calling them to the back.

"It's showtime. Bring yo' ass on."

Sunshine couldn't help but laugh at how excited he was. He acted like his mama ain't already tell them it was a little girl. Everybody knew them grandmas be knowing the situation before the doctors and parents did.

Monsta stood there watching the doctor rub over Sunshine's stomach after squeezing that gel shit on it. He couldn't help but get worried as she pressed her belly.

"You pushin' kind of hard. That's not gon' hurt my baby, is it?"

"Oh no, Dad. I'm not hurting your little one at all. Right now, I'm getting some measurements out of the way so I can tell you guys the gender if you wanna know. I know nowadays it's a thing to have a gender reveal, so I like to ask before I tell."

Monsta was all smiles. "Yeah, we wanna know. We wishin' for a boy."

"No, we not. I promise you this a girl just like your mama said."

The room fell silent as the doctor took her measurements. As Monsta watched his baby on the screen, he knew he was gonna love his seed with everything in him. One thing he knew was that he would never walk out on his girl or baby.

"OK, happy parents, are you guys ready to find out the sex of your baby?"

"Yeah," they said in unison.

They were growing impatient as the doctor took her time going over Sunshine's growing belly.

"You playin'. What you see?" Monsta snapped.

"Monsta, calm down and let her do her job," Sunshine said, giving him a crazy look.

"My bad. I'm just so excited about this."

Dr. Ahmad didn't pay him any mind. "OK, you guys are going to be the proud parents of a beautiful baby girl."

"I told you, baby."

Monsta's smile left his face, but only for a quick moment. "Man, I just knew it was a boy."

He then turned his attention back toward the doctor. "Aye, you sure that's a girl?"

"Yes, I'm sure," Dr. Ahmad said, handing him a pink envelope containing the ultrasound pictures of their baby girl.

After getting cleaned up, Sunshine climbed off the table to fix her clothes. "You ready, baby?"

Monsta stood there just looking at the picture of his daughter. Sunshine could tell he was in his feelings.

"You all right, Monsta?"

He turned her way, then grabbed her neck. For a minute, she was terrified and wondered what she had done wrong. That was, until he pulled her in for a passionate kiss.

"I love you so much, and I really appreciate you giving me a baby."

"Baby, you don't have to thank me. Our daughter was made out of love. She's a gift for the two of us," she replied.

After leaving the doctor's office, Monsta stopped to get them something to eat.

"I can't wait to get home to eat and take a long nap."

Monsta looked her way with a smirk on his face. "Don't think I forgot about our bet. I should drop your ass off at the bus stop."

"Whatever. I saw a tear in your eyes when you were staring at that ultrasound picture. You happy about that baby girl?"

"Yeah, you right, I'm happy. I just hope she's as beautiful as you, but thugged out like her daddy. My daughter can't be no punk-ass crybaby like you."

"Whatever, Monsta. I'm not a crybaby. I just be in my feelings when I know I deserve better," she explained.

Before turning up his music, Monsta shook his head, then mumbled, "Crybaby ass."

Hearing her son pull up, Ms. Caldwell ran to the door. All she wanted to hear was that she was right about having a granddaughter on the way. She prayed she was right, hoping this would soften Monsta's ass up just a little. Seeing him help Sunshine out of the truck put a smile on her face. She can say that lately, he'd been acting like he had some fucking sense. She loved the way he treated Sunshine now, but couldn't help but wonder when he would go back to the old him. If he were really like his daddy, he was a time bomb waiting for the time least expected to explode.

"So, what'd the doctor say?"

"Damn, Ma, let us get in the door good."

Sunshine walked in with a huge smile on her face. "You were right. It's a girl."

Ms. Caldwell hugged Sunshine before walking over to her son. As she hugged him, she whispered in his ear. "I'm so proud of you. Do right by your daughter."

"I am, Ma. I love my baby with everything in me, and she ain't even here yet."

"That's so sweet, Monsta," Sunshine added.

"Y'all got this one, but I promise, I'm putting about four more in you, and they all gon' be boys."

Sunshine looked at him like he was crazy. "I think the fuck not. Who about to have all those kids?"

Monsta took a seat to eat. "For every girl, you owe me four boys. So, if I were you, I'd get that shit together."

Ms. Caldwell playfully pushed her son. "Boy, you is something else. Be happy she gave you that one."

"Shid, she ain't have no choice."

Sunshine fixed her mouth to say something back, but his phone went off again. She watched as he ignored the call, then picked up his fork to finish eating. She tried to ignore it the first few times, but her curiosity was killing her as the calls came in.

"Who is that, Monsta?"

Turning his phone on silent, he glanced up at her with a crazy look on his face. "I don't know."

"How the fuck you don't know, and they keep calling you?"

"Come on, y'all two, don't start this shit. This house been quiet for just about a month now," Ms. Caldwell said as she sat at the table texting her brother. She could feel that some bullshit was about to jump off, and he was needed.

Monsta kept eating, trying to ignore Sunshine. He really wasn't even in the mood to go there with her ass.

"Monsta, give me the phone," Sunshine demanded.

"Get the fuck on with that bullshit, Sunshine. Finish feeding my baby and chill out."

Acting out like him, Sunshine stood up to snatch his phone out of his hand. "Really? So, you still keeping in touch with this bitch?" she yelled, seeing Keisha's number across the screen.

"Nah. To be honest, I haven't even talked to the bitch," he said nonchalantly.

"Y'all need to cut that shit out," Ms. Caldwell yelled out.

"Nah, fuck that. He needs to tell me why this bitch still calling his phone after I already beat her ass a month ago," Sunshine yelled.

Monsta grabbed his dick. "Why the fuck you think she still calling? What else do you think she want?"

"So, shit funny, nigga?"

Monsta put down his fork. He tried to be calm, but he couldn't just sit there and let her yell in his face, especially when he really ain't been doing shit wrong. Since their last argument, he'd been good to her and even came home at a decent time every night.

"Look, muthafucka, you got my phone in your hand. Can't you see I haven't even been talking to her? Every call from her is a fucking missed call. That bitch ain't got shit I want."

It was Sunshine's time to act out because she was sick of his bullshit, and in a way, she felt threatened by Keisha. Jumping up from the table, Sunshine disappeared into the room before quickly returning. Swaddling his lap, she pulled his gun out on him.

"You still fucking with that dirty bitch?"

"Look, I'm giving you a fair chance to start all over. Now, go put my gun back 'cause I swear, if that bitch goes off, Jesus Christ himself won't be able to save you," Monsta calmly said.

Sunshine wanted to scare him so badly the way he frightened her, but he just didn't give a fuck about the role she was playing.

"Come on, Sunshine, we get the point. You tired of his shit, but you need to put that gun away. You know, like anyone else, that he don't play these type of games."

Sunshine started to cry. "I'm so sick of him lying to me about these other bitches and just doing me any kind of way."

Ms. Caldwell understood where she was coming from, but she still stood by her son's side. "Look, Sunshine, put that gun down and just leave. He'll still help you with the baby, but leave if it's to the point you wanna pull out guns and shit."

Sunshine couldn't believe her. She'd been around and heard everything that went on between them. Now, she was trying to blame her.

"He started this gun shit the day he jumped on me and raped me while holding this same gun to my head."

Now, Ms. Caldwell was all confused. "What?"

"You ain't gotta get into all that. Just put that gun up. Matter of fact, for your safety, keep it because soon as you drop that bitch, I'm fucking you up. You wanna be treated like a regular bitch so bad, I'm about to show you how those hoes get treated," he warned.

Sunshine kept a grip on the gun, but the sound of someone walking in the door made her lose focus.

"Bitch!" Monsta yelled as he slapped blood out of Sunshine's mouth.

Ms. Caldwell and her brother, who was walking into the house at the time, tried to grab him. But when Sunshine spat a mouthful of blood on him, they couldn't control him. He was like a wild beast attacking her. Dwayne was usually able to calm his nephew down, but that day, Monsta gave him a run for his money. It took everything in his power to pull him off Sunshine.

"Go get your ass in the car, boy!" Dwayne yelled as he tried to pull Monsta out the door.

"Let me go. I finna kill that bitch," he yelled, trying to get his hands back on Sunshine.

Ms. Caldwell helped Sunshine get up from the floor. Looking at her face, she actually felt bad for the girl. "His uncle got him out of the house for a minute. If I were you, I'd use this time to leave. I was only mean because I didn't want you to be comfortable here. You and my son need to part ways. Can't you see he's not right for you?"

Sunshine was crying so hard she couldn't even get her thoughts together enough to speak. After helping her into the room and getting her a warm towel for her face,

Ms. Caldwell started grabbing her clothes and placing them in her bag.

"You still have Monsta's phone?"

Sunshine nodded.

"Call your mama, girl, and tell her to come get you now before he gets back."

Although Sunshine's whole body was in pain, she managed to do as told.

"What the fuck you want, stupid-ass boy?" Ms. Mathews yelled into the phone, expecting Monsta to be on the other end of the line.

"Ma, it's me. Please come get me," Sunshine cried into the phone.

"I don't have time for this shit, Sunshine. I'm not about to come over there just for you to stay with that nigga. It's a waste of my time *and* my damn gas."

"Ma, please come get me before he gets back. If I'm still here when he gets back, he gon' kill me," she whispered into the phone.

Hearing that alerted her, and she was rushing out of the house, ready to get her daughter away from his crazy ass. Never hanging up, Sunshine cried and rushed her mom to hurry the whole time.

"Ma, where you at now? I'm really scared," she cried.

"I'm coming, baby. Mama's coming. I'm almost there."

Ms. Caldwell grabbed Sunshine's bag. "Come on, Sunshine, let me help you get out of this damn house."

As they made their way into the living room, Ms. Caldwell hugged Sunshine. "Listen, I don't care if you never fuck with Monsta again, but don't keep me out of this baby's life."

Sunshine nodded her head in agreement just as her mama pulled up and jumped out of the car.

"Sunshine, you all right?" she asked before her daughter turned around with a face full of tears and bruises. For a second, the sight of all the blood frightened her.

"Get that girl away from this house before he gets back."

Ms. Mathews grabbed her daughter's bag and helped her get into the car. For a moment, she couldn't even drive away. All she could do was hold her daughter.

"I love you so much, Sunshine. Lord knows I shouldn't have let you leave with that boy."

"Ma, just get me away from here before he come back. I don't want him to kill me."

Hearing the fear in her baby girl's voice made Ms. Mathews break down in tears. She hated that her daughter was around a muthafucka who scared her so much.

Pulling up to the emergency room, Ms. Mathews killed her engine. "Come on, Sunshine. Let's go in here and let these doctors take a look at you."

Sunshine took the towel off her face to look around. "Ma, no."

"What you mean, girl? You and that baby were attacked by his crazy ass, so let's make sure y'all are OK."

"No! Please just take me home. I can't let him find out I was here. He gon' think I was telling on him," Sunshine cried.

"You gotta stop protecting him and get his bitch ass locked up for what he did to you."

Sunshine continued to cry. "Ma, that's just gon' make shit worse. If the police go to his house, he not gon' go without a fight. They will kill him, Ma."

"Good, now, get out of the car."

Sunshine understood her concern for her and the baby, but she just wanted to go home without getting the police involved. She knew how much he hated the police, and in her eyes, he would really hurt her if she told on him. There won't be shit they could do to stop him from touching her.

Ms. Mathews walked into the emergency room without her daughter but returned with a nurse pushing a wheelchair, and the two officers who were on duty that afternoon.

The officer opened the passenger door. "Ma'am, can this nurse take you in to check on you and your baby?"

Sunshine was scared, and with each teardrop, she felt like she was digging herself deeper in a grave. "I just wanna go home."

The nurse helped her out of the car and into the wheelchair. "I promise, after making sure you and the baby are all right, we'll let you go home."

Sunshine felt a little better after hearing that.

While the nurse examined Sunshine, her mom tried to talk to the police about Monsta and what he did to her daughter. The problem with that was that Sunshine refused to say anything to them about him. It pissed off her mom, but she tried her hardest to understand the mindset her daughter was in.

"Ma, I can't believe you let her leave me," Monsta said, not realizing that he was wrong.

Ms. Caldwell was tired of trying to explain herself to his ass. "You damn near beat that baby out of that girl. She don't need to be around you right now."

"Just tell me who came to get her, so I can go get her and bring my baby back to me."

Dwayne was tired of all the bullshit. "What you need to do is go lay your ass down somewhere, and let that girl be. I can't believe what I saw today. You need to be ashamed of yourself."

Ms. Caldwell had a smirk on her face, happy somebody was finally getting in his ass.

He turned his attention to her. "I don't know why you smirkin'. I'm pretty sure this shit been going on, and your ass just now calling me to handle him."

"I thought I had it under control, Dwayne, but you know how he can get. He's just like his damn daddy."

Monsta stood up from the couch. "I really don't want to hear this shit right now. I just want my babies back here with me."

"You just beat the shit out of that girl. Do you really think she wanna be around your ass right now? One minute, y'all was happy about having a baby girl. Then the next, you tryin'a kill her and that baby. Let her be, Monsta."

He stuck to his story about not wanting to hear shit else they had to say. He quietly walked into his room, slamming the door behind him. When he used to say nobody understood him, he meant that shit. Sunshine was the only one close enough to his heart who understood that he acted out when his feelings were hurt.

As he lay across the bed, it dawned on him that she still had his phone. He now knew how he was gon' get in contact with her. Getting up to look through his top drawer, Monsta pulled out his trap phone. After the third ring, he heard Sunshine's voice answer the phone.

"Hello," she mumbled into the phone. She didn't recognize the number and only answered, thinking it was a bitch calling for Monsta.

Monsta knew that if he started talking, she might hang up, so he stayed quiet.

"Hello?" she repeated into the phone.

Monsta still didn't say shit. Although she pissed him off, he now blamed himself for everything that happened that day. For a quick second, he wanted to hang up to give her a chance to move on, but his selfishness and pride couldn't picture life without her.

"Look, if this one of Monsta's bitches, go find something else to do. Y'all bitches kill me chasing after this nigga like y'all don't know he keep his face buried in my ass. I'm starting to think y'all hoes just wanna fuck me at this point."

Monsta hung up. When she did shit like that, it always made him laugh because she was crazy too. How could he still not love her?

Sunshine slid the phone back under her pillow. Now she was pissed off again. For one, she hated being stuck in the hospital. And two, she just went off on a bitch over a man she couldn't be with, stressing her baby out. Thanks to her and Monsta's bullshit, the doctors thought it would be a good idea to keep her there for a few days.

Lying there, she had time to think about her life. Here she was, just months away from bringing another human being into the world, and she still didn't have her shit together. She knew that if push came to shove, she had to figure out how she'd take care of her and her daughter without Monsta. She never wanted to be a single mother, but it was time for her to grow up and handle her business. No more living off Monsta's street money.

Over the next few days, Monsta tried to keep his cool without Sunshine, but he found himself driving past her mama's house daily, praying to catch her walking out the door or something. He even tried to tell himself that if he did see her, he wasn't gon' try to force her to come back to him. He told himself he could live with just seeing her and knowing she and his daughter were all right.

Every day that Monsta couldn't hold Sunshine was another day he didn't speak to his mom. Now, his mind was telling him that no matter what Sunshine did or how he reacted, it was his mama's fault for letting her walk out the door.

"You still not talking to me, boy?" Ms. Caldwell asked, standing in his doorway.

He sat there, lost in his thoughts for a second, before looking up. "I think you need to get outta my face and go get my girl."

"You bein' upset and acting out ain't gon' bring her back. Give her some time to get her life in order. She'll be back if it was meant to be."

"What the fuck you talkin' about, Ma? She had her life together here with me."

"Keep telling yourself that bullshit if you want to. That whole relationship was toxic as fuck. You stayed cheating, bring all types of bitches up in here, and then wanna play house when you knocked up her ass. If she still stuck on stupid, she'll be back. Hopefully, she'll learn to love herself and that baby more than she loved you."

"If you done, get the hell outta my room."

Ms. Caldwell turned to walk out.

"Muthafucka," Monsta yelled before throwing his shoe at her.

"That's why that girl gone now, crazy ass."

Ms. Caldwell went back into the living room with her brother.

"I blame you for all this shit."

Lighting her cigarette, she gave him a crazy look. "And how is that?"

"You know that boy not all there in the head, and you keep going in there to let him know he's fucked up in the head, and that girl ain't coming back. You should've been got his ass some real help. While he was growing up, your ass sat back collecting those crazy checks for him but never tried to get him the proper help he needed. Now look at him," Dwayne tried to explain.

"Why the fuck you ain't let him stay with you then, since you care so fucking much?"

"'Cause you and Big Monsta raised that boy to believe he didn't have to answer to anybody. That boy ain't really start listening to me until his daddy was killed. If I knew he was gonna be this bad, I would have got him from your ass."

"Whatever. Everyone walked out on my son when his daddy died. I couldn't handle him, and yeah, I let him do whatever the fuck he wanted to do just to keep the peace in the house," she yelled in her feelings.

Dwayne stood up from the couch. "Let me get the fuck from here before you go and piss me off."

"You go and do that then. I got my son like I been had him, without any fucking help."

Walking out the door, Dwayne mumbled, "And that's why he fucked up now."

Monsta appeared in the doorway. "Ma, you know I'll put that nigga on his neck if you want me to."

"No, baby, that's all right. Just let him leave and be on his way. We don't need him over here in our business anyway."

Chapter 5

"Sunshine, you all right in here?"

Sunshine turned around to face her mama, who was standing in the doorway. "Yeah, Ma. I was just about to jump in the shower and get dressed."

"Oh, really? Where you on your way to?" she asked, hoping her daughter wasn't planning on hiding in the house for the rest of her life.

"I need some fresh air. I was thinking about just sitting on the porch or something."

"All right," Ms. Mathews said before walking away.

Sunshine had been out of the hospital and home with her for three weeks now, and for the first time, she wasn't trying to stay locked in the house. Ms. Mathews was relieved she wasn't acting scared, as she had been just weeks ago.

After getting dressed, Sunshine sat on the bed to put on her shoes. That's when she heard Monsta's phone vibrate from under her pillow.

"Hello."

Monsta smiled, hearing her sound better than the last time he called. He still couldn't find the right words to express how he really felt, so he hung up. Laying down the phone, she finished putting on her shoes before going downstairs and out the door. For some reason, the sun shone just a little brighter that day, and she loved it. For the first time in a while, she felt free and happy within herself. After spending all her time locked up in her room, she began to appreciate the outside world.

"I'm off to work. You gon' be all right?"

"Yes, Ma. I think I'm gonna walk to the store and enjoy this sun," Sunshine said, smiling at her mom, so she knew everything was good.

"All right. Zoey in there if you need her."

"Ma, I'm good. Go to work and stop worrying about me."

Ms. Mathews gave her a tight hug before getting into her car. She was proud of how strong her daughter was acting now.

After a while, Sunshine got up to go back upstairs to grab her bag. She couldn't go nowhere without any money on her. Right when she was about to go back upstairs, she rushed to use the bathroom.

"Damn, girl. You be right on Mama's bladder."

Finally walking back outside, she felt the phone vibrate again. She planned on ignoring it, but it kept going off.

"Hello. Are you gon' go ahead and ask for the nigga or keep playing on the phone?" she asked, standing on the porch.

"I'm glad to see you and baby girl all right. I left some money in the mailbox for y'all."

Sunshine's mouth dropped open, hearing his voice. "Monsta? How did you know where I was?"

"I'm not trying to bother you or nothing. I just wanted you to know that I love you, and I'm sorry for not showing you when I had the chance to."

Sunshine wanted to cry while holding the phone, but she needed to be strong. Monsta's car was parked a few houses down from her mama's house, and he could see how hurt she was. He hated that she was no longer cheerful like she was before he called her.

"I'm sorry if I ruined your day. Get your money and buy whatever you and the baby need." Not waiting for a response, he hung up.

Sunshine was still at a loss for words, even when she saw him drive past the house. She wished she could explain to her mind what her heart felt. She still loved him, and it was clear he loved her and their daughter.

After leaving Sunshine's house, Monsta went back to the block. Her leaving him had him in a fucked-up space, and he'd been slacking on work. It was time for these niggas to remember who the fuck he was.

"What's up, bro?" he said, pulling up on Lamar.

Lamar gave him some play. "What's good? Where the fuck you been? I tried hitting you up a few times."

Monsta laughed it off. "You know, man, I've been here and there. But yeah, I got a new number and shit. Give me yo' number so I can call you."

Monsta and Lamar exchanged numbers before he got to the business part of their meeting.

"Aye, bro, you got that bread?"

"Now, you know the answer to that, nigga. We go way back, my baby. Shoot me to the crib right quick."

After Lamar jumped in the truck, they rode just a few blocks over to his crib. Jumping out, he went into the house to get the money he owed Monsta. Those niggas' daddies used to roll together, so if nothing else, Monsta knew he wouldn't have to question Lamar twice about having his bread.

Lamar climbed back into the truck with a bag. "Here, bro, it's all there."

Monsta flipped through the money. From what he could tell, it was all there like he said from jump.

"Aye, I need you to do me a favor, bro."

"What's up? I got you."

"Go pick up that bread from Shawn and Mike for me. I'll get you later. I gotta shoot a move right fast."

"All right, cool. Just shoot me back to the block so that I can get my car."

Seeing Keisha's car drive past threw him off his square. He really didn't want to take Lamar to his car, but he went ahead since he was looking out for him on that money tip.

As soon as Lamar jumped out of the truck, Monsta sped off. He wasn't sure where Keisha went, but he was for sure going to catch her ass.

After riding around and turning a few corners, Monsta parked his truck a few blocks from Keisha's apartment building. As he walked to her building, the angel on his shoulder begged him just to go home, but the devil yelled louder, begging him to fuck her up one last time before putting her out of her misery.

Monsta made it to her door without being seen. Picking her lock was easy as hell, especially since he'd done it before. He took a seat on the couch to wait for her to return home.

Keisha had just come from seeing one of her niggas before dragging her ass home. Her bed was calling her, and she was all for it. Plus, she needed to rest up so she could have enough energy to clean up before Brandon came to visit later that night.

"What the fuck you doin' here?" she yelled at Monsta, at the same time, ready to run out the door.

"Bring yo' ass in here and have a seat. We have some catching up to do."

Keisha was scared but listened. The last thing she wanted to do was piss him off even more.

"I tried calling you, but you act like you can't answer the phone."

"You know I'm not the type for all that talking shit, but why the fuck was you blowin' up my phone like we go together or somethin'?" Monsta asked while pacing the floor.

"I really needed to talk to you."

"Nah, you ain't have shit to say to me after telling Sunshine we been fuckin' around behind her back."

Keisha had a smirk on her face. "I believe we do."

Not liking that she was playing in his face, Monsta snatched her up by her shirt. "Do you know how bad you fucked shit up for me?"

Before she could answer, he snapped as his mind went back to the way he left Sunshine's face. He had really fucked her up, and Keisha's stupid ass was in his face, looking clueless. Monsta let her go only to make her think wasn't shit wrong before he slapped her to the floor.

"You fucked up my whole fucking life, bitch," he yelled, giving her a hard kick.

Keisha managed to scream out, "Stop, Monsta, I'm pregnant!"

Monsta stepped back just to laugh in her face. "Fuck you telling me for, bitch? Fuck that baby. I know for a fact that muthafucka ain't mine."

"Why else would I be telling you this?" Keisha cried.

"Because you slow as hell," he laughed.

"I swear this baby is yours."

"Come on now, Keisha. We both know this not my baby. Only muthafucka that had this dick raw was Sunshine," he explained, laughing and shaking his head at her.

Keisha needed him to hear and believe what she was saying. "Do you remember that night we were drunk as hell, chilling at the spot, and you wanted a quickie before anyone else came?"

"Bitch, even if I were a custo in the spot snorting twenty lines, I would never forget to strap up with your ass. You the bitch we pass around at the spot and never take home to meet Mama."

Keisha's feelings were hurt, but he was telling the truth. Her past behavior had him doubting everything she said.

"What the fuck I got to lie for?"

Monsta continued to laugh. "Maybe because you a ho and need somebody to help you take care of that muthafucka."

Keisha shook her head, trying to get her story together. "Look, we done fucked plenty of times without a rubber."

Monsta reached out and slapped her again. "You really gon' stand in my face and keep lying? Bitch, I even make you suck my dick with a runner on."

"I'm not ly—"

Before she could even get the sentence completely out, Monsta was tagging her with blows straight to her face. Since she wanted to be a fucking liar, he was going to treat her as such.

When Monsta finally walked out, Keisha was balled up in the corner of her living room, crying her eyes out. She knew she had done some fucked-up shit in her life, but this time, she knew she was right about him getting her pregnant. Lying there in a puddle of blood, Keisha blamed herself for being so stupid. Just months ago, she put together a plan to make Monsta all hers finally. Now, she realized everything that glittered wasn't always gold.

Before Sunshine and Monsta got together, she used to trick with him. He paid good, and because she thought that one day, he would be hers, she sometimes sucked him off for free. She loved the attention he paid her when they were alone, and deep down inside, she thought he felt the same way. It wasn't until he started fucking with Sunshine that she realized he didn't give a fuck about her.

Still, every now and then, they would link up to fuck, or she would just suck him off. Over time, she got jealous of Sunshine and couldn't understand why he picked her. Keisha tried to talk to Monsta about how she felt, but he pushed her feelings aside and then passed her to his team. She never thought that coming up with the plan to make him hers and only hers would have her calling for an ambulance and praying they got there fast enough to save her unborn baby.

"So, are you gon' have a baby shower or have you even thought about that?" Zoey asked Sunshine as they sat on the couch watching TV.

"To be honest, I think I'm just gon' buy my baby whatever she needs. Forget that baby shower shit."

Zoey caught an attitude. "You always actin' funny. Maybe the family wanted to help you out and buy that baby something. You know everyone heard about what happened between you and Monsta."

Sunshine tried to be cool, but she knew deep down inside it was only a matter of time before Zoey jumped on that bullshit train.

"This baby don't need shit from this fucked-up-ass family. You act like they don't sit and turn they nose up at us. Fuck I look like asking them for shit? My daughter gon' forever be good."

"You confident as hell with no job and a crazy-ass baby daddy. But do you, boo."

"Bitch, my baby daddy might be crazy, but he serves your nigga an eight ball every other day. That's why he can't find a job. He a fucking junky."

Zoey jumped up from the couch. "Bitch, you lucky you pregnant with my niece because I'd do you dirty. You thought that nigga beat your ass, but I'd do worse."

Sunshine busted out laughing in her face. "Pregnant or not, you can't fuck with me. Monsta the only one that's ever beat my ass."

Zoey busted out laughing. "Bitch, you proud of that shit, ain't you?"

"As proud as you when you on the bus with your junky-ass nigga."

Zoey stomped away. She really hated Sunshine. Just her presence in that house irked her nerves. Once Zoey went into the basement, she picked up the phone to let her mama know just how much Sunshine hated their family.

Sunshine sat on the couch, rubbing her belly. It seemed like every time Zoey came around, her daughter started kicking her harder.

"It's OK, Mya Caldwell. We won't be around that miserable-ass bitch for much longer."

Just as those words slipped through her mouth, Monsta's phone started to vibrate. Now that she knew it was him calling, she kept it on her. They didn't talk every time he called. Sometimes they just held the phone, listening to each other breathe. Sometimes, she would cry, and he would do the same. It was clear they loved each other, but just couldn't be with each other.

"Hello."

For a good five minutes, they played the silent game before Monsta finally said something.

"Aye, can you do me a favor?"

"What?"

"Just step on the porch so I can look at you and my daughter."

Sunshine gave it a quick thought before she got up to walk to the porch. She looked a few houses down and saw his truck.

"You look beautiful, like always."

Sunshine started blushing. "Thank you," she shyly said.

"Damn, my daughter got you glowin' like a muthafucka."

Sunshine took a seat on the porch swing. "She is very active too. Her ass stays kicking my bladder."

Monsta laughed before getting serious. "I feel like shit not being able to feel her move around. I know I fucked up, but I'm trying to make shit right with us."

Sunshine didn't want to piss him off or fuck up the moment, so she chose her words carefully. "We need to work on everything so that when Mya gets here, we can coparent without all that toxic shit."

Monsta nodded in agreement. "You right about all that shit. Hold up, you said, 'Mya'? That's gon' be her name?"

"Yeah. Mya Caldwell. I haven't come up with a middle name yet."

Monsta was all smiles. He was surprised she was still giving his daughter his last name, but overall, he loved the name.

"Baby M.C. I can't wait to meet her."

"I feel the same way. I tell her all the time I can't wait to hug and kiss all over her precious self."

Just talking about baby Mya, Monsta couldn't help but get emotional. He might have been pushing it, but he had to try his luck.

"Come ride with me for a second."

Sunshine's smile left her face. "Now you know I can't do that."

"Why not, Sunshine? I just wanna rub on your stomach and feel my baby move around."

Sunshine held the phone, knowing just how wrong she would be to leave her porch to be with him after all they'd been through.

"Please, Sunshine. You know deep down inside I love y'all for real. I need and want to be a part of this. Don't you think I deserve to be a part of this with you? I did help make her," he said, trying to plead his case.

Sunshine stood up to shut the door before walking off the porch. Walking toward his truck, she hung up the phone before placing it back inside her purse. Turning

back to give her house one last look before jumping into
Monsta's truck, Sunshine prayed she wasn't making a big
mistake.

Monsta smiled like a kid in a candy store. They sat in
the car for a moment, as he gently rubbed her belly and
told baby Mya how much he already loved her. Sunshine
knew he was telling the truth because he was damn near
in tears. She knew he was a hurt man who did love her
and Mya, but she only wanted to work things out so their
baby girl would never see them going through all that
toxic shit.

"I know I fucked up, but I'm not the same without you
by my side. I can't force or rush you to take me back, but I
swear I'll do whatever it takes to have you back in my life
completely. I changed, Sunshine, I really did."

Sunshine started to cry. She still loved Monsta with
everything in her, but at the same time, she didn't want
to run back to the same shit as before. The last thing she
wanted her baby to see was her getting her ass beat by
him.

Monsta pulled her in for a hug. "I love you, and I know
you still love me. Everyone in our business was our real
problem. We can start all over and have our family."

Sunshine sat there still crying and in her feelings. He
was right about them still loving each other, but going
back to him so quickly didn't sit right with her. She knew
that it would be stupid, especially if he fucked around
and beat her ass again. Monsta could tell she was in her
feelings just like he was.

"What you doin'?" she asked when he started the truck.

He had one hand on the steering wheel with the other
on her stomach. "Chill. I did ask you to take a ride with
me."

Sunshine tried to calm down as they turned the block.
She kept telling herself that he loved her and wasn't on

no bullshit. After grabbing some food, Sunshine was surprised when they pulled up to his house.

"Is your mom here?"

He could sense that she was scared. "Nah, but I promise you in good hands."

Monsta helped her get out of the truck and into the house.

"Close your eyes. I got a surprise for you."

Sunshine shut her eyes, then felt his hand grab hers.

"Keep them closed until I tell you to open them. You gon' love this," Monsta said as he led her to the other bedroom in the house.

Typically, they never used the room for anything but his extra clothes and shit. So, she was surprised when he told her to open her eyes. She looked around the room with her mouth wide open. Monsta had the room decorated with all the Disney princesses.

"You think Mya will love it, or did I overdo it?" he asked with a grin on his face.

"Oh my gawd, Monsta, it's beautiful. I can't believe how good it looks."

Monsta opened up the walk-in closet. "Look, she got clothes, diapers, and everything that she'll need."

Sunshine was shocked at how he went all out and beyond for Mya. Not only was the closet packed with stuff for Mya, but both dressers were also full of clothes. There was even a wall with boxes of diapers and wipes for her.

"Monsta, I swear you're gonna be the best dad ever."

Pulling her into a hug, he whispered in her ear, "I'm gonna be the best man to you from now on. Just give me another chance."

Not giving her a chance to answer, he kissed all over her neck and lips. She was just as soft as he could remember. Sunshine didn't know what came over her, but she couldn't hide her true feelings for him. In a hot second, they were in his bed with his face buried between her legs.

As Monsta made his way back up and entered her, he whispered in her ear again, "You gon' always be mine."

Being caught up in the deep strokes she was receiving, Sunshine nodded her head in agreement. It was clear she was truly a fool in love.

"Where your sister at? I done called that girl to talk to her ass about that bullshit between y'all, and she not answering."

Zoey was in the kitchen washing the dinner dishes when her mom walked in. She saw Sunshine jump into the truck with Monsta and couldn't wait to run her mouth about it.

"Ma, tell me why, right after she cut up on me, she ran outside and left with that boy?"

Ms. Mathews set her purse on the counter. "I know you fucking lying."

"Nope, Ma. I told you she just as crazy as him. Ain't no way she would've left if she wasn't," Zoey added to the story.

Ms. Mathews pulled out her phone to call her youngest daughter and check her ass.

"Hello?" Sunshine answered, still half-asleep.

"You got to be the one on whatever that boy selling in the streets. Are you fucking crazy?"

Sunshine sat up. "Ma, please calm down and let me explain everything."

Ms. Mathews wasn't trying to hear anything she had to say. "Are you with that boy?"

"Yes, Ma, but it's not what you think."

"You and that baby have a good life over there. I told you that as long as you were in this house, I needed you to be done with him for good. I shouldn't come home and hear you jumped into the car with him. I have to work tomorrow. Come get your shit then because I don't wanna look at your ass." With that being said, Ms. Mathews hung up.

Monsta sat up. "What's wrong?"

Sunshine threw down the phone with a face full of tears. "Everything's so fucked up. I should have just stayed home. Now, I don't have a home."

Monsta sat up to hold and calm her down. "You act like you don't got me. Do you think I will let y'all be out here without shit?"

"I wasn't trying to move back over here."

Just that fast, Monsta's whole mood changed. "What the fuck is that supposed to mean?"

Sunshine could tell his mood had changed, but she still tried to explain her side of the story.

"Monsta, when I got in your truck, it wasn't so I could run back over here. I was being nice and considering your feelings. We fucked, but that didn't mean I was ready to move back in."

"We fucked, huh? Damn, I thought we were making love." He laughed. "People always calling me crazy and shit, but to run back to you, crying and begging for you to take me back had to be the craziest shit I ever did. You said it yourself, it was just a fuck. So that's what you do now? Just out here fuckin' niggas, huh?"

"Monsta, calm down, baby," Sunshine said, touching his arm.

He snatched away from her. "Get dressed so that I can drop your ass off somewhere."

Sunshine watched as he climbed out of bed and put on his clothes.

"You a stupid-ass bitch, I swear. A nigga works hard to give you and that baby the fucking world, and you just wanted a quick nut. Bitch, get dressed before I throw your ass out butt-ass naked like I did the last bitch that played in my face."

Crying, Sunshine climbed out of bed. Her emotions were everywhere, and she didn't know what to do.

"Monsta, how were you just telling me how much you love me and miss your family, and now, you callin' me bitches and putting me out?"

Not even replying, he walked out of the room. He was pissed and trying so hard not to fuck her up. He hated to say it, but she was the type of bitch who liked getting fucked up from time to time.

After freshening up in the bathroom, Sunshine got dressed and grabbed her bag before going into the living room, where Monsta was sitting. She looked at him and could tell he was frustrated.

"You ready to go? Where am I taking you?"

Sunshine sat beside him. As she began to rock back and forth, she burst out in tears. Monsta tried to keep a mug on his face, but seeing her break down affected him.

"What's up? Talk to me."

"I don't know what to do. It's like I have no control over my life. If I stay, then my family will be against me, but if I go, then you'll hate me. Either way, I won't be happy."

"I can't tell or force you to do anything. What you need to do is think about what feels right. If you love me the way you were just hollerin' in the room, then stay. If you don't, let me take you to where you really wanna be."

Sunshine buried her head in her hands as she cried. She couldn't understand why she had to make this choice anyway. Of course, she loved her mom, but she also loved Monsta. She thought it was wrong for her even to have to pick a side.

Monsta knew she wasn't gonna pick him because it was taking her too long to decide. Snatching the phone from her hand, Monsta called her mama's phone back.

Ms. Mathews answered the phone with a lot of attitude. "Yes, Sunshine?"

"This Monsta. I really need to talk to you, so please don't hang up."

He was surprised when she listened.

"What's going on? Is Sunshine all right?" she questioned.

Monsta placed the phone on speaker so Sunshine could hear everything.

"Aye, look, I talked Sunshine into getting in the car with me before I drove back to my house. She was against it because she didn't wanna piss you off. I just wanted her to see the nursery and all the baby stuff I've been buying. She wasn't trying to move back over here or nothing. I think you tryin'a put her out because of that is wrong, and the way she over here crying and shaking is stressing my daughter out."

Although he tried to talk like he had some sense, she still didn't like him and refused to show any type of respect toward him. "Listen here, boy, I told Sunshine the day she got out of the hospital from you jumping on her that I wasn't about to play that back-and-forth shit with y'all. She promised y'all was done and now she back over there with you. In my eyes, she picked over there to call her home."

Monsta shook his head. "You wrong as hell. Didn't I just tell you I forced her into the car and then tricked her into coming over? She was against all this shit."

"Look, little boy, I just got off work, so I don't have time for this shit. Tell her she can come get her stuff in the morning."

Monsta looked at the phone, pissed that she had hung up before he had a chance to snap on her ass.

"I tried to fix the situation."

Sunshine wiped away her tears. "I know, Monsta. Sometimes, she can be hard to deal with."

Monsta took a seat next to her. "I know you don't wanna be here, and I can't force you to stay. Whatever you wanna do, just let me know."

Deep down inside, he didn't want her to leave, but he also knew that if he tried to force her or flip out again, she would really hate him.

"I just need some time to think."

Sunshine hated how just that fast, he flipped on her, then tried to help her. She didn't know how she should really feel at that moment. Monsta got up and walked back to his room. Once she thought she was in the clear, she picked up her phone to text the only person she knew could save her.

Sunshine: Hey, wyd?

Kyrah: Nothing. Just got home from the shop. What's up?

Sunshine quickly texted back, scared Monsta was about to walk back in.

Sunshine: Long story. I really need you right now. Can you come get me?

Kyrah sat up on her couch to put on her shoes.

Kyrah: Where you at, boo?

Sunshine: I'm at Monsta's house, but you can't pick me up from here. I'll call you when I'm somewhere safe. Please just be in the area.

As soon as Sunshine sent that last message, she was creeping out the front door. She knew not to use an Uber to get to Kyrah's house because it was all connected to his account and card.

Monsta finally got up to check on Sunshine. The last thing he wanted to do was stress her and the baby out, so he gave her some space. Besides, he blew up at her and really hurt her for nothing. Since losing her the last time, he tried to look at things from her point of view.

"Baby, you alr—"

He stopped midsentence, seeing her ass was gone. He rushed back into his room to grab his truck keys and phone.

"This sneaky bitch," he said, jumping in his ride.

She wasn't sure how much time she had until he found out she ghosted him, but this was the only time Sunshine wished she weren't pregnant. She found herself running out of breath really quickly, trying to get to the major street in the neighborhood.

She had only made it two whole blocks down when she heard the music coming from his truck. Thinking fast, she ran into someone's backyard to hide on the side of their garbage can. Since it was dark, he didn't see her and ended up driving right past her. Sunshine waited until she could no longer hear the music before she ran from the backyard. Just then, the phone went off.

"Hello," she said out of breath.

"I'm at that Coney Island a few blocks up his street. Where are you?" Kyrah asked.

"I'm a block down. I'm not sure if I can make it. Monsta driving around looking for me. I'm so scared," Sunshine admitted.

"I'm about to drive down there. Be ready to jump in the car."

Just as Sunshine hung up the phone, she could see his truck coming back up the street. She wished she had stayed put 'cause instead of hiding in someone's backyard, she was now hiding around a vacant house that had caught fire some time back. She was so scared that she started shaking and crying.

Monsta knew for sure that she was around that area, but since he really didn't know where she dipped off to, he parked his truck and then stood there looking around.

"Sunshine, come out here. I know you around here somewhere. I'm not gon' hit you," he yelled.

At this point, he was so pissed that instead of beating her, he wanted to shoot her ass.

"Sunshine," he yelled again.

His voice sounded like it was getting closer, and she couldn't stop crying. She prayed he didn't find her.

Feeling the phone vibrate, Sunshine quickly pressed ignore, but Kyrah called right back. Sunshine was scared that he would find her, so she promptly texted her.

Sunshine: I'm hiding in the burnt-down house. Monsta is around. Please stop calling, he gon' find me.

Kyrah: Go to the backyard and leave from the gate. I can get you through the alley.

Sunshine cried harder, thinking this move would be her last, and he would for sure find her.

"Calm down, girl, you got this," she mumbled to herself.

Since she was already toward the back of the house anyway, she tried to tell herself how simple it would be. Just as she ran out to the gate to hit the alley, she heard Monsta call out her name.

"Bitch, I swear the next time I see you, I'm killing you."

Monsta took off to catch her ass, but by the time he hit the gate, the car that she jumped into was in reverse and backing out of the alley. He tried to identify the vehicle and the driver, but the bright-ass headlights made it impossible.

"Stupid-ass bitch."

As they got away from Monsta's neighborhood, Sunshine's tears slowly went away. She was surprised and happy as hell to be still alive.

"You good, boo?"

Sunshine nodded her head. "I can't believe I made it. I've never been so scared in my life. Oh my gawd, thank you so much, Kyrah."

Kyrah continued to drive to her house. She was willing to help Sunshine as long as Monsta didn't come to her with no bullshit. Once they got to Kyrah's place, Sunshine took a long, hot bath to relax her body. Mya was kicking her ass for doing all that fucking and running around. Kyrah gave Sunshine something to sleep in and a sheet for the couch.

"What's your plan?" Kyrah asked as they chilled in the living room.

Her tone gave Sunshine the impression that she really wasn't wanted there. "Kyrah, I have to be honest. I really appreciate you and everything that you have done for me, but I know I can't stay here."

Kyrah changed her tone and tried to play it off. "Girl, you are more than welcome to stay here until you get on your feet."

Sunshine shook her head. "Thanks, but I know just like you know that if Monsta finds out where I'm at, he's gonna pull up and act a fool. I don't wanna bring all that drama to your house. In the morning, if you can just take me to my mom's house, I'd appreciate that."

She might not have been brave enough to tell Sunshine to get the hell on, but Kyrah was happy she was thinking straight. The last thing she wanted to do was have to deal with *his* wild ass.

"What the fuck is going on?" Ms. Caldwell yelled as she walked into the house and heard a bunch of banging and screaming coming from the nursery.

Walking toward the room, she peeked in to find Monsta completely tearing the room apart.

"Boy, what the fuck is wrong with you? You done spent all that money for this shit, and now you fuckin' up everything for your daughter."

"Fuck her and fuck her bitch-ass mama!" he yelled.

Not knowing what happened while she was away, Ms. Caldwell tried to calm her son. "Whatever's going on, you can't say fuck your baby. She a part of you, and you gotta respect that."

"She part of her bitch-ass mama too, so fuck her. I swear to God, if I ever see Sunshine again, I'm murking her ass. I was too nice to that bitch and let her get away with too much. I thought I loved that bitch, but I should've just fucked and passed her to the team."

Ms. Caldwell shook her head. "You upset, I get that, but don't ever let that stupid shit come outta your mouth. Now, clean this shit up. Your daughter will be here in two months."

Walking off thinking she did something, she felt like the big dog of the house . . . that was . . . until Monsta yelled out, "Fuck both of them muthafuckas. I hope they both die during birth if I don't catch her ass first."

Ms. Caldwell went upstairs, praying nothing happened to Sunshine or her granddaughter. She thought it was crazy that she had to explain to the big man upstairs not to pay her son any attention because something was really wrong with him.

The next morning, as promised, Kyrah dropped Sunshine off at her mama's house and wished her the best of luck. Sunshine walked into the house, surprised to see that her mama was home and not at work like she said she would be.

"Hey, Ma."

Ms. Mathews gave her a strange look before giving her a dry, "Hey."

Sunshine sat on the couch. "Ma, I know you're pissed at me, but I don't wanna leave this house with any ill feelings."

"I told you I didn't want you dealing with that boy while living here. I don't like him, and I know he ain't wired right."

"I understand all that, but—"

Ms. Mathews cut her off. "You must not understand shit because you wouldn't have left with him."

"Ma, I do understand what you're saying, but he *is* the father of my child. He's gonna be in her life."

Shaking her head, Ms. Mathews was pissed at her daughter. "I remember before you got with that fool. Fresh out of high school, you took that class to get your license to do hair and shit. Then you got with him right after that and ain't did shit with your life since then but chase behind that boy."

"I still got time to do what I dreamed about, Ma."

Seeing that her daughter was still so naïve behind Monsta, she tried to scare her to get her shit together. "I want you to think about the road your life is headed down now. Do you think you'll be alive long enough to follow your dreams and live off the fruit of your labor?"

She was surprised when Sunshine broke down crying. Although she was trying to show her tough love, Ms. Mathews felt bad for her. Getting up from the couch, she walked over to sit beside her daughter. For the first time in a while, she held her daughter and just let her cry in her arms.

Zoey walked in with Darryl and instantly got a crazy look on her face. They had been out dropping the kids off at their grandma's on their daddy's side. Walking in and seeing Sunshine getting attention from their mom didn't sit right with her.

"Ma, what she doin' here?"

Ms. Mathews released Sunshine so she could address Zoey. "Girl, mind your own damn business."

"I'm just saying that she did say fuck us when she went back to crazy ass."

Sunshine stood up, ready to knock her ass out, but Ms. Mathews was quick on her feet. "Y'all not about to do this shit. Why y'all two can't never be in the same room without all this bullshit? You two are sisters, not rival gang members."

Sunshine wiped her face again. "Ma, this is your fault. I blame you for why we can't get along."

Ms. Mathews looked at Sunshine like she was out of her mind. "Excuse me? Please go ahead and explain. I need to hear this bullshit."

"Ma, while we were growing up, you always made everything between us a competition. Now that we're older, we can't get along because we're too busy trying to outdo each other instead of trying to uplift each other," Sunshine tried to explain.

Ms. Mathews turned her attention toward Zoey. "Do you feel the same way?"

"No," she lied.

"Girl, you lying. You stay kissing ass, and for what?" Sunshine asked.

"Mama ain't did nothing wrong but made sure we were good. It's not her fault you wanted to be grown and fuck with that boy. Now you don't know what to do with your life."

"This is a good example of why there's a problem in this house. Whenever I disagree with whatever, y'all bring

Monsta up. If me and you have a problem and get to the bottom of it, we'll see that Monsta wasn't the cause of it all."

Zoey only heard what she wanted to hear. "Girl, bye. You bring up Darryl all the time."

"But only when you bring up Monsta. Our real problem is that we were raised to always compete with each other and not be real sisters."

Ms. Mathews was growing tired of Sunshine. "I don't wanna hear this shit. I did the best that I could, raising y'all on my own."

The sisters watched as she headed up the stairs.

"You always starting shit. That's why you gotta leave now. Mama shouldn't have had to call off work for your drama."

Sunshine shook her head. "Bitch, fuck you," she said as she got up to go to her room.

She didn't know where she was going, but she was tired of crying and begging to be somewhere she wasn't wanted. One thing's for sure: she was going to use the money Monsta gave her to make sure she and her daughter had somewhere to go.

Sitting on her bed, Sunshine thought about everything that had just taken place. It's crazy how she and her mom had that time to bond, but as soon as Zoey came home, it all turned into drama. Then all the bullshit with Monsta was too much even to process all the way.

"Everybody fucking toxic," she mumbled.

Ms. Mathews knocked on the door to Sunshine's bedroom before opening it.

"Yes, Ma?"

"I thought about what you said about everything being my fault. I just wanted to tell you I won't completely agree with that, but I can see where you're coming from. I wasn't always right in a few situations that happened between you two, but I wanna make things right now."

Sunshine stood up from the bed to hug her mom. She knew it took a lot just for her to come to her and say that.

"Ma, I love you."

"I love you too, Sunshine. I really want the best for you and my granddaughter."

"I know, and I promise you, I'm gonna get my act together. I now understand clearly that I'm about to be someone's mother, and there's certain toxic shit I just can't have around her."

Ms. Mathews smiled, listening to her daughter speak. She knew it would only be a matter of time before she opened her eyes.

"Sunshine, you can stay but get your shit together before that baby gets here. I know you can do it in the next few months." With that being said, she turned and walked away.

Sunshine sat on the bed thinking about what all she needed to do to get her life back in order. She wasn't sure yet what road she would take, but she knew for sure she was leaving Monsta for good. The first step she needed to take was to get rid of his old phone.

Just as she pulled out the phone to copy down Kyrah's number, she saw that it had over twenty missed calls and messages from Monsta. Shaking her head, she couldn't believe it had taken this long to realize he really had a fucking problem.

Sunshine looked through the photos of her and Monsta one last time before feeling like she wanted to cry. There were so many photos of them, happy as hell just to be together. Then there were a few of her caught off guard, and even just asleep. Once upon a time, there was so much love between them. She wasn't sure what changed, but that love was gone, and she knew for a fact she didn't need to rekindle shit.

Turning off the phone, Sunshine made her way into the garage to get a hammer. The only way to get over Monsta now was to stop all communication between them for good. Ms. Mathews watched out the back window, and for the first time in a minute, she was actually proud of her baby girl.

Chapter 6

Bang! Bang!

Ms. Caldwell jumped up from the couch to see who was banging on the front door as if they had lost their damn mind.

"Who is it?"

"Ma'am, it's the police. Open up," she heard an officer yell.

Her heart raced, and her mind instantly started to wonder what Monsta could have done.

"What y'all want?" she asked as she pulled open the door.

"We're looking for Montez Caldwell Jr. Is he here?" the officer asked.

Ms. Caldwell never wanted to see her son in any trouble, but with the thought of him harming Sunshine and their baby, she wasted no time leading the officers to Monsta's bedroom.

"Mr. Caldwell," Officer Thomas yelled, causing him to jump out of his sleep.

"Fuck y'all want? Ma, you did this? You called these muthafuckas on me?" he questioned.

"Monsta, what the fuck did you do?" Ms. Caldwell yelled.

Before he could respond, the officers were placing him under arrest for the assault on Keisha Freeman. Monsta didn't want to leave without a fight. In his mind, she needed her ass beaten for coming to him with all those bullshit-ass lies she told him.

"Man, let me go. I didn't do shit to that bitch," he yelled as they tried to pull him out of the house.

"Monsta, just stop trying to fight them before they kill your ass," Ms. Caldwell yelled.

One of the officers stopped walking, then turned to face her. "Ma'am, we're not trying to kill anyone today. Can you please back up?"

Not wanting to bring any more attention to her home, Ms. Caldwell stopped in her tracks and allowed them to continue to do their job. As they drove off, she sat on the porch even more confused than before. She didn't know who the fuck Keisha Freeman was. After smoking her cigarette, she got ready to go check on what mess her son done got himself into.

Keisha waited for her Uber at the entrance of the hospital. After almost suffering a miscarriage from when Monsta jumped on her, she was surprised her baby was a fighter and survived.

Returning home, Keisha lay across her bed, lost in her thoughts. She couldn't believe she had come up with a dumb-ass plan to get Monsta for herself. Thinking over her decision to steal sperm from Monsta's condom didn't seem like a good idea anymore. The day he came over, Keisha figured she would be able to convince him they fucked without a condom one night when they were drunk. But he was smarter than she thought and knew she was full of shit.

How did she even think all this was a good idea when he'd explained to her plenty of times that she was a ho, and he loved his girl, who was her best friend? Even when her girl came to her, either happy about Monsta or crying over his bullshit, why did she still want to know what it was like to be his girl? So many questions ran through her mind, but not one answer. Everything she thought of was never a good answer.

Now that her plan was blown to hell, she started to doubt if having his baby was even worth all the pain and bullshit to come. Times like this, she wished she had a good friend to talk to. How could she even start a conversation with Sunshine? *"Hey, girl. So, I'm having Monsta's baby too, but let me tell you what's going on."* Just thinking about it made Keisha shake her head.

Hearing her phone ring, Keisha rushed to answer it.

"Hello."

Keisha listened to Detective Marshall give her details on Monsta being arrested earlier that morning for her assault.

"Wait a minute. When I talked to the police at the hospital, I told them I didn't want to press charges against him."

"Ma'am, you do understand your and your unborn child's lives are in danger with this guy on the streets."

"Oh my gawd. If he don't stay in jail, he will certainly come after me," Keisha cried into the phone.

The detective smiled. That's exactly what she needed Keisha to believe. "Ma'am, can I come pick you up and bring you down to the station? I believe I can help you out."

Keisha shook her head as she thought about what was happening. Being intrigued by what she was saying, she finally told her that it would be OK. As long as they could keep her safe from Monsta, she was willing to help them out with anything.

Sunshine woke up from her nap, hearing her mama calling her like there was a damn fire or something. Jumping out of bed and making her way down the stairs, she could see her mom standing there with Ms. Caldwell.

"She stopped by to speak to you. If you need me, I'll be in the kitchen," she said, giving her a look that said she better not fall for Monsta's mama's bullshit.

Ms. Mathews went into the kitchen, leaning against the wall to hear everything. She'd be damned if she allowed Sunshine to get pulled back in that family's shit when their family had enough issues of its own.

"What's up?"

"I tried calling you on Monsta's old phone, but couldn't get through. The police came to pick him up this morning."

Sunshine's heart dropped, but she kept her cool. "Oh, all right. What happened?"

"They talkin' about him beating some girl's ass and some other shit about her being pregnant."

"Pregnant?" Sunshine questioned, trying not to cry.

"Yeah, but fix your face, honey. He says the baby isn't his."

Sunshine wasn't sure what to believe at this point. She knew he cheated, and his mama played both sides from time to time.

"Oh, all right. Well, I was about to help my mom in the kitchen. Thanks for letting me know."

Ms. Caldwell rolled her eyes. "Oh, so you one of those?"

Sunshine was confused. "Huh? One of what?" she asked.

Ms. Mathews was now in the doorway. She knew exactly what that lady was getting at, and she dared her ass to say that bullshit.

"You were just so in love, and them legs stayed cocked open and wide for the money train. Now he's locked up, and you giving a fuck about your mama's kitchen? Y'all females all the same."

"First of all, bitch, you can get the fuck outta my daughter's face with that bullshit before I drag you out by that little-ass ponytail. My daughter put up with enough of your son's shit. She don't have to give two fucks about him being locked up. If it was up to me, his ass would have been locked up or dead somewhere long ago."

Sunshine was shocked but happy her mom had her back.

"I never dragged a bitch in her own house, but today will be the day. Bitch, try me," Ms. Caldwell said, ready to fight.

"Y'all, please stop this shit right now."

They both looked at Sunshine, who was fighting her tears.

Looking at Ms. Caldwell, Sunshine got honest with her. "Look, you know just like I know what all took place in that house. Whatever me and your son had is over now. My main concern right now is my daughter. Whatever he did to end up in jail, that's on him."

Ms. Caldwell turned to walk out the door, but something in her needed to break Sunshine just one last time. "Oh, I forgot to ask. Ain't your friend's name Keisha?"

"Yeah, and? What about her?"

"Y'all babies gon' be siblings," she said with a smirk on her face.

Sunshine's whole face dropped right along with her tears.

"OK, bitch, you got a reaction out of her. Now you can take your stupid ass on," Ms. Mathews said, holding on to her daughter.

Ms. Caldwell left, wishing she felt a little better about herself. Truth be told, she knew Sunshine had had enough of her son's shit, and she really needed this break from him to make sure she and that baby were gonna be all right.

Sunshine pulled away from her mama. "I can't believe he did me like this. I swear I never did anything wrong to him. I hate him and Keisha so much. I can't believe I called that bitch my best friend. I was so stupid."

"Stop all that, girl. Fuck them. You have a family in your corner that's gon' help you with that baby. You don't need them people."

Sunshine cried a little longer before walking away and going back into her room.

Although she knew they'd been fucking around, hearing that a baby was made between them really hurt her to the core. She blamed herself and even questioned how she could be so stupid as not to see what was really going on between them. So many times, she heard them talking shit about each other and never put it together that they were really fucking on the low.

Eventually crying herself to sleep, Sunshine slept the day away with only thoughts of bettering her life for Mya and herself.

"Sunshine, Sunshine, get up."

Sunshine opened her eyes to see her mom standing over her. "What's up, Ma?"

"Baby, you been in this bed all day. I know you hurt, and there's probably nothing I can say to change that right now, but can you at least get up and feed my granddaughter?"

"Yeah, Ma, I'm about to get up now."

"Good. I cooked dinner, and it's ready."

Sunshine followed her mom downstairs to the dining room to eat. Seeing Zoey at the table made her roll her eyes. She hoped she wasn't going to be on no bullshit 'cause she wasn't in the mood.

"Hey, sis. How you and my niece feeling?"

Sunshine had to give her a double look to make sure it was really Zoey. She hadn't heard shit nice come out of her mouth in so long.

"We're doing all right. Thanks for asking."

Zoey heard everything when she was in the basement and kind of felt bad for her sister. She was forever telling her Monsta would do her wrong, but damn, he really *did* play her sister wrong. She knew Sunshine didn't deserve any more hurt than what she had already gone through.

It had been a minute since the three sat at the table and ate dinner in peace, but that was a moment well overdue.

"Sunshine, I know you were against a baby shower, but while I was out today, I couldn't help but buy Baby Mya a few things."

"Thank you, Zoey. I would love to see them after dinner."

Ms. Mathews was pleased with what she saw. She knew her daughters could get along.

"Thank you, Jesus," she mumbled before finishing her dinner.

Sunshine tossed and turned all night. Once she convinced herself to let all that hurt go and that it was time to let Monsta go for good, she slept like a baby.

The next morning, she lay in bed thinking about what she was gonna do next. She loved that her mom was understanding and let her stay there, but she also wanted her own place for her and her daughter. She really wanted to use the money Monsta gave her to pay for a place, but she knew the money would only last for a few months, and she needed more to add to it. Being seven months pregnant and big as hell, she knew finding a job was out of the question. After thinking everything over, she smiled at her final plan.

Sunshine jumped in the shower to start off her day. She was gonna be one busy mama that day if everything went her way.

"Ma, I really need to use your car," she said, racing downstairs.

"Oh, hell nah. Your ass ain't about to go looking for that girl to fight."

"Ma, I promise I'm not even on that tip. I need to go handle something else right quick."

Her mother hesitated before handing over her keys, but the desperation in her daughter's eyes told her she was on a mission.

"Here, but whatever tip you on, please, be careful."

Sunshine hugged her before grabbing the keys and running out the door.

Although she was hurt behind their betrayal, she decided that instead of going to beat Keisha's ass again, she would get her revenge another way.

Pulling up on one of the blocks Monsta's boys ran, Sunshine put her plan into action. Lamar was surprised to see her out and about without Monsta.

"What's up, Sunshine? What you doing on the block? That nigga Monsta not out here."

"What's up, Mar? Monsta sent me to pick up his bread," she lied.

"Oh really?" he questioned.

Trying to play it cool, Sunshine pretended everything was all good. "Yeah. Why? Is there a problem? Should I call him and let him know you don't have his shit?"

"Nah, sis, calm down. Let me go get that right quick."

Sunshine watched as he walked off. At first, it pissed her off seeing him on the phone, knowing he was calling Monsta to verify her story. Then she thought about how he wouldn't get an answer, so she was good. Lamar soon walked back with a few black bags.

"Tell that nigga to hit me up later," Lamar said, tossing the bags into her backseat.

Sunshine grabbed the bag and checked to make sure the money was really in it. She wasn't sure how much was supposed to be in the bag, but it looked like enough to handle her business.

"It's all there, sis."

"Just had to check. Anyway, Monsta got some new shit, so he'll be hitting you up soon."

Lamar nodded. "All right."

Sunshine drove off, wondering if she should make a few more rounds and pick up more of Monsta's money, but she decided not to. Lamar had more business coming his way, so she hit up the big bank.

After Sunshine drove off, Lamar pulled his phone out to call Monsta one last time. Something in his gut told him Sunshine was on some bullshit. Monsta never sent her to do his job. He hated for her to even be in his business. He only gave over the money just in case his ill feelings were wrong, but if they were right, Monsta would handle her ass.

Sunshine pulled up to the shopping plaza to get a new phone. After finding a parking spot, she took out a knot. She couldn't help but smile as she thought about spending Monsta's money. He broke her heart, so she was gonna break his pockets.

After placing the bag in the trunk, she was ready to start her shopping spree. The first stop was at the phone store. With a new number, she would be able to communicate with those she gave the number to and not have to worry about Monsta getting in contact with her for shit.

It's crazy how she tried to make shit work between them and stayed around just so her daughter could have a father. Just months ago, she was pissed when Keisha told her she needed to find her baby a new daddy. Now she finds out their babies share the same father. Sunshine shook her head, trying not to think about the shit. She wasn't about to let her thoughts of them fuck up her mood.

"Hey, Ms. Lady, can I talk to you for a second?"

Sunshine turned around to see a guy standing there. "What's up?"

Jonas handed over a business card. "How you doing? I'm Jonas Bentley, the owner of Bentley Cuts and Styles," he said, pointing to the shop behind where they stood.

"Hi, I'm Sunshine."

Jonas was a little shy but tried to keep up a conversation. "When I first opened the shop, it was just for barbers, but over the last year and a half, I decided to change it up some. I hired a few stylists and nail techs to do hair and nails."

"That was a great idea. I see business is booming," Sunshine said, wondering why he stopped her to tell his life story.

Jonas could sense she was slightly bothered. "Anyway, I was just stopping you to see if you would like to check out my place of business. My cousin Meka could hook your hair up before you go into labor," he said, giving her a full look-over.

"I'll think about it. I need to go get me a phone first."

Jonas took that as she didn't have enough money for both. "Let me see that card right quick."

Sunshine handed over the card, then watched as he wrote something on the back.

"I'll be here to help make your appointment, and when the day comes, just hand over the card."

Sunshine looked over the card and saw that he had written "50 percent off" with his signature. She smiled.

"Thank you, Jonas, but you didn't have to."

"Yeah, I didn't, but I wanted to. Just make sure you come back this way after you grab that phone."

Sunshine smiled. "I'm gonna do that."

Jonas smiled as he watched her walk two doors down to the phone store. Although she was pregnant, he still liked what he saw.

"Hey, cuz, don't get your hopes up," Meka said, standing in the doorway.

"Fuck you talkin' about?"

Meka shook her head. "That girl got a man."

"How you figure that?" he said with a straight, serious face, making her laugh.

"You ain't blind, nigga. I could see that baby bump from inside the building. Don't tell me you ain't see it."

Jonas opened the door so they could walk back into the shop. "I saw it, but she not fuckin' with that nigga like that."

"And how you know?" Meka asked.

"I was in her face too long. If she had a man for real, she would have tried to walk away."

Meka shook her head again. Her big cousin Jonas always thought he knew women better than a woman. "OK, cuz, don't get your own feelings hurt."

"I'm not. She pretty as fuck. I want her."

Meka laughed. "OK, do what you gotta do then."

"I am, and you're gonna help."

Meka didn't wanna go against him because he always looked out for her and the rest of the family, so she was down.

"I got you. Just tell me what the plan is."

"Let me put some other shit in motion, and then I'll let you know."

It took Sunshine a good twenty minutes before she came to the shop.

"Hey, can I help you?" one of Jonas's other cousins asked.

Meka jumped up. "I can help you."

After telling her current client she would be right back, she walked off to help Sunshine.

"I wanted to schedule an appointment to get my braids done," Sunshine said, holding the business card in her hand.

Meka took Sunshine's information down in their appointment book. "I'm Meka, one of the braiders here."

"I was told you were one of the best here. I want my appointment to be with you."

"OK, no problem. I have a slot available on Thursday. Is that all right with you?"

"Sure," Sunshine said before walking out of the shop.

Jonas stood in the office doorway at the back of the shop. He didn't want to embarrass himself, so he let Meka take over. He hadn't given her a plan but knew she was smart enough to pull off some shit.

Once Sunshine left, Meka got back to her client's head. She planned to tell her big cuz about her idea later.

Chapter 7

Monsta picked up the phone, ready to hear his mama tell him she got all the money to help him out.

"What's good, Ma? Tell me you got my bread."

"No, Monsta, I got some bad news. Lamar said Sunshine came to pick up the money. He said he didn't even know you were locked up until I came to talk to him."

"What the fuck you mean that bitch got my money?" he asked.

He was trying to keep his cool, but hearing that Sunshine had collected his bread from Lamar pissed him off. The day Sunshine picked up the bag, Lamar had just made some rounds and picked up the money from the other spots, as Monsta had asked him to. Now, hearing that Sunshine had all his money, he really wanted to get out and kill her *and* Keisha.

"I can go by her house and talk like I got some sense. Maybe she'll give it up," Ms. Caldwell suggested.

"Fuck . . . All y'all some fuckups. Y'all can't do shit right," he yelled.

The guard walked over, which prompted Monsta to sit back down.

"Ma, go get my fuckin' money from that bitch. If you gotta fuck her up, then do it. I can't be in here any longer."

"You crazy as fuck. I'm not touching that girl."

"Well, you figure out how to get my shit back," Monsta firmly said before hanging up and walking away.

After talking to her son, Ms. Caldwell drove straight to Sunshine's mother's house. She was going to try her best to talk her into handing over the money, but she wasn't about to get herself in any trouble and jeopardize *her* freedom. Sunshine rolled her eyes as she saw her car pull up in the driveway. She was chilling on the porch with Zoey while the kids played outside.

"You want me to go get Mama?"

"Nope. I'll handle this."

Ms. Caldwell got out of the car and approached the porch. "Sunshine, I need to talk to you for a minute."

"What's up?"

"I went to see Lamar today to try to get my son's money, and he told me you picked it up already. Now, I know you and Monsta had some problems, but now you've gone too far playing with his freedom. You need to give me back his money so he can come home."

"I'm sorry, but I don't know what you're talking about."

Ms. Caldwell pulled out her phone. "Let's see if you gon' be singing that same story," she said as she dialed a number and put it on speakerphone.

"Monsta, I'm standing right in front of Sunshine now."

"Baby, I need you to give my mama that bread so I can come home and help take care of my baby," he said, trying to sound like he gave a fuck.

"I don't have no money, Monsta. Maybe you should check with Keisha."

"It's not the right time to play with me, bitch. Go get my fuckin' money, you stupid bitch," he yelled.

Usually, Sunshine would be in tears, but this time, she laughed at him and his threats.

"That shit no longer bothers me. Sit back, do your time, and make sure you don't drop the soap with yo' stupid ass."

"All right, bitch. You talkin' all that shit 'cause I'm locked up. You act like you forgot who I am. Bitch, I can still get yo' pregnant ass touched, behind bars and all."

"Do what you gotta do, Monsta. I'm so over you and your shit."

"Wait, Sunshine. I know you only trippin' 'cause that bitch said I got her pregnant. I swear she lyin' on my dick."

Sunshine laughed again. "Boy, fuck you and her. I no longer care about that shit. How long did you think I'd be your fool?"

"I'm gon' kill you as soon as I get out," Monsta said with a tone that made her believe this threat.

"OK. Well, let me let them boys know you smuggled a phone up your ass and keep calling, making threats toward me and my unborn baby."

"Stupid bitch, how the fuck I'm supposed to take care of you and my baby while I'm locked up?"

"She don't need you, boy. We gon' forever be good. Now, tell your mama to leave her alone."

Ms. Caldwell shook her head listening to their conversation. It's clear they both were crazy. And from their conversation, there were still some type of feelings between the two.

"Ma, beat her ass and get my money," Monsta ordered.

"I told you I'm not fighting this girl."

"Fuck her and that baby. Ma, I can't be locked up. They trying to do a nigga in," he begged.

Yeah, she never wanted him locked up, but maybe a little sit-down wouldn't hurt him.

"Monsta, I have to go."

"Ma, please," he begged again before she hung up the phone and placed it into her pocket.

"Sunshine, I'm sorry. I really shouldn't have brought my ass over here in the first place. I really just wanna be in my granddaughter's life. I don't care about all that other shit."

"I'll think about it," was all Sunshine would say before walking back to the porch.

Ms. Caldwell got into her car to leave. She could only pray she didn't fuck up with Sunshine and the baby. Monsta was grown and would be OK. She just needed to pick a side and stick to it.

Later that night, Monsta lay on the hard mattress, waiting to get the text that everything had been handled. Muthafuckas were playing him like a fool, so it was time to send out messages to let the streets know he was still running shit. Just as he began to shut his eyes, his phone vibrated.

Quan: It's handled.

Monsta: Good looking.

Monsta turned off the phone and tried to go to sleep, but his mind kept going back to the last conversation he had with Sunshine. She really was letting people put shit in her head. She was ready to throw away everything they had worked so hard for. He wished he had moved her far away from her mama 'cause she wouldn't have been so quick to say fuck him.

Lamar was in tears as he watched his family's home burn to the ground. He knew Monsta was behind it, and it was an attempt on his life because he handed over that money. Since finding out his boy was locked up and Sunshine was on that bullshit, he snuck his family away just to be on the safe side. He had a feeling it was only a matter of time before Monsta showed his ass. He wasn't the type to put hands on a bitch, but Sunshine was about to meet a side of him she'd never seen before.

Sunshine was up, getting ready for her hair appointment. She was happy to have an early appointment. That way, she could relax the rest of the day. As she got dressed, she listened to the morning news. She stopped in her tracks upon hearing them mention a fire that had occurred in the middle of the night. Hearing the street address is what caught her attention.

"Oh my gawd, Lamar," she mumbled.

For a minute, she wanted to blame herself for his death. That was, until the news reported that no one was at home during the time of the fire. Since Sunshine's mom had to work and her sister was still knocked out, she set up her Uber. She was gon' try to go about her day without letting Monsta's shit disturb her peace. Jumping into her Uber, Sunshine had no idea Lamar was parked right up the street, waiting to catch her ass.

Lamar followed her to the shopping plaza. Since it was still early, he wasn't worried about nobody really being up there to stop him from fucking her up. Sunshine jumped out of the backseat, ready to sit in the chair for at least two hours. It had been awhile since she had braids, but she couldn't wait to get them done and over with.

"Aye, Sunshine, let me holla' at yo' ass right quick."

Sunshine turned around to see Lamar standing there. She had no idea what was going through his head, but by the look on his face, it wasn't good.

"What's up? I'm sorry about your house. I saw that shit on the news this morning."

Lamar got close enough to grab her. As he snatched her up by the shirt and tossed her onto the car, the Uber driver began to honk his horn and yell out the window. "Aye, let her go! Let her go!"

"Bitch, what the fuck you tell Monsta?"

"I didn't tell him shit. Now, let me go," Sunshine yelled.

The Uber driver pressed the horn, praying someone would come to her rescue because he was too scared to get out to help her himself. The noise alerted Meka, who was in the shop preparing to open up.

"Jonas, come out here. Something's going on with that girl Sunshine."

Before Jonas left his office, Meka was already running out with the metal bat she kept in the shop.

"Get the fuck off her, muthafucka," she yelled, busting Lamar in the back.

Lamar turned around and saw Meka standing there with her bat and Jonas walking out the door with his gun. Before anyone could say anything else, he looked back at Sunshine. "You better fix this shit with Monsta." Then he ran off.

Jonas rushed over to Sunshine's side. "Are you all right?" Sunshine nodded.

The Uber driver rolled down his window a little more. "Are you all right, ma'am? I called the police, and they're on the way."

"Come into the shop and have a seat."

Jonas helped Sunshine to a chair in his office while Meka went to get her a bottle of water. He had a million questions for her, but he wanted her to settle down first.

"Was that your child's father?" he asked.

Sunshine shook her head. "If it was my child's father, you would have been picking me up from the ground instead of chasing him off so easily."

Jonas quickly caught on to what she was saying. "Damn, I'm sorry to hear that. Is there anything I can help you with? Are you all right?"

"I'm gon' be all right. My feelings were hurt more than anything," she admitted.

"I don't understand how a fucking man can lay hands on a woman. Especially one as beautiful as you."

Sunshine was flattered but didn't want to get Jonas mixed up with her shit. So, instead of responding, she stood up to get to her appointment.

"Hey, Sunshine," Jonas called out before she made it out the door.

"Yeah?"

"You know ain't shit gon' happen to you while you're in this shop, right?" he asked.

She smiled. "I hope not. By the way, I apologize for bringing this shit to your place of business."

"It's all good. Now, go let Meka hook you up."

Sunshine walked out, then went over to Meka's work area. "Thank you."

"Girl, it's nothing. I don't play those types of games. He lucky the whole family wasn't here to fuck him up. He got off too easy if you ask me."

"So, your family runs this place?"

Meka smiled as she started Sunshine's hair. She noticed Sunshine was now asking questions, and she could easily plug in Jonas.

"Yeah. Well, really, this is Jonas's business. Instead of hiring strangers, he paid for everyone interested to attend school and complete their paperwork. Then he hired us all in. He's all about family."

"Is that so?"

"Yeah, he a good guy, for real."

Just as she said that, Jonas walked out of the office. Sunshine looked his way, and they smiled at each other. Thinking about the bullshit she was already in and not wanting to get him caught up, she put her head down. Jonas wanted to go over to her and lift it back up, but didn't want to make her feel like a charity case or something. He went to his barber chair and started working on his clients for the day.

It took long enough, but the police finally showed up. To keep the rest of the clients out of the mix, they stepped into Jonas's office to ask Sunshine a few questions. By the end of the conversation, she had given them Lamar's name. They left with a promise to keep her updated on the case. Sunshine sat back down to finish getting her hair done. Once again, Meka asked if she was all right. Sunshine explained again that besides snatching her up and him talking shit like his boss, Lamar really didn't do any harm.

A whole three hours passed, and Meka was just now getting done with Sunshine's hair.

"So, how do you like it?" she asked, spinning her around to face the mirror.

Sunshine looked over her head. "I love these braids. You do have the magic touch."

Sunshine pulled out her wallet to pay Meka. "Here you go."

"Hold up. Come over here with me," Meka said as she went over to the front desk.

"Gotta keep the books right."

Jonas walked over to get a better look. "Those look nice on you."

"Thank you."

Jonas saw the money in her hand. "Where's your card?" he asked Sunshine.

Meka looked at him, wondering what he was talking about.

Sunshine looked into her purse, then pulled it out. "Here it go."

Meka watched as her cousin took over the register, wondering what the fuck he was thinking, giving her 50 percent off her hairdo.

"Thank you," Sunshine said to Jonas before turning her attention back to Meka. "I really appreciate you for everything today," she said, giving her a hundred-dollar tip.

"Thank you, girl."

Sunshine walked out the door. Jonas had to think of something quickly to stop her from leaving.

"I'll be right back."

"Jonas, she comes with drama. You sure you wanna be bothered with all that shit?"

"Just call me a fucking actor 'cause I'm ready for the drama," he said as he rushed outside.

Meka shook her head. She didn't want anything to happen to her cousin, but she will forever have his back.

"Aye, Sunshine!"

Turning around, she saw Jonas trying to catch up with her. "What's up? Did I forget something?"

"Not really, but I was wondering if you needed a ride or something. I notice you came in an Uber earlier."

"Look, Jonas, you really seem like a nice guy, but I don't need you getting mixed up in my bullshit."

"Maybe I believe you'll be worth it."

Sunshine tried not to blush. "And what makes you think that? How you know I'm not still with my child's father?"

He chuckled. "If your child's father was in the picture, no other nigga would be putting their hands on you, and you wouldn't be jumping in and out of an Uber. Well, I know if you were mine, I wouldn't be letting none of that shit go down. Especially while carrying my child."

Sunshine stood there blushing. She could not long hold it in. Jonas was saying everything right.

"Besides, I've been holding your hand all this time, and you haven't snatched away yet. Just let me treat you to lunch or something."

"I don't know about all that, Jonas."

"Look, it's not a lifetime commitment. It's just two friends going out to lunch."

After thinking it over, Sunshine agreed to the invitation. "All right, I'm down for that."

Jonas walked Sunshine over to his car. "Let me go tell Meka I'm leaving. I'll be right back."

Sunshine waited in the car as he went back into the shop. She prayed she wasn't making a terrible mistake with Jonas. She wondered if she should've just taken her ass home.

"Aye, Meka, let me talk to you right quick."

Meka followed Jonas into his office. "What's up, cuz?"

"I'm leaving for the day. Can you close up for me?"

"I guess I can do that," she said with a smirk on her face.

Jonas pulled some bills out of his pocket. "Thanks for everything."

"Yeah, yeah. Just be careful, Jonas."

"For sure," he said before walking out.

Jonas wasn't into that whole street life bullshit, but he was never afraid to handle his business. He wasn't gonna go out asking or looking for a problem, but he would solve shit quickly.

"So, what do you have the taste for?" he asked Sunshine as he got into the car.

"Tacos."

Jonas laughed. "We can do that, but it won't be none of that Taco Bell bullshit. Let's go get some real shit."

"All right," she said, sitting back for the ride.

That day turned out better than she thought. They ended up eating at a Mexican restaurant. Over lunch, they had the opportunity to discuss just about everything. At first, she tried not to bring Monsta up and keep the conversation on her, but Jonas kept beating around the topic. It's as if he were trying to place himself in her life, but he was also making sure Monsta wouldn't be a problem.

"Jonas, my daughter's father is locked up right now. I really don't wanna talk about him."

"So, you're saying if I wanted your number and wanted to ask you out again, he wouldn't be a problem?"

"I told you he was locked up."

"I heard that. I'm just trying to see if we were to get closer eventually, I wouldn't get pushed to the sideline so you two could rekindle what y'all had before when he gets out."

Sunshine sat up in her chair. "I thought what we had was good at first and looked over his bullshit. But after finally walking away, I can't see myself running back to that toxic shit. I'm just trying to live my life in peace and take care of my daughter."

"I feel you. Ain't nothing wrong with that either. I just wanna be part of your life."

Sunshine was a little confused. "Huh?"

"I didn't mean to say that out loud, but I guess it wouldn't hurt for you to know how I really feel."

"Jonas, you're a nice guy, but I'm not trying to rush into anything when I just got out of a bad relationship. Besides, I don't want it to seem like you're a rebound guy. I hope you understand that."

He smiled at her. "Yeah, I do understand. I also like how you're not telling me hell nah or get lost. I guess I still stand a chance with you."

Sunshine giggled. She saw he was letting her pass him by. As they continued to talk, she could easily feel herself liking him even more, especially when he talked about business and the love he had for his family.

"So, I planned to open up another shop this fall, but some bullshit popped off and pushed my plans back."

"What happened?"

"I moved my cousin here and was waiting for him to get his license to cut hair. I guess the process was taking too long, and he came up with this stupid-ass plan to sell drugs. One day, some nigga shot him down and killed him right on his block. I wish he had let me know he didn't have shit. I would've given him any amount of money before I let him turn to the streets."

"Damn, I'm so sorry to hear that."

"It's cool. My family and I help his baby mama out with the kids and everything as much as possible. It won't bring my cousin back, but hopefully, his sons will never end up making the same mistakes he did."

After lunch, Jonas drove around with Sunshine. He enjoyed the conversation so much that he didn't want her to go home.

"Where are we going?"

"I don't know, just riding. You ready for me to drop you off?"

"I'm full and getting sleepy," she admitted.

She tried to protect him and act like she wasn't trying to start anything with him, but her actions told him she was feeling him. Sunshine had to admit to herself that Jonas was not only handsome, but he was, in fact, a good guy. It's crazy how she thought Monsta was a boss because he made moves in the streets, but then there was Jonas. He was the real boss. He had his own business and plans to grow his family name. Upgrading to a real boss didn't sound like a bad idea.

"So, this is where you live?" he asked as he pulled up in her driveway.

"Yeah, for now, but I'm looking for a place for me and my daughter. Staying here with my mom and sister is cool, but I need my own space."

"If you need any help, I can help you out. I could talk to the people I bought my building from. That's if you're trying to buy property."

"Yes, that's exactly what I wanna do. I swear you stepped into my life at the right time."

"I hope that's a good thing."

"It is."

Jonas stared at her as she undid her seat belt. He didn't want her to get out, but didn't wanna rush shit between them. In his mind, she was gonna be his one day.

"Sunshine, you got my number. Make sure you use it."

"I will," she said, jumping out of the car.

Jonas sat there and waited for her to step into the house safely. She had no idea how happy it would make him if she decided to give him a chance. He didn't even mind playing daddy to another man's baby, either.

Sunshine had just gotten out of the shower and climbed into bed when her phone went off. She didn't wanna answer it at first because she hadn't given anyone her number yet. Whoever it was kept hanging up, just to call again, so she decided to answer, thinking that maybe they were trying to reach whoever had the number originally.

"Hello."

"I had to kill my best friend over your ass."

Sunshine shook her head, regretting that she had answered the phone. "Monsta, how did you get this number?"

"I heard Lamar tried to get tough with you. He dead now. See, baby? Even locked up, I'll always protect you."

"Oh my gawd, Monsta. What did you do?"

"I told you ain't shit stopping 'cause I'm in here. If I really wanted to hurt you or your people, I could."

Sunshine started crying. "Monsta, leave my family out of this. If you mad at me, then deal with me. Leave them alone."

"That's the thing. I wanna beat your ass so fucking bad, but you still got my heart. I love you, Sunshine. Can you just say it back so that I can have a good night's sleep for once?"

Sunshine knew this act all too well. This was the part where she'd play forgive and forget because he was talking nicely. Good thing she was finally tired of his shit.

"Monsta, you don't love me, so stop saying that shit. You got a whole side family. Go love on them."

"I told you that bitch lying. I never fucked any other bitch raw besides you. How long have we been together, and how many times have I admitted to the shit I did? I might be a lot of shit, but never no liar."

Sunshine hated to admit it, but he was right. He always admitted what he'd done, no matter what he did or who he hurt. When he was mad, throwing up that he got her best friend pregnant would have made him feel better about himself, and she couldn't see him passing up that opportunity.

"How did you get my number?" she asked again.

"You my baby. Why wouldn't I have your number? Did you really think it was gonna be that easy to get rid of me?"

Sunshine shook her head at his foolishness. "Monsta, you really hurt me in so many ways. I need you to let me go and live my life without you."

"Bitch, you sound stupid as hell. You gon' be mine forever, especially since you havin' my baby."

"You have a lot of nerve. You wish death on me and Mya every other day. Now, you wanna act like a family man. I don't want this shit anymore. I deserve better."

"I'm the best out here, bitch. Do you ever wonder why you never heard from your ex since we been together?"

"No, Monsta. I thought he just got over me like I want you to do."

"After the first night we fucked, I killed him. I never wanted another nigga to say they had you the way I had you. Can't you see I'm not gon' let you go? Bitch, you mine for life."

Monsta didn't give Sunshine a chance to respond. He hung up, leaving her in her thoughts. Because of his love for her, Lamar and her ex-boyfriend were dead. Monsta was just that—a fucking Monsta.

Chapter 8

"Damn, cuz. You look lost over there. What's on your mind?" Meka asked Jonas.

Jonas put his phone on the table. "Nothing much. Wondering if I should've listened to you about Sunshine."

"What's going on? What happened?" she questioned.

"I haven't heard from her ass since I dropped her off two weeks ago."

"Cuz, I told you she had drama and needed to get her shit together. Let her deal with that shit before you jump straight into it. I know you think you really like her, but maybe she just wasn't the one."

Jonas got up to unlock the door. The shop was about to get busy with everyone trying to get fly for the weekend. Hearing the bell above the door go off made Meka and Jonas look up. To their surprise, Sunshine walked in. Meka didn't like how her cousin felt played and couldn't wait to say something to Sunshine. She didn't play about family.

"How can we help you?" she asked with much attitude.

"Hey, Meka, I really need to speak to Jonas."

Meka was ready to go off, but Jonas stepped in. "I got it, Meka. Everyone else should be pulling up soon."

Meka rolled her eyes at Sunshine as Jonas walked her into the office.

Taking a seat across from him, she began to apologize. "I wanted to apologize for being missing in action."

"You don't owe me shit."

"I don't, but I felt it was only right that I explain everything to you."

Jonas tried to act like it didn't matter to him, but he was happy to see her again. "I'm listening."

"I told you I had a crazy ex, and right now, he is locked up. He's been doing a lot of shit from behind bars, and it scared me. The guy who attacked me that day was his best friend, and he killed him that same day for touching me. I bought a new phone and somehow, he found out my number. He made threats against me, our daughter, and even my family. For the last few weeks, I have moved and changed my number three times. I'm at the point where I just threw the phone away 'cause I don't wanna be bothered, and that's why I couldn't call you."

Jonas got out of the chair and went over to her. Sunshine cried in his arms. She wasn't sure if he could save her from Monsta, but it would be nice if he could.

"I got you. I'm not gon' let nobody hurt you."

Sunshine wanted to believe what he was saying. There had to be some good guys left in this world.

"So, what now?"

"I had my mom call up there, and she reported him for having a phone so that he won't be a bother anymore," Sunshine admitted.

"OK, cool. For now, let's put this shit behind us and actually build us. How does that sound?"

"I like that plan. I can't keep letting that boy run my life."

Meka didn't bother to knock as she opened the door. "Jonas, they're starting to pile up. Your service is needed out here," she announced before looking down at Sunshine. She could tell she'd been crying. "What's wrong, Sunshine? Is everything all right?" she asked with a whole new attitude.

"Let's give her a minute. She'll be all right," Jonas said before pulling Meka out of the office. "She had some shit she had to work out, but I'm gonna help her out."

"OK, cool. She's a sweet girl, and it was gon' kill me to act up on her. You know I'm all for having my family's back."

"Yeah, and I appreciate that, but she gon' be around for a minute."

"OK, Jonas. I'm following your lead on this. As long as you like it, I love it."

The two cousins went to their booths ready to work. Once the shop started to calm down, Jonas made his way to the store to purchase Sunshine another phone. Since she was pregnant, she didn't need to be riding around without one. When he went back into his office, he saw that she was lying on the couch, sleeping. He didn't want to wake her, but from napping on the couch plenty of times, he knew it was very uncomfortable.

"Get up, sleepyhead," he said, giving her a shake.

"I'm up," she said, sitting up. "Dang. I didn't even realize I fell asleep."

"Here, I got you this. I can't have you out here with no phone. I'm not sure how that nigga keeps finding out your number, but that one's in my name. He shouldn't be able to do shit with that one."

"Thank you, Jonas. You know you didn't have to do this."

"Yeah, I really did."

The two shared a kiss. Sunshine was happy. Not a single bone in her body felt guilty about liking someone other than Monsta. He was now old news. For the first time in a minute, Sunshine believed everything would be all right, and she would remain happy.

***

For the next two weeks, Jonas kept his promise about helping her find a home for her and her daughter. She was delighted. Since packing and moving from the old house, she hadn't unpacked everything 'cause she hated moving and all the work that came with it.

Ms. Mathews thought Sunshine was crazy for calling herself having a new boyfriend, but after meeting Jonas, she could see he was the complete opposite of Monsta. After dinner at Sunshine's new house, he quickly got her and Zoey's approval.

"Ma, what do you really think? Over the last few months, I've learned to really appreciate your opinion about these guys out here."

"He's one of the good ones, Sunshine. Any man who's gonna stick around a girl in your situation is an angel in disguise. Just make sure you do right by him."

"I am, Mama. I really do like him."

After her mom and sister left, Jonas helped Sunshine clean up their dinner mess.

"I gave y'all some free time to talk about me. What's the verdict?"

Sunshine turned to face him and placed a kiss on his lips. "Let's just say my mom likes you and actually told me to make sure I take good care of you."

"Oh, OK. I guess we locked in," he said, wrapping his hands around her.

Sunshine enjoyed the way he kissed on her and the way his hands touched her.

"Jonas, why don't you take the trash out and meet me in the shower?"

"Fuck that trash," he said between kisses.

"Jonas, we can fuck after the trash is out of the house."

Jonas hated to stop after getting in the mood, but finally being able to have her in that type of way was a gift in itself.

As promised, Sunshine allowed him to make love to her from the shower to the bedroom all night long. She had never been the type to rush anything with a guy, but everything about being with Jonas felt right.

The next morning, Sunshine woke up feeling great. Jonas had what her body cried out for.

Feeling her eyes burning a hole in him, he opened his eyes. "Good morning."

"Good morning."

"You sleep all right?"

Sunshine smiled. "Yeah, I slept great and woke up feeling even better."

Jonas smiled, knowing he was the reason she felt good and wore a smile on her face. He pulled her in closer, wrapping her in his arms. After placing a kiss on her lips, he whispered in her ear, "I wanna be the reason you're always smiling."

"I believe you're doing exactly that, Jonas."

He gave her another kiss, then kissed her belly. "You want some breakfast?"

Sunshine rubbed her round belly. "You already know," she said, giggling.

After a hot shower, Jonas left to pick up their breakfast from Coney Island. As he got into his car, he never knew he and Sunshine were being watched.

"Aye, Monsta, you called just in time. That nigga just pulled off."

Monsta was hurt. "She got that nigga spending the night and shit? I'm gon' kill that girl. I let her play with me for too fuckin' long."

"Tell me the next move."

"When I give you a callback, light up that bitch. I don't give a fuck anymore," Monsta said before hanging up.

While Jonas was out getting food, Sunshine jumped into the shower, although she wished she could chill in bed with him all day. Just as she was getting dressed, her phone started to ring.

"Hello."

"You letting niggas bust all on my baby head and shit? You a nasty bitch like your friend. I told you that both you hoes were the same," Monsta yelled into the phone.

Sunshine hated how this nigga kept finding her.

"You hear me talkin' to you, bitch? You know I can't let that nigga live, right?"

Sunshine felt sick to her stomach hearing Monsta's voice over the phone. She quickly hung up. Just as she was on her way downstairs, she could hear Jonas shut the car door. She ran into his arms at the door, panicking. "He knows about us!" she said.

"What?"

Before she could explain anything, shots rang out, tearing holes in the windows and front door. Jonas quickly got Sunshine down to the ground.

"You all right?" he asked, but all he could do was hear her screaming.

What seemed like forever really turned out to be a hot five minutes of nothing but gunshots entering her home.

"Jonas, I think they gone. The shots stopped."

Sunshine gave him a minute before she finally tried to sit up. Jonas's arm stayed wrapped around her tightly, making it difficult.

"Oh my gawd, Jonas, get up! You gotta be all right, Jonas," she yelled out, noticing the blood rush out of his shoulder.

She quickly grabbed his phone that was lying on the floor. It must've fallen out of his hand when he was saving her.

In no time, an ambulance was pulling up, thanks to the neighbors who helped call.

***

Sunshine sat in the waiting room, crying and praying for Jonas. He was a good guy and didn't deserve what being with her brought him.

The police were there, in her face, asking her a million questions. "Ma'am, if you know who did this, we can go pick them up now and have them locked up. We just need you to say something."

Just then, Meka and a few other members of Jonas's family showed up.

"Ain't no point in talking because y'all not gon' do shit. I put in many reports and even told y'all about the mastermind behind all of this shit having a phone behind bars. Y'all not trying to help me out. I might as will let him kill me, so he can stop killing everyone else," she cried.

Hearing her say that, Meka walked over to Sunshine. "I don't fuckin' think so. My cousin is gon' be all right, and these officers are gon' go do their fucking job. You not about to give up that fast."

Sunshine buried her face in her hands. She was so hurt that she couldn't stop crying. If Jonas didn't make it out of surgery, she didn't know how she could live with that on her conscience.

"Aye, shorty, you can't sit over there beating yourself up. We know this wasn't what you wanted for you and our cousin," Kyrie said, taking a seat next to Meka.

"I just can't believe Monsta did this shit. I wish he would just let me go," Sunshine mumbled.

"Monsta?" he asked.

"Yeah, that's my ex."

Kyrie eyed his brother, Mason, and then they both eyed their older cousin, Jayson. Meka tried to stay on top of shit but was so out of the loop.

"What's that for?" she asked.

"We'll talk to you later," Mason said before pacing the floor.

"OK," she said, turning her attention back to Sunshine.

"I just want y'all to know I never wanted this to happen to Jonas. I have done so much to keep all my personal business and stuff a secret so that I wouldn't be found. I hope y'all aren't mad at me."

"As long as our cousin good, we cool. Just pray he pulls out of this shit," Jayson firmly warned her.

Ms. Mathews walked into the waiting room. "Oh my gawd, Sunshine, are you all right?"

"Ma, it was Monsta. He found me again."

She held her daughter and allowed her to cry until she couldn't cry anymore.

"How is this boy finding you and able to do as he please while he's locked up? I don't understand why the police can't do anything about this shit."

"Ma, I don't know. They were here asking me questions, but it felt like they were playing in my face. I don't even want to deal with them anymore."

"Don't worry about all that shit. Our family gon' handle all this shit," Kyrie said before texting on his phone.

Meka pulled her phone out after hearing the notification sound go off. She quickly read the message Kyrie sent.

Kyrie: Aye, cuz, her ex the one that killed Trevor. We gotta do him in.

Meka put away her phone without saying a word.

Knowing they had a big family, Sunshine let them do whatever and didn't give a fuck. All she wanted was to have a healthy baby and for Jonas to be all right.

After another hour and some change, the nurse came into the waiting room to let them know Jonas was out of recovery and now back in his room. His family rushed to see him, leaving Sunshine sitting in the waiting room with her mom.

"You gon' go see him?"

"I can't, Ma. What if he blames me and hates me now?"

"Come on, girl. You sat here all this time waiting to see how he was doing. Now, you act like you scared to see him."

Sunshine stood up. "Can you just take me home? I need to figure out some shit."

Just as Ms. Mathews stood up, Jonas's cousins walked past the waiting room. Everyone kept walking, but Meka.

"Jonas is asking for you."

"I was just about to leave."

"No, you weren't. He doesn't blame you for nothing. Now, go talk to him," Meka said.

Once Sunshine walked off, Meka told Ms. Mathews she would take Sunshine to her house to make sure she was all right.

"You ain't wanna come see me?" Jonas asked as soon as she walked into the room.

Sunshine took a seat. "I was scared you were gonna blame me for everything. I'm so sorry about all of this, Jonas. I swear I never wanted this to happen."

Jonas shook his head. "Nah, never that. I could never blame you. If anything, I knew what I was getting myself into when I decided to still fuck with you after you told me about your ex."

Sunshine started crying. "I'm just so sorry you got shot. I never wanted this shit to happen."

"Come sit up here with me," he said, patting a spot on the bed.

Sunshine hesitated at first, but she got up to join him in the bed. As she sat on the edge, he tried his best to hold her without hurting his shoulder.

"You mine now, and ain't shit gon' change that. I'm not on no shit like your ex, but I'm not about to give up without a fight."

Sunshine managed to lie on his chest. She felt safe in his arms, and he hadn't lifted a finger or even made a move yet. Just his tone made her feel better.

Meka figured she had given them enough time to talk. Besides, she was ready to go home. She was surprised to walk into the room and find them both knocked out, asleep. She smiled, knowing her cousin was happy despite what happened.

"Aye, Sunshine, come on, girl. It's time to get up."

Sunshine sat up, still half-asleep. "All right, I'm up."

As she climbed out of bed, Jonas woke up. "What's going on?"

"We about to go, cuz, I'll bring her back tomorrow."

Sunshine hugged Jonas. "I'll see you tomorrow."

Jonas gave her one last kiss.

"OK, lovebirds, it's time to go," Meka announced, making everyone laugh.

The following week flew by, and it was finally time for Jonas to be released. It was Meka's idea for Sunshine to pick him up from the hospital, and Sunshine couldn't have been happier to do so. As they drove off, Jonas told her over and over again how glad he was to be able to come home to her finally.

"Jonas, for the last few days, I've been between my mom's house and Meka's house. I really ain't been back to my house."

"Let's go by it and see what's up," he suggested.

"Hell nah. I don't even wanna see how fucked up that house is right now. Besides, it's gonna bring up bad memories."

"Go over there right quick. I need to see it for personal reasons."

Sunshine gave him one last look before making her way toward her house. She didn't know what was so important that he needed a reminder of what happened in that house, but she listened. As they turned on the block, Sunshine could see a lot of activity going on.

"What the hell?"

Jonas sat there with a grin on his face, knowing his family had come through just as he asked them to.

"Jonas, what the hell?" Sunshine parked in the driveway.

To her surprise, her house was back to normal. She gave up on the house after the shooting and even started looking for a new one. She had no idea Jonas had his family fix the house up while he was in the hospital.

Before getting out of the car, he leaned over to kiss her. "I told you I wasn't giving up on us that quickly."

Sunshine started to open the door, but stopped in her tracks. "I just wanted to tell you that I really appreciate you, and that I love you, Jonas."

"I love you too," he said, meaning it from the bottom of his heart.

Jayson came over to the car and opened Jonas's door. "Can we have our cuz now?"

Sunshine laughed. "Only for a second."

Jayson laughed as he helped Jonas out of the car. Sunshine was also helped out of the car and couldn't help but smile at her home. Someone even took the time to plant flowers in her yard. Everything was just so beautiful. After looking over the house, the tears couldn't stop falling from her eyes. It had been a minute, but she was actually crying tears of happiness. Between Sunshine's mama, sister, her sister's kids, and Jonas's family, the house was packed with nothing but good energy and positive vibes. Sunshine felt love coming from everyone there. She couldn't help but love his grandma, who kept bringing her plates. She kept telling Sunshine to "feed the baby."

"Granny, you just brought her some food."

"I don't need another skinny-ass grandbaby. Your mama ain't wanna listen to me. Now look at your skinny ass."

She had everyone in the house laughing at her. Sunshine laughed for a minute before she realized his granny thought she was carrying Jonas's baby.

Meka pulled Sunshine aside. "I told you that if Jonas was down, our whole family was down, and I mean that shit."

Sunshine hugged Meka. She couldn't even lie or act like they didn't have her back.

"Before we all fuck up this food, I wanna make an announcement," Jonas yelled, getting everyone's attention.

"What's up, nephew?" his Uncle Buck asked.

"I wanted everyone to be here to witness this day. I'm really counting on my family to support my every move."

Sunshine looked around and saw that just about everyone was smiling while she waited to see what he was talking about. It wasn't until he stood in front of her, then dropped down to one knee that she figured it out.

"Oh my gawd, don't do it, cuz," one of his cousins yelled out as a joke.

"Sunshine, will you make me the happiest man alive and take my hand in marriage?"

Sunshine was crying as she looked over at her mom.

"I can't answer the question for you, girl. Answer that man," Ms. Mathews yelled out. She was happy for her daughter, although their relationship was moving fast. Just after a few months, her daughter was finally getting what she had spent years trying to get from that fool Monsta.

Through her crying, Sunshine was able to tell Jonas she would marry him. She loved him, so she didn't see why not. Besides, tomorrow wasn't promised, and there was no need to put her life on hold. Sunshine helped Jonas get up after he placed the ring on her finger. What she didn't know was that he had made this plan before he got shot.

For the rest of the night, everyone congratulated them and helped celebrate their engagement. Everything was going great, and Sunshine couldn't help but pray that things stayed that way. That night, once everyone left, Sunshine started cleaning up whatever her mom and his granny didn't do.

"Oh nah, leave that shit alone."

"Baby, I can't just leave this stuff everywhere."

Jonas grabbed the trash bag from her. "Let me get this."

"Fuck," he yelled, dropping the bag.

"I got it, Jonas. Don't fuck up your shoulder."

"You not about to lift that shit while you're pregnant. Just leave that shit. I'll have my li'l cousins come clean up in the morning."

Sunshine looked around. "I can do it if you get out of my way, Jonas."

"No fiancée of mine is about to be lifting trash. Let's go to bed." This time, he grabbed her hand.

After a shower, the couple chilled in bed, holding each other.

"You just don't know how happy you made me today. I prayed you didn't turn me down in front of everyone."

Sunshine giggled. "Now, why would I do that? In the short time I've known you, you've been nothing but good to me. I never feel like I need to question or doubt anything you say. Jonas, I really do love you."

"I really do love you too. I'm willing to do whatever it takes to keep you safe, happy, and anything else you need. Not only do I wanna be in your life completely, but I also wanna be here for Mya. I want her to have a real man in her life. Every child needs a father in my book."

"You're right about that, Jonas. That's exactly why I'm happy I found you to be part of our life."

Sunshine fell asleep on his chest like she would typically do, but Jonas couldn't sleep. His mind was focused on his future with Sunshine and Mya.

Two weeks later, Ms. Caldwell went to visit her son. Like any other time, she didn't bring good news.

"Hey, Ma. What brings you here after ignoring me for so long?"

Shaking her head, she cut straight to the chase. "Sunshine had the baby. Mya is finally here. I'm surprised she made it through all y'all bullshit."

Monsta smiled. "My baby, Mya Caldwell," he said with a big Kool-Aid smile.

"They let you smoke dope in here, boy?"

"Fuck you talking about, Ma?" he questioned.

"Mya *Bentley* is finally here. Did you think that girl was gon' give that baby your last name?" she asked, laughing at her son.

Monsta jumped up. "You lying. Tell me that bitch didn't give my baby that nigga's last name."

The guard walked over to calm him down. "You gotta sit down, boy, or your visiting hour is over."

Monsta stood there in his feelings. "Get the fuck away from me, bro."

"Monsta, sit your ass down. You deserve this hurt for everything you did to that girl."

Monsta slammed his fist on the table. "Oh, you think this shit funny? Fuck you, fuck Sunshine, that fuckin' baby, and especially that nigga who was supposed to be dead. Fuck everybody," Monsta yelled, picking up his chair and flinging it toward his mama.

She was grateful for the glass that divided them.

The guard grabbed him, and Monsta went crazy. Next thing Ms. Caldwell knew, more guards were jumping on her son. They pulled her out of the building. She wanted him to hurt, but never wanted nobody to lay hands on him. She drove off, once again blaming herself and her fucked-up way of thinking that caused her son to get hurt.

Chapter 9

"I don't know what your problem is, boy, but you gotta learn to let all that hurt go and serve your time without going to the hole every time we let you out. What's wrong with you? What type of person wanna be in the hole for weeks and months at a time?"

"A muthafuka that just don't give a fuck," Monsta calmly said.

The guard shook his head, not understanding Monsta's way of thinking. "Maybe you can talk to someone about getting you some help," the guard suggested.

"Help me out by shutting the damn door before I fuck you up, bitch-ass nigga."

The guard slid the door shut before walking away, confused about it all. He knew being locked up could be tough on someone, but Monsta had spent most of his time in the hole. Just four months ago, Monsta received some bad news from the outside world, and ever since then, he has spent most of his time in the hole. Whenever it was time for him to join the prison population, he would beat a prisoner's ass or jump on a guard, just to go back to the hole. He took a few ass beatings from the guards, but nothing seemed to faze him because he stayed on his bullshit every time he was freed.

Monsta sat with his back against the cold wall. He was hurting deep down inside over the way Sunshine played him and gave his daughter Jonas's last name. For one, she really ain't even know that nigga like that. On top of that, the way his mother laughed at his pain tore him down even more on the inside. He had no other choice after that day but to take her off his visitors' list and stop responding to her letters. He didn't give a fuck how she was gonna get by without his help. He had to wash his hands of her petty ass. That dark, cold room and his thoughts were all he had left.

Monsta tossed and turned, thinking about his pops. It wasn't long before he felt his eyes getting too heavy to stay awake.

"Look at cha', son, just look at cha'. I left my legacy for you to keep our name in these streets. I'm not proud of what I see, Monsta. All I see is you running our name into the damn ground."

With tears in his eyes, Monsta replied, "I'm sorry, Pops. I'm sorry."

"Never be a sorry nigga. Just do better," Big Monsta firmly said.

"I am, Pops. I promise I'm gonna do better."

Before vanishing, Big Monsta gave his son one last look, hoping he was helping him out.

"I died a fucking legend. Don't kill off our family name by being locked up for some bullshit. I taught you better than that. You get outta this muthafucka and get your bread and title back in these streets. Fuck all that other bullshit."

Monsta jumped up, reaching out, hoping he could at least get a hug from his pops, but Big Monsta was gone. The whole situation had him in his feelings. He cried out for his pops, knowing his father was the only one who truly understood him besides Sunshine.

The next morning, Monsta thought back to what the guard and his pops told him and decided to look into it. The first thing he had to do to get his plan popping was act like he had some fucking sense when he got released from the hole again in three weeks. Maybe it was time to admit he did, in fact, have problems so he could get the help he needed.

"Hey, my Mya Pie," Sunshine said as she played with Mya.

Ever since she had Mya, her smile never left her face. It was a blessing to have such a happy baby. Mya's face lit up every time she saw her mama and daddy. Sunshine knew what love felt like, but with Mya, it was something stronger than love. Mya had her whole heart.

Besides getting so much love from Mya, Sunshine also had to admit Jonas had been by her side every step of the way, and he was really a good help with Mya. When she was pregnant, he made so many promises. She had to admit that he was truly a man of his word. At first, she thought maybe they were moving too fast, but when the feelings were real on both ends, time didn't mean a thing.

Jonas stepped into the room fresh out of the shower.

"I thought you said you were putting her to bed."

"I am, baby," Sunshine said, still playing in Mya's face.

"You know all that keeps her wide awake and wanting to stay up longer," Jonas said, picking up Mya. He walked over to his side of the bed. "Hey, Daddy's princess."

Sunshine giggled. "And you were just talking about me. She got you wrapped around her baby finger."

"As she should. Y'all two know where my heart is. It's my job as her dad and your future husband to make sure y'all want for nothing," he replied.

Sunshine blushed. "Aww . . . You're such a sweetheart, baby, but I think you just wanted to take her from me to play with. You not trying to put her to sleep, either."

"I think you're right," he said, placing a kiss on Mya's cheek, causing her to giggle.

Since the birth of Mya, Jonas had stepped up as a great father and provider. He made sure she and Mya never went without. He never knew about the money Sunshine stole from Monsta, but that still wouldn't have stopped him from being the provider in the home. He told Sunshine since day one that he would step up, and he did exactly that. Never in his life did he think he'd find a wife who came with drama, but he was glad he was able to look past it all because Sunshine and Mya had his heart completely.

Jonas lay Mya down on his chest as he got comfortable in the bed. She was tired and was ready for dreamland.

"How was your day?" he asked.

"It was going good until I bumped into Ms. Caldwell at the market."

Jonas sat up, damn near waking up Mya. "I know she didn't try any slick shit."

"Nah, baby, she didn't. It was weird. To my surprise, she acted like everything was all good between us."

"Really?"

Sunshine didn't say anything else, and her quietness alerted Jonas.

"Why do I feel like you're not telling me everything?" he questioned.

They had only been together for a few months, but Jonas knew the look Sunshine gave when she wasn't being completely honest about everything. She had a cute, telltale sign and didn't even know it. Sunshine looked down, hesitant to tell him everything. At the same time, she didn't want to lie to him, either.

"Baby, we stood in the aisle and talked. She even played with Mya for a minute. She also told me she wanted to be a part of Mya's life."

Jonas wasn't feeling all that shit, but before he gave his opinion, he decided to see where her head was. "How do you feel about that? What did you tell her?"

Sunshine sat up, trying to choose her words carefully. "Honestly, I wouldn't mind her being in Mya's life. I told her I would talk to you first since you're her father now."

Jonas leaned over to kiss her. One thing he could admit was that she was loyal to his position in their life.

"What makes her think it would be cool if all she gon' do is run to her son about everything? We haven't heard shit from that nigga in months, so let's leave it that way."

"She said she hasn't spoken to him, either. Supposedly, he said fuck her, removed her from his visitors' list, and stopped responding to her letters. I told you that boy ain't all there in the head."

Jonas buried his head in his hands before looking back up at Sunshine. "So, what do you wanna do about this situation?"

"I don't know, baby. Would it be right just to say, 'Fuck her'? I mean, whatever happened between me and Monsta wasn't her fault."

"Hell nah. Fuck her, him, and whoever else out there played a role in me getting shot. I don't trust the bitch."

"Jonas," Sunshine called out.

Jonas got out of bed with Mya. "Forget it. Just do whatever you wanna do, Sunshine. It's clear as hell this nigga still got a part of your heart, and you desperately need him in your life. I guess I'm just the loyal, good nigga sitting around, loving you like a dumbass."

"Why would you say that? Do you really believe that bullshit?" she yelled as he walked out of the room.

After storming out of the bedroom, Jonas went into Mya's room to lay her down. Standing over her, he spoke softly to her. "You my baby, and I'm not about to let your mama fuck shit up dealing with those toxic muthafuckas."

Sunshine didn't mean to piss him off. She was only trying to be honest about the whole situation. Making her way downstairs, she saw Jonas lying on the couch. If he'd rather lie on the sofa than sleep in the bed with her, they had a problem.

"Baby, please come back to bed. We need to talk about this."

"I'm good. Go ahead and go to bed. Don't you have plans to go see your mama in the morning?" he replied.

Sunshine sat at the end of the couch. "Forget all of that, Jonas. Can you please listen to me? Yes, we did move fast with our relationship, but you shouldn't have any doubt in your heart that I love you and only you. Why would you ever question your place with me?" she asked with tears rolling down her cheeks.

"Mya got a fucking daddy. My whole family loves her and treats her no differently from the other kids. What the fuck you need his family for? Where was these muthafuckas when he was beating yo' ass and making you cry every fuckin' day?"

"Jonas, baby, calm down. You ain't have to say all that. Besides, I told you she was there and, for the most part, stopped a lot of that bullshit from happening. You act like I'm talking about taking Mya to go see him while he's locked up."

Jonas turned his back on her. He was over the conversation.

"Go ahead and do what the fuck you wanna do, Sunshine. If you think she needs to have a relationship with that lady, then it's clear a part of you still wants to have an attachment to him."

Sunshine sat there in her feelings and silently cried. She hated that he didn't understand how she felt. No, it wasn't about pleasing Monsta. It was about Mya knowing her family, whether it was hers, Jonas's, or even Monsta's family. With her way of thinking, she didn't see any wrong being done.

"Jonas, can we try to come to an understanding about this? I hate for us to go to bed mad at each other."

Jonas sat up. "I'm not mad. Go get some sleep."

Sunshine wasn't giving up that easily. "No, talk to me, Jonas."

"Look, I don't give a fuck about Monsta or his mama. You act like you forgot about him having someone shoot up this very house like a fucking month before you gave birth to Mya. I don't trust them muthafuckas. What more proof do you need not to trust them too?"

"Jonas, it wasn't her who was doing wrong. It was her fucking son."

"You can't trust her either. That's all I'm trying to say."

"And why do you say that?" she asked, confused by the statement.

Jonas sat up. "Why have you been riding around for months with a newborn and no fucking phone?"

Sunshine didn't respond. Instead, she sat there with her head hanging low. Jonas allowed her a second to get her thoughts together.

"I understand what you're saying about him, but what about her? I'm not asking you if he can be in Mya's life because she has you, and I know you're all the father she needs."

"And you don't think that lady wasn't the one giving him all your fuckin' information? How else did he find out where you stayed or your phone number every time you got a new number? Come on, Sunshine, use your fuckin' brain, and think about this shit."

"Really? Use my fucking brain? For your information, she didn't have my new information to give out."
Sunshine jumped up from the couch before storming
upstairs. At this point, she was beyond hurt; she was
pissed. She thought they could work shit out before bed,
but he was just as stubborn as she.

As she climbed back into bed, she couldn't help but be
in her feelings. Although their relationship did start off
fast, Sunshine really did love Jonas. But she didn't like
how he continued to say she still loved Monsta whenever
they disagreed. She allowed Jonas to take over the relationship to prove she loved him and only him. Running
back to Monsta would make her the biggest fool ever.

Since Mya's birth, Jonas has played the role of a loving
father to Mya and a great fiancé to Sunshine. Having
them around completed his whole life. Still, whenever
Monsta's name was mentioned, he felt insecure. He
never said anything to Sunshine, but there was always a
look in her eyes that rubbed him the wrong way when she
talked about her ex. He hated to admit it, but it was there.
For a while, he tried to ignore it. Still, every time they
argued, he made sure to let her know she still wanted to
be with Monsta. Sunshine denied it, but there had to be a
reason why she still needed to be attached to his ass.

Jonas stood in the bedroom doorway listening to
Sunshine cry herself to sleep, something he never wanted
to be responsible for. He also never thought he was the
jealous type, but feeling like Monsta still held a piece of
her heart fucked with him daily. Climbing into bed, he
pulled Sunshine in closer to him.

"I love you, and I'm sorry for trippin'," he whispered.

Sunshine stared into his eyes. "I love you too, Jonas. I
just need you to trust and believe that it's only you I want
to be with. The relationship I had with Monsta is in my
past. You're my present and future. I'd never go back to
him."

Jonas smiled as he placed a kiss on her lips. "Damn, girl, you're telling me everything I wanna hear," he jokingly said.

"You're so silly, baby, but I'm serious about this. I want you to believe me when I say it's only you."

Sunshine and Jonas shared another passionate kiss before he flipped her on her back and positioned himself between her legs.

"I don't think I can do this shit," Keisha cried in the interrogation room.

The lead detective, Detective Marshall, was getting sick and tired of Keisha's shit. She needed her to pull herself out of that crying shit and help build the case that would bring Monsta and his family down for good. Growing up, Detective Marshall could remember hearing her dad speak so much about bringing this crime family down before he died in the line of duty. Now she dedicated her whole career to bringing them down herself and making her father proud.

"Look, Keisha, this guy almost killed you and your unborn baby. You have to help us build this case and keep him locked up for good."

"I'm scared. Y'all can't protect me from him," Keisha yelled.

"You've been alive these last few months, so what you're saying doesn't make any sense. We've been protecting you all this time. Now, wipe them damn tears, and let's get this muthafucka together."

Keisha just sat there crying and rubbing her stomach, wishing she'd never told on Monsta in the first place. She never thought they would talk her into being a star witness in bringing him down. If shit went left and Monsta found out she helped in any type of way, she knew it would be on her head, and there's nothing they could do about it. She was a dead man walking.

"So, he doesn't know I'm helping y'all build this case against him?"

"No, Keisha. Right now, he is locked up only for your assault. But if he gets out, there's no telling if he will fly off somewhere and get ghost. We need to keep him locked up while we get all our paperwork together."

Keisha sat there thinking over things. "What if I only wanted to get him in trouble for hurting me? I don't think I wanna help out with the other part. I don't wanna die behind this shit."

Detective Marshall slammed her hands on the table. "He's already locked up because of you. Do you want him to get out in a few months and kill you for real, or would you rather help us keep his ass locked up?"

"Calm down. Just give her a minute to think," Detective Fisher finally said, not liking the way his partner was handling things. He understood how badly she wanted to take this family down, but he didn't want her to get out of character behind it all. The last thing he wanted for her was to get herself thrown off the case.

Keisha stood up.

"What are you doing?" Detective Marshall asked.

"I can't do this shit. I need to get the fuck away from Detroit before y'all get me killed."

"Sit your ass down. You're gonna help us, or I'll fix it and you'll go down as an accomplice in all his bullshit."

"You can't do that!" Keisha yelled.

Detective Marshall jumped in Keisha's face. "Yes, the fuck I can. Now, sit your ass down so we can discuss how we're gonna take that muthafucka down."

Detective Fisher couldn't believe what he was witnessing. It wasn't much longer before he walked out of the room. He wanted no parts of the shady side of business.

Chapter 10

"Hey, Ma," Sunshine said, walking into her mom's house with Mya in her arms.

After receiving numerous threats from Monsta months ago, Sunshine used some of his money to move her mom and Zoey into a new house.

"Hey, Sunshine. Hand over my grandbaby," she ordered, taking Mya out of her arms.

Sunshine sat on the love seat. "Ma, I need to talk to you about something."

Ms. Mathews took a seat on the couch. "What now, girl?"

"I think I'm fucking up so badly with Jonas. I'm scared I'm gonna lose him."

Not being able to control herself, Ms. Mathews laughed. "Girl, that man loves you and Mya. I'm willing to bet any amount of money he ain't going nowhere. You are overreacting and doing too much for me."

"Ma, can you really be sure of that?" Sunshine questioned.

Although Ms. Mathews didn't like to put her two cents in her daughter's business, the desperate look on Sunshine's face worried her. She knew her baby girl needed help. "What's going on, Sunshine? What did you do now?"

"We got into it last night. I told him I ran into Ms. Caldwell, and she wants to see Mya. He is against her knowing Monsta's family, but I think she should at least know her grandma. Ma, you always tell it like it is. Was I wrong?"

For the first time in a minute, Ms. Mathews was at a loss for words. She sat on the couch, giving her crazy-ass daughter the death stare. She couldn't believe how stupid she sounded. Then again, Sunshine had always been a fucking fool for Monsta.

"Ma, say something."

"Are you sure you ready for what I have to say?"

Even knowing her mama could be a little too real at times, Sunshine still wanted her help. "I need help, Ma. I don't want him to leave me. Was I wrong?"

Shaking her head, Ms. Mathews chimed in on the situation. "You must be on dope or something. Ain't no fucking way you think it's all right for my grandbaby to be around that bitch. Truth be told, I still owe that ho an ass whipping. For real, sometimes a stepfather can be more acceptable than the real family."

Sunshine didn't respond. She couldn't understand how or why she was the only one who saw no wrong in Mya getting to know her other grandma. No matter what she and Monsta went through in the past, she didn't want to hold that against Ms. Caldwell.

Ms. Mathews shook her head at her daughter. "You finally got you a real man and stuck on fuckin' stupid. Fuck Monsta and fuck his bald-headed-ass mama. My granddaughter is not about to be in their muthafuckin' faces."

At this point, Sunshine was pissed off. It was her fault because she asked for advice, knowing her mom had no chill, and there was a chance she wouldn't be able to handle it. Without saying a word, Sunshine jumped up from the couch, grabbed Mya from her mama's lap, and then stormed out the front door.

"It's a damn shame how quick your ass is to run away from the truth, but took your damn time running away from Monsta and his bitch-ass mama," Ms. Mathews yelled as Sunshine walked out the door.

Sunshine bumped into Zoey as she rushed to get to her car.

"Damn. Excuse you. I know you saw me," Zoey yelled.

Sunshine didn't even bother to respond. At this point, she was beyond pissed, and Zoey was the best candidate to get her ass beaten.

"Ma, what's wrong with your daughter?" Zoey asked, walking into the house.

"Jonas about to leave her stupid ass because she still wanna be in Monsta and his mama's face. Sike! Nah, she trying to get Mya to be around them people."

"Wow, are you fucking serious? That girl loves learning the hard way. You would have thought Monsta knocked some sense into her ass," Zoey said, shaking her head.

"She's just as crazy as that nigga Monsta," Ms. Mathews stated.

Darryl stood in the doorway listening to them talk. It was always some bullshit with them. He really wasn't in the mood for all their drama when he knew he and Zoey had their own problems.

"What's up, Darryl?"

"What's up, Ma? How you doing?" he responded.

"I'm all right, just dealing with my crazy-ass daughter. Nothing new."

Darryl chuckled. "Yeah, I'm used to how things are with y'all."

Zoey said what she had to say about Sunshine's situation, but she was also in a fucked-up mood. She loved it when she seemed to be her mama's favorite, but she knew that if her mom found out the news she had recently learned, she would become the new topic of discussion.

Earlier that week, Darryl had a job interview. They just found out he didn't get the job because he tested positive for drugs. Although wasn't shit funny about the situation, Zoey found it amusing that Sunshine had been saying he was on drugs for the longest, and she never listened.

As soon as they made it to their bedroom, Zoey went off.

"So, how long have you been a fucking crackhead, Darryl?"

Sitting on the bed, Darryl buried his head in his hands. "I'm not no fuckin' crackhead. I told your ass in the fuckin' car that the test had to be wrong."

"Oh my gawd. So you *really* about to sit and lie to my fuckin' face, nigga? We have been living off my mama for the longest because you ain't been able to get a job. I thought it was just a case of bad luck when, all along, you been dropping dirty pee."

"I'm stressed out right now. I wish you would just shut the fuck up. You got too much fuckin' mouth."

Zoey continued to yell. "I just found out the father of my kids and the man I love is on drugs. How the fuck do you think I'm supposed to act? If, for a minute, you think I'm gonna be calm about this shit, you crazy as hell."

Darryl knew he had fucked up, and his secret was no longer his secret. That was the main reason he hated it when she wanted to tag along with him or be all in his business. Ain't nobody tell her ass to go through his emails to find out shit.

"Zoey, calm down, baby. It's not even that fuckin' serious," he yelled, jumping up from the bed.

At this point, Zoey was in tears. "How can you say that when we can't even afford to get our own place? We've been living with my mom, and she's been paying the bills and helping us take care of the kids. My little job at the restaurant ain't doing shit," Zoey cried as she paced the floor. "All this time, I've been giving you money just so you can have some pocket change, and you've been giving it to the dope man."

Not only was Darryl embarrassed, but he was also tired of hearing the truth about his habit.

"Man, fuck you," he yelled before storming out the door.

Zoey didn't bother to chase after him. On top of being embarrassed, she was hurt.

As Darryl sat in the car, he thought about his next move before he finally drove off. He had no intention of letting Zoey go, but he knew she needed time to process the information she had just learned.

Zoey was hurt as she lay across the bed, crying her eyes out. It hit her that she wasn't sure if his being on drugs hurt her more than his begging her not to leave him.

Once Sunshine got home, she put Mya down for a nap. She only had a few hours before Jonas got home from the shop, and she wanted dinner done and the house nice and clean before he walked in the door. As she prepared dinner, she pictured Jonas walking through the door looking handsome as always and smelling good. She just knew she wouldn't be able to keep her hands off him. Although they had been together the night before, she felt like she hadn't been with him in a while, and her body missed his touch. Sunshine made up her mind that she was gonna do whatever Jonas thought was right. Although her mama pissed her off earlier that day, she decided to listen to her as well. There was an old saying that mother knew best.

After making plates and lighting candles, Sunshine waited patiently for her soon-to-be husband to walk in. She had plans to feed, bathe, and fuck him to sleep so he knew it was real and all about him. She never wanted him to question her love for him. Looking at the clock on the kitchen wall, Sunshine realized Jonas was running late. It was unlike him, but she figured maybe he had a few extra heads to cut.

Sunshine went into the bedroom to fetch the phone Jonas left in the drawer, just in case of an emergency. She called him twice, but he never answered.

"Man, what the fuck?" Sunshine mumbled as she received Jonas's voicemail again.

Since this was out of the norm, she panicked.

"Baby, you got me worried. If I don't hear from you in the next ten minutes, I'll be on my way to the shop to find you," she said to his voicemail.

Although she was dead serious and worried, she tried to make a little giggle at the end of her message just in case she was tripping for no reason. She hated how badly her nerves were waiting for him to call back or pop up at the house. Finally, Sunshine sat at the table to start eating her food. Food always helped her calm down. Then she picked up the phone and dialed Jonas's number again. But like before, there was no answer. This time, she didn't leave a voice message.

Later that night, as she climbed into bed, Sunshine couldn't help but shake her head as she thought back to the night before. After their little disagreement blew over, they ended up making sweet love. She thought they'd made up. Seeing that he didn't decide to come home or bother to respond to her numerous calls and texts, she realized that the night before was nothing more than a fuck. Sunshine prayed she was only overreacting as she cuddled up with Mya in her bed.

Jonas tried his best to get comfortable in the bed in his own apartment. He had been at Sunshine's house for so long that he couldn't fall asleep without holding her. Everything felt so different in his own place. He couldn't believe he had ever been truly happy being on his own before meeting Sunshine. On top of missing her soft body lying on his, he never missed a night of kissing Mya good night. He wondered if she was still up, waiting on her daddy to tell her good night.

Jonas shook his head at the situation that had him torn. On one hand, he wanted to do whatever it took to make Sunshine and Mya happy. On the other hand, getting Monsta's people involved in Mya's life wasn't something he wanted to do. He took on the responsibility to be in her life as her father. It was his job to protect her from any harm that came her way. He didn't understand how Sunshine didn't see how crazy she was acting or thinking. She gave muthafuckas too many chances to prove to her they weren't shit, and he hated that about her.

As he lay across the bed, he picked up the phone, only to place it back down. He wanted so badly to call her, but just the thought of her being on that dumb shit made him wanna give her some space. They both needed some space and peace of mind.

Meka sat around listening to her cousins act a fool. At least three times a month, they tried to meet up for a family day. And just like any other gathering, they were having a good time.

"Nakia, go check on the hamburger for those tacos," Meka yelled out.

Nakia, lost in her thoughts, got up with no problem. Once she returned to the living room, she took her seat before looking down at the carpet. Family was everything to her, but things just weren't the same without having her brother there, enjoying life with them.

"What's up, cuz?" Kyrie asked, noticing Nakia wasn't the life of the party that night.

Nakia looked up with tears in her eyes. "Shit's just not fair. I miss my big brother so much. My baby should be here with us, not buried in the fuckin' dirt."

Jayson killed his shot. "Yeah, somebody took a real nigga from us, but believe, we on that nigga Monsta's ass."

"I know Trevor was family, but let that shit go. That nigga Monsta locked up, and it ain't shit we can do to him now," Meka tried to explain.

"Meka, shut the fuck up with that shit. Trevor was *my* fuckin' brother, and you act like we not supposed to go after that nigga. The fuck you mean let that shit go?" Nakia snapped.

Meka snapped right back. "He locked up. If you ain't trying to be Ms. Big Badass and bring that shit to his mama's house or whoever else, then shut the fuck up."

Nakia jumped up. "Bitch, you know I ain't never been scared. Fuck him and whoever."

Mason stood up. "Y'all two, chill the fuck out. That nigga gon' get his, please believe that. I don't give a fuck how long we gotta wait, he gettin' his. I have a long life ahead of me, and I'm gon' get my payback for my brother's death. Y'all better believe that."

As Nakia sat back down, she started to cry. "I hate that nigga so fucking much. He took my brother from me, and that shit hurts every time I think about it."

Meka walked over to her cousin and hugged her. "We family, and I'll forever have your back. I just want you to think smart about shit. Let them deal with that shit correctly. I don't want you out here trying to handle shit yourself and end up locked up somewhere."

"Hey, has anyone heard from Jonas? I thought he was gonna drop by for a little bit," Jayson asked, trying to change the subject.

"When we closed the shop earlier, he said he wasn't feeling too good and didn't know if he was gonna come this time around."

"I bet that bitch Sunshine got his head buried in her ass," Nakia said, taking another sip of her drink.

"Come on, now, Nakia, don't start that bullshit. We all know he loves that girl. Besides, she's mad cool, if you ask me," Meka said, taking up for Sunshine.

Nakia rolled her eyes. "Whatever. I just think it's funny how her baby daddy killed my fuckin' brother, and y'all just invite her in the family like it wasn't shit. Since that bitch nigga Monsta locked up, I should just beat her ass every time I see the stupid bitch."

"Chill out, cuz. Why don't you go lay your drunk ass down somewhere?" Kyrie suggested.

Nakia was pissed that no one agreed with her. "Fuck y'all. I'm about to go lie down, but when I get up, all y'all muthafuckas better be outta my house. And y'all better save me some fuckin' tacos."

As Nakia stumbled to her bedroom, everyone laughed at her except for Mason.

"Low key, I don't think she was playing. Y'all know how hurt she was when they found Trevor dead on the block," he warned his family.

Meka didn't want to think about Sunshine being an enemy, especially since she had lots of love for her and Mya. Besides, she knew Jonas would flip the fuck out if he knew anyone planned on laying hands on his soon-to-be wife.

Nakia lay across her bed. Yeah, she was buzzing, but she was dead serious about getting her revenge. If she couldn't touch Monsta, somebody else was gonna pay.

Chapter 11

The next morning, Sunshine was in her feelings seeing that Jonas never came home the night before. This was the first time since forever that he hadn't come home to her, and her feelings were hurt. She wasn't sure if he was still pissed off like she thought the night before or if he was somewhere hurt.

After feeding Mya and getting dressed, Sunshine jumped into her car to pull up on Jonas at the shop. One thing's for sure, he would never miss work unless something were seriously wrong. Sunshine needed answers, and she needed them now. She wasn't in the mood to be played with, and he needed to know that.

Sunshine took Mya out of the car and walked into the shop to find Meka setting up before they opened up for the day.

"Good morning," she said, trying not to sound angry.

"Hey, Sunshine, what are you doing here so early?" Meka said, grabbing Mya from her arms.

"I was looking for Jonas. Has he got in yet?"

"Yeah, girl, he's in the office lying down. He must've had a long night," Meka said with a smirk on her face.

Sunshine didn't want her to think things weren't all good in their relationship. With a smile on her face, she walked off toward the office, leaving Meka with her own dirty thoughts about what had happened between them the night before.

Hearing the door open, Jonas jumped up. "What's up?" he said, rubbing his eyes.

"I don't know. You tell me, Mr. Bentley. I've been up all night waiting for you to show up. You didn't get any of my calls or texts?"

"Yeah, I got them," he admitted.

Sunshine slammed her hand down on the office desk. "So, let me get this straight. You got my calls and texts and just decided to ignore me?"

"Yeah," Jonas honestly replied.

Although he was being honest, he was pissing her off. "What's the problem, Jonas? Or are you letting me know you're the type of guy who gonna be running in and out of my life? If so, keep the shit real 'cause me and Mya don't need that shit."

Jonas chuckled. "You being a little dramatic, don't you think? I do have my own spot, and last night I decided to go home. What's wrong with that?"

Sunshine rolled her eyes as she smirked and sat at the desk. "I guess I'm doing too much. I was just worried about you last night. You've never not called or texted me back when I tried to reach you. With everything we've been through, you can't be doing shit like that, Jonas."

"I wasn't trying to scare you. I just needed some space to clear my mind. I wasn't feeling that whole situation with that boy's mama. That shit had me up all night thinking about keeping Mya safe. I even tried to look at things your way so we could come up with a solution, but I'm still not sure about this shit."

"Jonas, I was thinking about it too. At the end of the day, I really want us to be on the same page when it comes to Mya."

Jonas got real with her. "To be honest, I never thought I would ever feel threatened by that nigga being in y'all life like this."

Sunshine gave him a strange look. "Jonas, you trippin', baby. He is my past for a reason. The years I shared with him could never compare to the months we spent loving each other. I really believe you are the one for me."

Jonas kissed Sunshine. "Don't just think I'm the one. I want you to feel that deep in your heart. I know exactly how I feel about you."

Sunshine smiled. "I know we met for a reason, and you were able to look past the toxic shit that I was dealing with at the time. I love you so much for being there to save me and to make me realize what real love is."

Jonas held her in his arms before getting back to the situation at hand.

"Baby, you've been drinking this early?"

Jonas quickly lied, then changed the subject. "Nah, that's not my style. Anyway, do you think she'll be safe with that lady?" he asked, although his mind was screaming, *hell no.*

"Her son was the problem. I think Mya would be all right just dealing with her."

"How about we play it safe and just take Mya to see her for a minute before she really keeps her on her own?"

Sunshine smiled at the idea. "Thank you, baby. I think that would be a good idea. Then we could see how she acts with her and go by her behavior."

Jonas was glad their beef was over 'cause he couldn't picture sleeping alone at home again. Sunshine was his baby, and the love he had for her and Mya was everything to him. After years of being alone and broken, Jonas could finally say he believed in love again. There was something about Sunshine that made him want her from the moment he saw her outside his shop just months ago.

As he held her in his arms, he whispered in her ear. "You know I love you and Mya, and I only want what's best for y'all."

"I love you so much too. I never want to sleep without you by my side again," she admitted.

Jonas placed a kiss on her lips. "Baby, I'm not going anywhere."

Just as they started to share another passionate kiss, Meka walked in with Mya. "I'm sorry to interrupt, Jonas, but there are like three people out there for you already."

Jonas grabbed Mya from her. "All right, I'll be right out there. Let me talk to my baby right quick."

Meka walked out to let the clients know he would be out soon.

"Hey, Daddy's angel," he said, placing a kiss on Mya's cheek. She missed her daddy and told him with a smile.

Just seeing them so happy with each other also put a smile on Sunshine's face. She loved her little family and wouldn't trade it for anything in the world. Jonas played with Mya for a few minutes before handing her over to Sunshine.

"I'm gonna get off early so we can spend some time together. It's Saturday, I'm pretty sure you can plan something for us to do."

"I'm kind of mad at my mom, so she's not gonna want to watch Mya for us."

Jonas chuckled. "Don't say that. You know she will watch Mya. Just say you don't wanna ask her."

"Well, you've been around long enough to know how we are with each other."

"I'll figure it out. Just plan something out and have her bag packed. Now, take my baby back home and get some rest so I can get to work."

Sunshine kissed Jonas before they walked out of the office.

He recognized two of the clients waiting for him, but the other one had his head down in the newspaper. Sunshine was so busy trying to get out of the shop that she didn't notice one of Monsta's friends waiting to get his hair cut by Jonas.

"Welcome home, my nigga," Roc said as Monsta entered the cell they now shared.

"What up, nigga? When you get in this bitch?" Monsta asked one of his favorite cousins.

"Shid, nigga, I got in here about two days after you got your crazy ass in the hole. Why the fuck niggas tellin' me you been in this bitch wildin' out and shit?"

Monsta laughed. "I been on some bullshit, but maybe not enough. These stupid-ass niggas in this bitch running they mouth about my fuckin' business."

Roc laughed. "Don't go looking for any more trouble in this bitch. My pops told me."

Monsta shook his head. "Uncle Roc talks too fuckin' much. So, what he got you watching out for me now or something?"

"Hell nah. I'm just doing my time and getting outta these white muthafuckas' faces. You can keep that bullshit up, and these white pigs gon' make sure you do your time, *plus* some."

After doing their little handshake, Monsta sat on his hard mattress. "I'm ready to get the fuck from outta here too, nigga. I gotta plan, but I'ma need some strings pulled from the outside."

"Say no more, nigga. I got you."

Monsta spent the next hour explaining to his cousin how he could manipulate the system to his advantage and get released early. Everything sounded so much better when it was out of his head and into the atmosphere.

"Cuz, you know you have to stay out of trouble for that shit to work," Roc reminded him.

"For sure, my nigga. I think I can handle that for my freedom. I miss my girl and wanna finally meet my daughter."

Roc chuckled. "Cuz, I thought things were over between you and Sunshine. Word in the hood is you got Keisha's trick ass pregnant, and Sunshine done moved the fuck on with one of the Bentley Boyz."

"Fuck that nigga. Just wait. I'm gon' get my family back as soon as I get out of here."

Just the mention of Sunshine's name made Monsta forget about the conversation he had with his pops a few weeks ago.

Roc shook his head. He already knew the backstory on Monsta and Sunshine's relationship and firmly believed she was better off without his crazy ass. Monsta didn't know how to love correctly, and the last thing he needed was to be around her and that innocent baby girl.

"Cuz, you know she happy and engaged to that nigga, right?" he tried to warn him.

Monsta looked up so his cousin could see just how serious he was about getting his family back. "I don't give a fuck about what they think they got going on. I know for a fact she only acting like she want that nigga because she think Keisha's baby is mine. Sunshine knows I'm the right nigga for her."

Roc chuckled. "Yeah, OK, if you say so."

"You don't believe me, nigga?"

Roc could sense that Monsta was about to be on all bullshit, so he changed the subject.

"If you believe it, then hey, who am I to tell you anything different?"

"That's what the fuck I thought, bitch-ass nigga. Ain't no nigga about to have my family while I'm alive, and you best to believe that shit."

***

Jonas stepped out of the shower, ready to spend the rest of the day with his future wife. It had been a good three weeks since they last went out and just enjoyed themselves.

"Damn, sexy, maybe we should stay in today," Sunshine said, lying across the bed.

Jonas chuckled. "That sounds like a good plan, but I wanna get out of the house and talk. We can do whatever you want once we get back home."

"All right, I'm down."

She could have gone for some long strokes before they left, but the way their bodies were set up, their plans of going out would've been canceled.

"So, who's gonna watch Mya tonight?"

"Nakia said she'll watch her. She usually didn't do the whole babysitting shit, but I told you my family loves her so much."

Sunshine was excited to hear the news. "I'm so grateful for you all. As you already know, my family's not close like that. Through it all, yours had my back, no matter what."

Her words made Jonas blush a little. "We're all about family. I told you this when we first met. Now that you and Mya are my family, y'all their family too."

Sunshine loved his family's way of doing shit. For the most part, her family didn't really fuck with each other like that since their grandma died. She had been the glue that once kept their family together.

"What's on your mind?" Jonas asked as he noticed her dazing off in her thoughts.

Sunshine lied. "Nothing, baby, I'm just ready to go."

"All right, I'll be ready in a minute," Jonas said as he grabbed his wallet.

Sunshine laughed to herself as she thought back to Monsta having money in a shoe box and how Jonas had a wallet with cards and a healthy bank account. It wasn't all about the money, but she really had upgraded to a real boss.

After dropping Mya off with Nakia, Sunshine and Jonas stopped by the mall to pick up a few items. Sunshine thought they were just doing some random shopping, but Jonas had a plan he hadn't discussed with her yet.

"Look at this. I think it'll look cute on you."

Sunshine looked over the swimsuit he was holding. "It's cute, but damn, that's a lot of money for something that's barely gonna cover my ass."

Jonas couldn't help but laugh at her. She was silly, but it really just told him what type of nigga she was used to fucking with. Since being together, he always had to remind her that prices didn't mean shit to him, especially when it came to her.

"Go ahead, get it, and stop tag watching. Stop acting like you don't deserve the best," he said, egging her on.

For the rest of their shopping trip, Sunshine didn't say much as Jonas picked out things he thought would look nice on her. Growing up in a house full of women helped him pick up on female style. Sunshine watched as he pulled out his card and swiped it without second-guessing the total. Just thinking to herself, she knew she had finally found a real one. This wasn't the first time he had taken her shopping and spent money on her, but something in her was waiting for him to switch up. That's probably because of all the damage Monsta had done to her in the past.

"Where to now?"

Sunshine giggled. "Why are you asking me?"

"You were supposed to plan something, goofy ass."

Laughing, Sunshine yelled out, "Feed me."

Jonas stopped at the red light. "You wanna eat for real or go home to get served this dick?"

"Both," she said as they laughed together.

"Your ass is something else, you know that, girl?"

Since the first time he took her to his favorite Mexican restaurant, Sunshine made sure that whenever they went out, they ate there. Jonas learned to deal with her taco-eating ass, but she made him hate their food.

"Baby, I'm not trying to be difficult, but let's grab this shit, then go so I can get something else to eat. You got me hating this place."

"All right, I'm cool with that," she said, laughing.

Sunshine sat in the car as he went into the BBQ restaurant to grab some ribs. Being caught up on social media, she never saw Kyrah sneaking up on her.

"Bitch!" she yelled as she opened the passenger-side door, then started swinging on Sunshine.

Luckily for Sunshine, she had taken off her seat belt as soon as they pulled up to get Jonas's food. Because of that move, she wasn't trapped in her seat, getting her ass beat. She was able to fight back.

"Get the fuck off me, stupid bitch!"

Kyrah wasn't letting up and was getting the best of Sunshine.

"Don't cry now, bitch. Your stupid ass got my brother killed!" Kyrah yelled as she continued to hit Sunshine in the face.

Jonas waited patiently for his ribs until a guy walked in, laughing, "Aye, it's two bitches out there fighting and the yellow one gettin' tore the fuck up. That big girl tagging her ass."

Jonas grabbed his food as the lady called his name, then rushed out of the restaurant. He had no reason to believe it was Sunshine fighting . . . until he walked out and saw a crowd around his car.

"Get the fuck outta my way," he yelled as he pushed his way through the crowd.

Finally making it to the passenger side of the car, he grabbed Kyrah off Sunshine.

"Bitch, get your ass back!"

Kyrah tried to swing on Sunshine again, but Jonas wasn't having that shit. He wasn't the type to hit a female, but he was strong enough to hold down her ass.

"Get the fuck away from my car."

With tears in her eyes, Kyrah looked Jonas dead in his eyes. "This dirty bitch is the reason my brother is dead."

"I told you I didn't have shit to do with that," Sunshine yelled, trying to defend herself.

Kyrah shook her head in disbelief that she was denying her part in it. "We all know the truth, bitch. We know you were the one who took Monsta's money and set my brother up. How could you do that when Lamar was always there to stop Monsta from beating your ass? Bitch, I was there to pick you up when your ass was hiding in that vacant, burnt-up house, sneaking through the alley and shit."

Sunshine never really got into a lot of details when she talked to Jonas about what happened in her past. The look on his face told her he wasn't pleased with what he heard.

"Jonas, let's go."

"Every time I see you, bitch, I'm whooping that ass, and I put that on your daughter too," Kyrah yelled.

Sunshine tried to jump out of the car, but Jonas wouldn't let her. "Let that shit go."

The ride home was awkward. For one, Jonas was asking so many questions, and Sunshine wasn't trying to put out any answers.

"What money was she talking about, Sunshine?" he questioned.

"Just leave it alone, Jonas. Forget about that bullshit she was talking about."

He shook his head. "I never ask too many questions about your past, but now I need you to tell me where the money came from."

"It's *my* money, Jonas. That's all that matters. Now, can we please drop the subject?"

"When we get home, I think we need to talk about this shit 'cause shit's not adding up."

Sunshine had an attitude. His trying to investigate Kyrah's story pissed her off. It was bad enough she just got her ass beat, but now, Jonas was looking at her all funny and shit.

"Look, we don't need to talk about shit that happened in my past. Just leave it there."

Jonas pulled into the driveway. "Look, if you took that nigga's money, this shit isn't just *your* problem anymore. Don't you think that shit has *everything* to do with why your ass is living like you in hiding now?"

Sunshine didn't say shit. She was fed up and embarrassed about everything.

"Open your mouth, Sunshine. Say something, dammit."

She sat there crying, which just pissed him off. Her actions clearly were the reason for him coming after her. Her keeping it a secret all this time put him in harm's way too. For all he knew, Monsta probably thought he was living off his money when he wasn't.

Jonas leaned over to kiss Sunshine. "Baby, I'm not trying to judge you or anything. I just need to know the truth so we can move around this shit."

"What do you *not* understand? I *don't* wanna talk about this shit, Jonas."

Jonas killed the engine. "We gotta talk about this, Sunshine. This the type of shit a nigga not gon' let die down. Not only is *your* life in danger, but *Mya's* is too. I thought shit was over, but hell nah, he wants that bread."

Sunshine opened her door. "Go get my baby, then you can stay at your place tonight."

As she slammed the car door, Jonas jumped out of the car. "You're being real selfish right now, Sunshine."

"Just go get my baby and leave me the fuck alone."

Jonas couldn't believe how she was talking to him. Since day one, he'd not only told her, but he also showed her just how much he cared for her. Now, it was fuck him just that quick.

"Leave you the fuck alone? That's *really* what you want?"

Sunshine never wanted him to leave her alone, but she wasn't ready to face the reality that she fucked up. If she didn't know shit else, she knew for a fact that if she talked shit and hurt his feelings, he would wanna get out of her face. Jonas watched as Sunshine walked into the house and slammed the door.

"This shit can't be happening right now."

On his way to pick up Mya from Nakia, Jonas decided at the last minute that he wasn't about to take her back to Sunshine. Something told him she needed some time to clear her mind.

"Hey, Jonas, y'all on the way to pick up Mya?" Nakia asked as she stood on the porch.

After pinching her for the fourth time that evening, Mya wouldn't stop crying, and Nakia didn't want Jonas to hear her over the phone.

"If it's all right with you, can you keep her until the morning?"

Nakia paused. With the way she felt about Monsta and Sunshine, she didn't trust herself not to fuck around and hurt or kill Mya's ass. Plus, she had started sipping.

"Damn, cuz, my boo is supposed to be coming over tonight. You think she'll be all right with some earplugs on?"

Jonas laughed and shook his head. "I'm on my way."

Going back to the locked bedroom where Mya was, Nakia started to feel bad. Mya sat in her car seat, damn near asleep from all the crying. She was innocent in all this, and Nakia had allowed the devil to take over her.

"I'm so sorry, Mya, I'm so sorry."

Getting her mind together, Nakia finally took Mya out of the car seat she had been in since being dropped off. She made sure to clean her off and change her dirty diaper before Jonas pulled up. Once she finished, she sat on the couch with Mya, feeding her a bottle. Mya kept her eyes on Nakia until she fell asleep. With that look alone, Nakia knew that Mya didn't like her anymore.

Nakia cried her eyes out thinking about her brother Trevor. He'd always been there to take care of her and Mason when their dad ran off and their mom got sick. When he moved away to go to school and start his family, Jonas helped out as much as possible. It wasn't until Trevor dropped out of school and moved back to Detroit that they realized he was the one now in need of family help.

Trevor wanted to be on his feet before he brought his family to Detroit. Having too much pride and too ashamed to ask for help, he ran to the streets, not knowing he was fucking around on one of Monsta's territories. Although Trevor was a good guy who made a bad decision, he didn't deserve to lose his life.

It was time for Nakia to realize that Mya and Sunshine had nothing to do with what a coward muthafucka decided to do.

"Damn, Trevor, why didn't you just ask for help? We had you, big bro," she cried.

Twenty minutes later, she heard the doorbell ring. Nakia wiped her eyes, then got up to open the door for Jonas.

"What up, cuz? How was the outing with your future wife?" she asked, trying to sound cheerful.

"It was all right," he lied.

Nakia gave out a fake smile. Jonas wasn't easily fooled and could tell she'd been crying.

"You good?"

"After playing, then eating, Mya went to sleep, and my mind got to thinking about Trevor. I haven't seen his kids in a minute."

Jonas shook his head. "Let me know when you wanna go down there to see them. I got you."

"Thanks, Jonas. I really appreciate that, but Chrystal be trippin', like it's our fault he's gone."

"Damn, she still on that tip? The girl just doesn't know how bad his death hurt us. Our family is too close for anyone ever to think we would want to see one of our own dead."

Jonas picked up Mya from the couch to place her in her car seat.

"I really appreciate you watching her."

"We family. Ain't we supposed to have one another's back?"

"For sure," Jonas said, hugging her before walking out to his car.

Jonas felt like it was only right to give Sunshine the space she needed and asked for, so that night, he took Mya to his apartment.

"Bring me my daughter," Sunshine firmly said into the phone.

Jonas wiped the crust out of his eyes. "Sunshine, it's two something in the fucking morning. We asleep."

"I don't care what time it is, I want my baby."

Jonas shook his head at how petty she was being. "Look, just go back to sleep, and I'll bring her home in the morning. Is that all right with you?"

Sunshine still had an attitude. Although it wasn't because of Jonas, she still took it out on him. For months, she had hidden the truth about the money, and now that he knew, she was afraid he wouldn't look at her the same anymore.

"Nah, it's not all right. I want my baby *now,*" she demanded.

"Damn, baby, stop trippin'. What the fuck is your problem? Didn't I tell you she was asleep?" he yelled, waking up Mya.

"I hear her, Jonas. Bring my baby home before I call the police."

"Your ass is *really* trippin' now. You gon' call the police on me because I have my daughter?"

"That's *my* daughter, Jonas—*not* yours."

Jonas wanted to hang up in her face for talking that dumb shit to him, but instead, he decided to put her ass in her place. "It's real fucked up how you would say that fucked-up shit to me when *I'm* the muthafucka who always had y'all fuckin' back. You know what, Sunshine? If you want her, drive your ass over here and get her."

Being pissed off and embarrassed, Sunshine let those hurtful words come out of her mouth and wished she could take them back as soon as she said them.

"I'm so sorry, Jonas. I'm so sorry. I didn't mean that."

"You said what the fuck you said, and I said what the fuck I said. Come get her since she not mine. Now you can let her meet her *real* people without hearing my mouth. Ain't that what you wanted?"

Those words left his mouth, but he didn't mean any of it. Just the thought of Mya and Sunshine being out of his life was killing him.

After he hung up on Sunshine, she immediately hated herself. Jonas was a good man, and here she was, sabotaging her own relationship. As badly as she wanted to call him back to apologize and beg for forgiveness, Sunshine got dressed to get her daughter. On the ride there, she thought about how Monsta always told her she was so fucked up and damaged that if he were ever to let her go, none of her relationships would work. She never listened to that shit, but now she could understand exactly what he was saying. She was damaged goods.

Jonas opened the door for Sunshine after hearing the second knock.

"Jonas, I'm so sorry. I don't know why I even said that shit. You are her father, and the only one she will ever know."

Something in Jonas wanted to forgive her because he loved her so much, but the damage was already done. She had broken him with those words.

"You can't be talking to me any kind of way 'cause the last nigga got you caught up in all this bullshit. That nigga locked up while my dumb ass out here loving the fuck out of you, and you clearly don't appreciate the shit."

"I'm sorry, Jonas. I swear it was a mistake."

"A mistake, Sunshine? *Really?* A fuckin' mistake is dialing the wrong number or something simple like that. That shit you just pulled wasn't a fuckin' mistake; it was your fuckin' truth."

The more Sunshine stood there crying, the harder it was for him to keep up his guard. His family was right about him being a sucker for her. But this time, she crossed a line he couldn't see himself forgetting.

"Here, it's late. Hurry up and get your daughter home," Jonas said as he handed Mya's car seat over.

Sunshine hesitated to take it. She couldn't believe how badly she fucked up with him.

"Jonas—"

"What she needs to know is the truth. Ever since you bumped into that lady at the market, you've been on some real bullshit. It's like you're trying to push me away and out of your life. What the fuck happened, Sunshine? Did she tell you her son is coming home?" he questioned, pissing her off even more.

Gently, Jonas placed a kiss on Mya's forehead.

"I'm sorry your mama bat shit crazy and doesn't realize a good man when he standing in her face. I'm sorry I can't be your dad anymore."

"Jonas, baby, please, forgive me. You *know* I didn't mean that. How many times do I have to apologize?" she begged.

"Do you know I just planned a surprise trip to Miami in a few days for our vacation? You just fucked up everything."

Sunshine was already embarrassed enough, and that shit only fucked with her mental even more. She snatched the car seat from him, then stormed out of the house.

"All this shit because she didn't wanna face her truth," Jonas said as he locked his door.

Sunshine sat in the car crying before she finally drove off. She wasn't sure how she was gonna fix shit with Jonas, but it needed to be done.

Chapter 12

"Let me get this right. After witnessing the terrible murder of your father, you were never able to get professional help from *anyone?*" Mrs. Howard asked Monsta as he lay on the leather couch across from her desk.

"No, ma'am. My mom actually said only white people seek help, and since we are Black and from the ghetto, the folks around us would only tease me and make matters worse."

Monsta loved that they gave him an older, white psychiatrist. It was so easy to run game on her.

"Oh wow, you poor thing," she mumbled as she jotted some notes down in her notepad.

"Yes, ma'am. After his death, I was really fucked up in the head thinking that his killers were gonna come back for me. That's why I don't like to be in the general population here. Every time I wake up, I have to pray to see another day. I'm scared here, ma'am, to be honest."

"Yeah, looking at your file, I see that since you've been here, you've been in the hole most of your time here."

"That's the only way I know I won't be killed in here unless a guard decides to take me out. Ma'am, I don't mess with anybody, but it seems like I'm being targeted because of the ghetto where I grew up. It wasn't my fault I was poor."

Mrs. Howard shook her head. She really felt that maybe Monsta deserved the help, and she could be the one to give him the right type of support.

"Mrs. Howard, I don't really like to fight these men here, but I just feel like if I'm angry all the time, I won't be messed with."

"Now, we've had three sessions already, and I do believe you have quite a few anger issues. The good news is that if I can get you to take these medications regularly and behave, it might be able to help your case."

Monsta gave her a shy smile. "Thank you, ma'am. Nobody has ever tried to help me before."

"Now, I have to run my plan by someone else, and it might take some time to get your medications. In the meantime, try to stay out of trouble."

"Yes, ma'am. I just pray no one messes with me."

For a whole hour straight, Monsta easily convinced her that he only acted out when he was forced to. He told her he did have a few anger issues, and when he did become angry, he hit people, but only because that's how he was raised. Growing up, he never received a hug when he cried for his dad. Instead, his mom used to punch him and call him a faggot for crying. Mrs. Howard soaked up everything and took copious notes, stating Monsta was a victim since birth, and with the proper help and medication, he could possibly be helped from years of abuse.

On his way back to his cell, Monsta wore a smirk on his face. He couldn't believe how easy it was to have his psychiatrist eating out of his hand in just a few weeks. Crazy thing is, while he thought he was getting down on the system, he was really about to get the help he truly needed.

"How shit go, nigga?" Roc asked as Monsta walked back into the cell.

Monsta looked down at Roc like he was crazy. "How the fuck you think, nigga? Don't you see I'm in a good mood?"

Roc laughed. "Yeah, bro, it's as clear as day."

Monsta took a seat. "Anyway, did you get that for me?"

"Yeah, Amber came to see me today and brought that. I told you them white bitches love my black ass and will do whatever a nigga want. She also found that nigga Darryl for you and put him on game like you asked."

Monsta nodded his head. "Good. I need my family waiting for me when I get out."

Roc didn't say shit else. He knew once Monsta had made up his mind, there was nothing anyone could say to make him change it. He spent so much time trying to convince Monsta to leave Sunshine alone and just let her be, but Monsta wasn't letting her ass go for shit in the world. He wanted his girl and baby, and that was it.

Later that night, Monsta woke up in a cold sweat. Once again, he had spoken to his pops, and shit wasn't pretty. His father accused him of still being a fuckup and chasing behind pussy instead of taking care of his business. Hearing what he believed was crying woke Roc out of his sleep.

"Aye, cuz, you good down there?"

"Yeah, mind your own fucking business," Monsta snapped as he wiped his tears away.

He'll never let another nigga know he cried. That shit would make a nigga think he was soft and would eventually try to test him. Little did he know, Roc had already heard him cry out for his pops before in his sleep, but never judged or told him what he heard.

"Ms. Freeman, open the door. It's Detective Marshall."

Today was supposed to be the day they linked up and discussed whatever news Keisha had for her. She thought she did her a favor by giving her time to think things over and realize she was doing the right thing. Detective Marshall banged on her door three more times.

"This is the very reason why I said we needed to watch this li'l bitch."

Detective Fisher shook his head at his partner in disbelief. "I told you from the jump this was a waste of time. You can't expect these folks to tell on someone they're scared of. You the fool for wanting his baby mama to help you out instead of doing your own work."

With that being said, Detective Fisher walked away. "I'll be in the car."

Not wanting to believe Keisha had played her, Detective Marshall banged on her door again.

"Don't nobody live over there no more," a guy next door to her yelled out as he peeked through his door.

"Do you know how long ago she moved?"

"Nah, I really don't be in other people's business like that." Finished speaking, he shut his door.

Detective Marshall felt like shit. She had given Keisha time to calm down and get her thoughts together. She wanted her to realize she was doing the right thing, while all along, Keisha had been plotting to get the fuck out of Dodge. She never planned on helping them build a case against Monsta. Anyone who knew of Monster and his people knew he was not to be fucked with. Detective Marshall walked away feeling played.

Meka walked into the shop an hour early, just like any other day, and noticed the office door was open.

"So, you just gon' keep sleeping here like you don't have an apartment? Jonas, you actin' like a real-life bum."

"I don't know why, but it's hard for me to sleep in my apartment or anywhere else. At least here, I know you'll wake me up for work."

Meka giggled. "You let that girl get the best of you, and I don't like it. And you're out of your mind if you

think I'm about to let you work today when you've been
drinking all night and probably this morning too. I'm
gonna have Mason or somebody come get your ass. Snap
out of this bullshit, Jonas."

"I did everything in my power to show her I was a real
nigga and that I really love her and Mya." His words
came out sluggishly.

Meka took a seat at the desk. For the last few weeks,
since he and Sunshine broke up, she'd been there keeping her cousin from jumping off the ledge. This wasn't
the first time he crashed because a bitch broke his heart.
The way she looked at it, he was too nice, and bitches
loved them rude, disrespectful-ass niggas.

Meka watched as her cousin could barely sit up on
the couch. He was back to abusing the bottle, and that
shit crushed her, seeing as his dad lost his life years ago
from drinking like a fish. Jonas had always been high on
family and a child having a father because he grew up
with an alcoholic father who died because he didn't know
how to put the bottle down.

"Jonas, just lie down and chill until Mason gets here."

"I gotta open the shop, you know that, Meka."

"I got it, Jonas."

Jonas lay his head back down, then closed his eyes.
"What the fuck did I do wrong, Meka?"

"Nothing, Jonas. I told you from jump she was gonna
be trouble and came with a shitload of drama. You were a
good dude for her. She'll learn that soon."

"I miss them so much, Meka. I can't go about my life
living like they never were a part of it."

"Come on, Jonas. Just like you got over Brandy, you
can get over Sunshine too," she tried to explain.

Jonas got loud. "You can't compare the two. Sunshine's
just a little damaged and need extra love, which I wasn't
giving her. And I learned Brandy is just a trifling bitch

looking for a nigga to pay her way through life. What me and Sunshine shared was real, and everyone knew that."

Meka couldn't lie; the drunk did speak the truth. She hated how Sunshine played with his heart, then spit him out like he wasn't shit. She also hated to admit her cousin needed Sunshine, no matter what bullshit she was talking about. For the most part, she actually liked Sunshine and knew he loved her ass.

"Man, where that nigga at?" Mason yelled as he entered the shop.

Meka rushed out. "He's in here. Why don't y'all take him home and let him sleep this shit off?"

Poppa shook his head. "We tired of his bullshit, Meka. He gotta stop letting these bitches get to him like this."

"Dog, shut the fuck up," Mason ordered.

Poppa was Jonas's little brother on his father's side. Jonas's mom took him in when he was a teen because he was having problems at home. Poppa is the one who found their father dead. He hated witnessing his brother having another downfall over a bitch. He felt like Jonas was playing with his own life.

"Come on, Poppa, your brother needs you right now. He needs his family to have his back and get him back on track. I'm gonna make sure the shop is good while he takes some time off."

Poppa walked over to the couch. "This nigga act like we didn't grow up around this shit. We hated our daddy, especially when he was sloppy drunk in the morning. This nigga a whole fuckin' bum."

"Just help me get him to the car," Mason said as he walked over to the couch.

"Get the fuck up, bro. Get your ass up with this dumb shit," Poppa yelled as they tried to pull Jonas up from the couch.

Meka could tell that the sight of his brother laid out, looking just like their dad, had him in his feelings. She understood his pain, especially since he was the one who found him dead.

"Poppa, I'm just gonna let him sleep the shit off," she said, digging in her purse. "Here. Why don't y'all go get the donuts and stuff since we're about to open up?"

Mason put the money in his pocket. "You sure?"

"Yeah, 'cause he's not getting up, and there's no point in trying. We're gonna have a crowd in a few, and everyone else will be showing up. Let's not give everyone a show."

"Come on, Poppa, let's go."

As they looked over to Poppa, he was sitting down with his face buried in his hands. They knew he was in his feelings and trying not to cry. They knew he needed some space. Mason didn't say anything as he walked out. Poppa and Jonas had a bond that only brothers could understand, and at that moment, Poppa prayed that he could get his brother clean again.

Mason didn't work at the shop but went to get whatever Meka asked for to make sure they opened up on time, like always. They were all raised to believe that family came first, no matter what.

Jonas woke up, looking around, somewhat feeling lost. Since Sunshine and he broke up, his new best friend was a bottle of Jack Daniel's. Growing up, that was his dad's best friend as well.

"Damn, I need to stop drinking so fucking much," he mumbled.

Jonas got up to take a peek out of the office door and saw business doing well and Meka holding shit down like always. Feeling embarrassed, he wasn't ready to face his family with his new lifestyle. He snuck out the back door before anyone noticed he was even up.

Jonas sat in his car trying to think about his next move. If nothing else, the first thing he wanted to do was go home and shower. He had been drunk on his office couch and hadn't washed his ass in two days, so he smelled like he'd been soaking in liquor for a month straight. Looking in the mirror, Jonas hated who he was becoming again. He never wanted to be like his dad, but when life wasn't fair in his eyes, the bottle made him forget about what was bothering him in the first place. The only thing was that when he finally sobered up, Sunshine was still heavy on his mind, which caused him to drink even more.

After taking care of his personal hygiene and another short nap, Jonas stopped by the phone shop to purchase a new phone before he made it to Sunshine's house. She had been avoiding his calls, and he needed to hear her voice again. He wasn't sure how shit would turn out, but he wasn't giving up without a fight. She had his heart, and he needed her to know it.

Sunshine jumped. "How did you get in?"

Jonas walked in the front door, still a little buzzed but sober enough to know how important this conversation was for him. He had the keys to the house, but never wanted to just pop up after their breakup. Since she hadn't answered the phone, he decided this was the time to use them.

"Hey, I really needed to talk to you, Sunshine."

Sunshine picked up Mya, then gave her the bottle she'd just warmed up for her. "I'm busy. Go away, Jonas."

Able to tell she was fronting like she didn't care about what they had, Jonas stopped all that. "Stop playing with me, Sunshine. You have no idea how this bullshit is affecting me. Can we talk as adults who love each other?"

"Jonas, I tried to apologize to you and explain that I said that bullshit out of anger. You're the one who wasn't trying to listen to me."

Jonas walked over to the couch and took a seat. Without saying anything else, Sunshine handed Mya over to him. "She misses you."

For the first time in almost a month, Jonas smiled. "Hey, my Mya Pie. Daddy missed you, baby girl."

Sunshine grinned as she watched him plant kisses all over Mya's chubby cheeks, making her giggle. Mya was nowhere in the talking stage, but her big, bright smile showed Jonas she wasn't lying about him being missed.

"I know we both have issues going on, and we probably need more time to heal before we move forward with everything, but I'm asking if it'll be all right if I can still at least be in her life while we work on fixing shit with us."

"Jonas, you are her father, so why wouldn't you be able to? I told you I was so upset that day that I said a lot of hurtful bullshit, but only for that reason. Mya is your child, and nobody can take the title of her father away from you."

Sunshine was happy to have Jonas there with her, but for some reason, the tears started and wouldn't stop rolling down her face. Jonas leaned over so he could hold her and Mya in his arms.

"It's gonna be all right."

"I'm a fuckup, Jonas. I'm so damaged," she cried in his arms.

He hated that she felt that way, but truthfully, they were both damaged in their own little way. Perhaps those who thought they were moving too fast in their relationship were right. Maybe they really didn't know each other well enough to be engaged and needed time to fix each other and themselves.

"Did you come over to make this breakup official?" she finally asked.

Jonas paused as he thought about her question. He also wanted to choose his words carefully because he knew words could cut like a sword.

"Sunshine, you know I love the fuck out of you and would do whatever for you and Mya, but I think we might have jumped the gun a little. Lately, we've been arguing more than normal over bullshit that should've been addressed early on in our relationship."

"Get out, Jonas! Get out!"

"No! We need to talk about this shit."

"Ain't shit to talk about. All this shit was fake. That's all I'm hearing from that shit you just said."

Jonas shook his head. "You know damn well that's *not* what I said, and I'm sorry if that's what you got from that. I just said we need time to get to know each other better before we get married. I fell for you quick as hell and put a rock on your finger within months. Wasn't shit fake about that."

Sunshine didn't say a word. The silence was killing Jonas. He finally got up from the couch and placed a kiss on Mya before laying her down next to Sunshine.

"I'll leave like you wanted. Just don't lie and say I never tried to fix shit."

"Jonas, wait," Sunshine yelled out before he could open the front door.

"What?"

"I do love you. Everything about us feels so right, and maybe that's why we rushed because it was real from the jump. Yeah, some things have never been brought up or talked about, but I'm not ready for this to be over. Whatever needs to be worked on or discussed, let's do it. Just please, don't leave me. I'm sorry, I'm sorry for everything," Sunshine cried out.

Hating to see her cry, Jonas rushed back over to the couch and pulled her into his arms.

"We're gonna work things out. You don't have to worry about me ever leaving you and Mya."

Sunshine cried her heart out as Jonas held her. Monsta had always made her cry. It made her hate him, and she always wanted him to go away. But with Jonas, she wanted them to be close and together forever. She wanted to be in his skin if that were even possible.

"Why don't you see if your mom and sister can keep Mya for a week so we can take that vacation I spoke about before? I think we need new scenery for a minute and to work on us."

Jonas walked in wanting to work on them, thinking maybe they just needed space and time. But the longer he held her, the more he hated thinking about the space between them. He wanted his family back. Sunshine hadn't talked to her mom since the last time they got into it, and she really wasn't ready to talk to her or Zoey.

"That sounds like a good plan, but we're still not talking."

"How long has it been?"

"Whew, a long-ass time. You know how we are with each other," she said, trying to play the hurt off.

Jonas shook his head. He reverted to the old version of himself that he hated when Sunshine wasn't in his life for a month. He couldn't understand how anyone who knew her could do without her being around for so long.

"Call them over, and I'll talk to them. You know your mom loves me and would never tell me no."

Sunshine knew he had a point. Her mom has treated him like a god since day one. Then again, any nigga who wasn't Monsta probably would've gotten the same treatment.

"I can't call her, Jonas."

"Yes, you can, Sunshine. Be the bigger person and reach out. I had to be the bigger person and just pull up on you today because I wanted things to get back on track between us."

Sunshine had a dumb look on her face as she told him the truth. "Jonas, I wanted to call you, I really did. The only reason I didn't is because the night I picked up Mya from your house, I tossed the phone out the window."

"I thought you might still be on that bullshit, so I bought a new phone so that at least Mya could Facetime me or something. I guess you need it now," he said, pulling out the new phone.

"Really? So, *Mya* was gonna Facetime you, Jonas?"

"Yeah," he responded, laughing.

Sunshine giggled. "I don't like us not being together. I feel so much better knowing when you get off work that you'll be walking through the door and embracing me with your love."

Jonas wanted so badly to tell her exactly how not having her in his life had a major impact on him relapsing and drinking, but he only told her how much he loved her. It was an embarrassing stage in his life that he needed to fight. "I missed my family too. I love y'all so much and never wanna be apart from y'all like that anymore. That month felt like a lifetime."

Sunshine felt like he was telling the truth and wanted nothing but the best for both of them.

Opening up the box that held the new phone, Sunshine took it out, then dialed her mama's phone number.

"Hey, Ma, what are you doing?"

Jonas sat there listening to Sunshine talk her mom into coming by the house to visit her and Mya. From the sound of the conversation, if Mya's name were never mentioned, she probably wouldn't have come. His family had their own problems, so he couldn't judge. Mya played with Jonas until she tired herself out and fell asleep on him. That was a feeling he never wanted to give up. Like Sunshine said, he was the father, and no one could take that from him.

Sunshine got up to straighten up before her mom arrived. She knew she would talk shit if she saw how her house looked. Since she never told her mom that she and Jonas broke up, she knew she wouldn't understand that when she was depressed and stressed, cleaning up was the least of her problems.

Ms. Mathews told Sunshine she was out and about, so it would take her a minute to swing by, but it was a whole two hours later when she finally arrived. Jonas laid Mya down on the couch so he could open the door for Ms. Mathews and Zoey.

"Hey," Jonas said as they walked in.

They both spoke as Sunshine walked into the living room.

"Hey, Ma. Hey, Zoey, where are the girls?"

"Girl, they're with their grandma like always. I swear it's like that lady doesn't know how to breathe without them."

They all laughed while walking into the dining room. Whenever they all got together at Sunshine's house, the dining room was the chill room. Sunshine wasted no time getting straight to the point.

"Speaking of kids with grandma, Ma, can you and Zoey keep Mya for about a week for me and Jonas?"

Jonas almost choked on his water at how she did that shit.

"Sunshine, I haven't heard from you in over a month, and now you finally hit me up because you want me to fuckin' babysit? That's my grandbaby, but you *not* about to use me, girl."

Sunshine rolled her eyes. "It's cool. You act like she ain't got another grandma. I was trying to be nice by asking you first."

Ms. Mathews shook her head. "Bitch, that shit doesn't work on me. Go ask that bald-headed ho if she can babysit for your ass, but I bet you any amount of money, if anything happens to my granddaughter, I'm coming for that ass."

"Ma, did you really just call me a bitch?" Sunshine asked, totally surprised.

"How else would you describe the way you acting? If you ask me, that was a straight-up bitch move," Ms. Mathews said, justifying her choice of words.

Jonas didn't like what was going on, and Zoey's laughing only irritated him even more. He'd be damned if this shit led to Mya being at Monsta's mama's house by herself for a week.

"Ms. Mathews, I would really love and appreciate you both if Mya could 'stay with you two for a week. There's something me and Sunshine need to work out. We really need y'all right now."

Sunshine waited to see if her mom would go off and call him out on his bullshit, but then she remembered he got treated better than blood.

"She got clothes and diapers at my house. Call me when you need me to drop her off."

Ms. Mathews wanted to cuss Jonas out, but then she thought back to the last time she spoke to Sunshine. Her daughter was scared she was losing Jonas, so maybe they needed some alone time to get their relationship together. The last thing she wanted was for Sunshine to be lonely and broken. When her first real boyfriend and she broke up, she became needy and ended up with Monsta's crazy ass.

Sunshine peeped how her mama didn't even ask when or nothing. She was ready to leave with Mya right then. She fixed her mouth to say some slick shit, but changed her mind. Besides, the look on Jonas's face told her she bet not fuck shit up. Instead, she went into the living room to grab the cell phone box.

"Jonas bought me a new phone. Take down my number just in case y'all need to call me."

Zoey and their mom typed her new phone number into their contacts.

"How long do you plan on having this phone?"

Sunshine giggled. "Forever."

Jonas smiled, hearing that. Maybe her being scared was over with.

After they left, Jonas told Sunshine he needed to stay there with her. She was all right with that, knowing she missed him fucking on her and just holding her while she slept. She never would have guessed he didn't wanna go home because his apartment was nasty and liquor bottles were everywhere. Besides living in an unclean apartment, he didn't wanna go home to be tempted to drink like that again. With Sunshine and Mya in his life, he never wanted her to know the true him.

"What do you want, Darryl?" Zoey asked, wiping the sleep out of her eyes, then looking at the big red numbers on her clock that read 2:47 a.m.

Darryl hadn't been able to talk to Zoey in a few weeks since she found out about his drug habit. It surprised him that she even answered the phone. He had been sitting in the driveway for the last hour, trying to figure out how to convince her to overlook his habit and take him back. His little secret fucked up their relationship majorly, but the way he looked at things, he had a lot more going on.

"Can you come outside to talk to me?" he asked, some-what begging.

Zoey couldn't believe he had the nerve to ask her that. "No. We don't have shit to talk about. I talked to your mom earlier, and the kids are good," she snapped.

"Please, baby. Besides, I'm already outside and need to talk to you badly," he pleaded.

Zoey held the phone in silence. She wanted to hang up and hate him in peace, but her love for him wouldn't allow her to.

"Zoey, baby, I need you. You are my only reason for living. I'm not shit without you in my life."

Those words rolled off his tongue so easily. He'd never been able to lie so well. After seeing the money that was deposited into his account earlier that day from Monsta, he knew he had to do whatever it took to make Monsta happy to keep the money flowing. Darryl fell out of love with Zoey over a year ago, but instead of leaving, he stayed. Who wouldn't want to live in a rent-free place? On top of that, he was added to Monsta's payroll and could just blow his money on whatever.

Zoey wanted to tell him her house wasn't the spot, and that's where he needed to be. She also wanted to tell him to go to hell. But being stupid in love, she climbed out of bed, making sure not to wake Mya.

As soon as she got outside, Darryl was all over her. "Damn, I missed you so much, baby."

Zoey broke loose from Darryl. "What do we need to talk about?"

"Come get in the car and talk to me," he ordered as he opened the passenger-side door.

Zoey got into the car, no longer putting up a fight. Something in her wanted to hear what he had to say. She wanted to hear that he was off that shit and wanted only her.

Trying to play it smooth, Darryl lifted Zoey's face so he could look into her eyes.

"Look, since you found out about my 'little problem' and kicked me out, I've been getting my shit together. Having you and my kids in my life is way more important than having that nose candy," he tried to explain.

Zoey ate up everything he said and was quick to forgive him for everything. "Darryl, can you promise that you're truly done with this shit? I can't have that type of shit around the kids."

"I promise, baby, all that shit is over with. That shit wasn't nothing for real. That shit's outta of my system."

Zoey leaned over to kiss him and show some love. "I believe you, baby. I believe you."

They talked for a while before Zoey realized she'd left Mya all by herself. "Me and mama babysitting for Sunshine and Jonas. I need to go in and check on Mya."

"Can I come in?"

Zoey smiled. "Yeah, baby. I'll just take her upstairs to my mama's room for the night."

As they got out of the car and walked toward the house, Darryl smiled at how easy it was to pull her back in. She and her sister were one and the same.

Zoey did as she said she would and took Mya to her mom's bedroom so she could have some quality time with her man. Determined to get his money while Zoey was upstairs, Darryl made it his business to snoop around. He made love to Zoey that night, making her feel like nothing in the world could come between them ever again. Happy to finally have her man back, Zoey took that good dick and was knocked out asleep in no time.

Darryl was usually ready to slide back into the wet pussy he once loved, but being on a mission that was gonna make him money and keep him supplied with the purest dope in Detroit, he let her ass stay asleep. Creeping out of bed, he snuck over to her nightstand. If he wanted to get paid, he had to bring Monsta anything on Sunshine. Learning that Mya was there is just a bonus. He knew a few photos of her would be worth a lot of bread.

"Got it," he mumbled as he strolled through Zoey's phone and found Sunshine's number. He couldn't believe she even had a phone. *Bitch must have thought shit was sweet and over with.*

Zoey flipped over. "What are you doing out of bed, baby?"

Before turning to face Zoey, he held the phone closer to his chest so she couldn't see the light coming from her phone. "I was about to go to the bathroom. Go back to sleep, baby."

Zoey turned around and drifted off, not knowing what she had just allowed to happen.

Chapter 13

"Don't get me wrong, I love Jonas with everything in me, but I'm really starting to not like Sunshine. That bitch had my cousin's head all fucked up and shit," Nakia yelled out as she took another sip of her drink.

Meka shook her head. "Here you go with this shit again. Sunshine ain't did shit wrong. If anything, she's the one who got him out of that dark hole he dug himself in."

It was cousin night, and once again, Nakia was buzzing and talking shit like she did every time they got together. Lately, her primary focus had been on her hate for Sunshine, and everyone was sick and tired of hearing about that shit.

"Nakia, stop speaking about my brother. At least he got off the couch at the shop, and he's trying to get back on track," Poppa said.

Nakia wasn't holding her tongue for no one. "I'm just saying that bitch pussy ain't made of gold. One minute, he's living like a real boss. Then the next, he acting like a fuckin' drunk on the streets. Why would he wanna throw away everything he worked so hard for to be like his fuckin' daddy?"

"Bitch, lay off my fuckin' daddy. I hated seeing my brother drunk and passed out looking like him, but you ain't about to sit up and talk shit about either one of them," Poppa yelled.

Everyone there knew the backstory of Poppa and Jonas's dad. They could feel the pain Poppa felt when

Jonas was out there fucking up again. Everyone had sympathy, but for some reason, Nakia called the whole thing bullshit and blamed Sunshine for everything.

"You mad and in your fucking feelings, so I'ma let that bitch word slide. Anyway . . . I'm just saying, he acts like that bitch pussy made of gold or something. She brought her funky ass back into his life, and *boom* . . . He don't need a drink, and he's able to go on a fucking vacation. He ain't even thinking about the shop."

"Shut up, Nakia. As long as he's trying to get clean and stay that way, what's the fucking problem? You really need to stop drinking too," Meka yelled.

"Bitch, whatever. We all drinkin' on something in this bitch, so fuck you talking 'bout?"

Meka really loved and understood Jonas, and she wasn't up for Nakia's shit.

Meka put down her glass. "We sip on cousin night. You drink to get pissy drunk at least four days out of the week. We are *not* the same."

Nakia rolled her eyes. "So, what are you trying to say? I'm gon' end up like my uncle?"

Poppa didn't like that his dad's name kept being brought up. "You need to chill the fuck out. I asked nicely the first time. What my pops did is in the past, and you, out of all people, not about to dog him or my brother out."

Nakia looked at Poppa like he was crazy. "I'm just speaking facts. Your brother is weak as hell for letting a bitch make him relapse again. He just showed us that if he don't have pussy, he's gonna slowly kill himself like his—"

"Chill out, Nakia," Mason yelled, cutting her off.

Mason and everyone else could see Poppa was ready to fuck her up. In the blink of an eye, Poppa slapped Nakia's glass out of her hand and choked her up against the wall.

"Let me go, Poppa!"

"Nah, bitch, this what you wanted. I asked your ass nicely to shut the fuck up about my daddy and brother, but you always want to push a nigga's buttons and shit."

Mason understood why Poppa was mad, but Nakia was his sister.

"Come on, Poppa, let her go."

Poppa slowly released his drunk cousin. "I'm gonna call it a night. I'll get back with y'all in a minute."

Although Nakia needed her ass beaten for all that bullshit she was on, nobody actually let him do it.

"Nakia, that shit wasn't cool at all. You know how hard they took their father's death, and you sat in his face actin' like you were talking about a fucking movie or something. You need to go lay your ass down or something," Meka said with much attitude.

"Fuck y'all. As a matter of fact, y'all can get outta my fucking house. This cousins' bullshit is over."

Mason hated the way she acted when she was drunk. "Nakia, chill the fuck out. Just admit you were dead wrong."

Nakia necked the last of her drink before slamming her glass on the coffee table. "It's time for all y'all Sunshine fans to get the hell outta my house. She got Jonas's head all fucked up, and y'all allowed it to happen, just like y'all let her baby daddy kill my brother. Now, Poppa wanna lay hands on *me* 'cause he probably heard her talk about when she was getting her ass beat all the time."

"Chill out, Nakia. Everything ain't that girl's fault."

At this point, everyone was tired of her shit.

"Baby, it's so beautiful out here. This view makes me never wanna go back to Detroit."

Jonas was all smiles seeing his woman so happy. "Really? I'm glad you're having a great time. You sitting here talking about never going back to Detroit, but what about Mya?" he asked with a smirk on his face.

Sunshine giggled. "I'll stay here while you go get my baby."

Although she was very grateful to be on vacation, she was still clingy when it came to Mya.

She grabbed the bottle of wine on the balcony table. "Baby, you want a glass?"

Trying to overcome his secret addiction, Jonas turned down the offer. He knew that anything, including wine, would be bad, especially if he was trying to quit cold turkey.

"I'm good, baby. The last thing I wanna do is get drunk and forget how beautiful you look in the Miami sun. That Detroit bullshit-ass sun doesn't do you justice."

Sunshine blushed. "Aww, that's so sweet, baby. I love you so much."

"I love you too, and I promise I'm gonna show it every day."

For the next few days, Sunshine and Jonas had the time of their life. Being away from home made Sunshine realize she wasn't living life to the fullest like she should've been. Being with Monsta, she got clothes, shoes, purses, and little shit like that. However, with a real boss like Jonas, he slowly showed her a better life.

"Babe, it's our last day here. What do you wanna do today?" Sunshine asked as she walked into the room.

Jonas stood up from the bed, putting on his drawers. "Let's get married."

"What?" Sunshine asked, surprised.

"You heard me. Let's get married. Why wait any longer when we can do that shit today?"

Sunshine was all smiles. "Baby, are you sure this is what you wanna do? I mean, we were just talking about taking time to get to know each other better and stuff like that. Now you're talking about getting married."

Jonas grabbed Sunshine's waist so he could hold on to his love. "Do you love me?"

"Yeah, I do, but you said there was some shit we needed to discuss and—"

Jonas wasn't trying to hear what she was talking about. He couldn't see himself moving on without her, and talking about his truth just might run her away. He couldn't chance it.

"Fuck all that. We're in love and don't wanna be with anybody else, right?"

Sunshine smiled, feeling that his love was genuine and that they could actually make this work. "It's a plan, baby."

His heart told him they were making the right decision, and there was nothing anyone could tell her about being in love. Sunshine wrapped her legs around him.

"I'm so ready to be Mrs. Bentley."

"That shit sound sexy as fuck."

Jonas knew Sunshine was the one and would be open to marrying him at the drop of a dime. He also knew some of his family might have tried to convince him to wait, so he didn't plan on speaking about it until after everything was said and done.

Their last night on vacation, they spent the day as Mr. and Mrs. Bentley. They were happy and in love without a care in the world.

"Wake up, my beautiful wife," Jonas said, shaking Sunshine's leg as they pulled up to their home.

Sunshine slowly opened her eyes and peeked around. The car radio said it was past midnight, and she was dead tired.

"I'm up, baby. Let's hurry up and get into the house so I can climb into bed."

Jonas grabbed their luggage. He was all for them going straight to bed because he was dead tired too.

Jonas set the luggage on the porch, then opened the door for his new wife, so she could go in while he went to get the rest of the stuff out of the trunk.

"Oh my God, Jonas!" Sunshine screamed.

Turning on the living room light, Sunshine was hit with a major surprise. It had been a minute, but once again, someone vandalized her home. Hearing her scream, Jonas was alarmed and quickly dropped the luggage in the yard as he ran into the house. The newlyweds stood in the living room, surprised at the extensive damage done to the home while they were away.

"Damn, man, what the fuck . . . Who the fuck did this shit?" Jonas asked, knowing neither one of them really knew the answer.

"Calm down, Jonas. Let's just clean up this shit."

Jonas gave his wife a strange look. He could sense she was hiding something.

"Somebody fucked up the house, and all you can say is, 'Let's clean it up'?"

Sunshine instantly caught an attitude. "What more was I supposed to say, Jonas? I'm tired and really just wanna go to bed so I can get my baby in the morning."

"Was it that nigga Monsta who did this shit?" he yelled, grabbing her.

"Let me go! How am I supposed to know? Wasn't I with you?"

Remembering what she went through with the last nigga, Jonas released her, then started pacing the floor. "I told you this nigga wasn't gonna stop until you dealt with that money situation."

"I don't wanna talk about that shit," she yelled, pissing him off even more.

"I told your ass this shit wasn't over as long as you had his money. What if we were home with Mya? What if I was at work and you were here by yourself with Mya? Shit fucked up and you don't wanna talk about it?"

Sunshine stomped up the steps. "Fuck this shit. I'm going to bed."

Jonas yelled, "You need to grow the fuck up, Sunshine."

Taking a seat on the couch, Jonas realized his cousin might have been right when she told him that sometimes love couldn't overpower someone loving toxic behavior. Sunshine was so accustomed to dealing with toxic people that she didn't know how to live without it, even if that meant creating her own problems.

Entering the bedroom, Sunshine couldn't believe how fucked up it was. Then she walked to Mya's room. Seeing the baby room was still how they left it, she knew Monsta was behind it all. It had been months since she heard from him, so she couldn't help but wonder what made him start fucking with her again after all this time had passed. When Sunshine turned around to leave Mya's room, she was frightened by Jonas standing there.

"Damn, you scared me, Jonas."

Jonas pulled her into a hug. "My bad, baby. Look, I don't want to fight or anything about this shit. How about I book you a nice room, with a Jacuzzi and all, for a week or so, and I'll start on the house as soon as the sun comes up. What do you think about that?"

Sunshine smiled. That right there is the very reason she loved him. She had just stormed away from him after giving him attitude, and now he was trying to make things right between them. He spoiled her, and that's all she ever wanted.

"What about Mya?"

"I'll pay your mom and sister to keep her longer, or I'll see if one of my cousins can get her for us. Stop trying to find a way to go against what I need you to do."

"I'm not, baby."

"Go pack your bag, and I'll call around to see who has anything available because it's so late."

Jonas went back downstairs to find his wife somewhere to stay while she got her things together. Sunshine had a few outfits in her suitcase already downstairs, but since she really didn't plan on doing too much of anything, she wanted to grab some regular clothes. Besides, when she was out of town, she was half-naked most of the time.

"What the fuck?" Sunshine said as she opened up her underwear drawer.

Inside was an envelope addressed to her. She knew by the handwriting that it was from Monsta. Although she desperately wanted to open it and read it, she decided to wait until Jonas took her to the room. The last thing she wanted was for Jonas to walk in while she was reading the letter.

Being anxious, Sunshine quickly grabbed some stuff and then rushed downstairs. "Jonas, I'm ready."

"OK, I found a spot downtown and booked the room for a week. I'm gonna call Poppa in the morning and see if he has time to help me get this shit together."

"All right. Come on, let's get out of here," she ordered.

Jonas made it downtown in no time. Sunshine was so tired and ready to go to bed that she damn near begged him to hurry up and get there. They checked in, and Jonas carried her bags to her room.

"I'm about to go back to the house and crash, but if you need anything, don't hesitate to hit me up."

Sunshine showered her husband with kisses. "I love you so much, baby. Go home and get some rest, my love."

"I love you too. I want you to get some rest too, and I'll handle everything like the house and Mya in the morning."

They shared another kiss before Jonas left to return home. He was going to ask his family for help, but he had a feeling that it wouldn't be as easy as the first time they helped.

After a hot shower, Sunshine threw on a T-shirt before grabbing the letter out of her bag. She was finally ready to read Monsta's letter and count how many times he called her a bitch. To her surprise, he wasn't as wild as usual.

> *Sunshine,*
> *Look, I really do love and miss your ass so much. I'm fucked up in here, not being able to hold or make love to you anymore. On top of that, I wanna meet my daughter. I don't care about the bullshit you did with that other nigga. Y'all my family, and can't anything change that. Do me a favor and go check on my mom. I fucked up with her again and haven't been able to talk to her in a while. I've changed for the better, and I want us to become a family again. From now on, I don't wanna be beefed out with you. I want nothing but love. Never forget that I was the nigga who kept that pussy soaked even when you made me mad.*
> *Love always and forever,*
> *Monsta*
>
> *P.S. I just got a new phone.*
> *Call me. 313-524-5555.*

Looking down at the rock that Jonas placed on her hand, she shook her head as she folded the letter again. He was trying to be nice, but she couldn't fall for that shit. As she lay down, she tried not to think about the letter, but when he said he kept her pussy wet, she couldn't help but think he was also the same nigga who kept her eyes soaked with tears.

"I hate you so much," she mumbled before closing her eyes.

Keisha lay across the bed, unsure of her next move. Whatever little money she did have was spent on her room and food, but things were getting tight for her. If she weren't so scared the detectives would find her, she would've gone to the hood to find one of her old tricks and made some money. One thing's for sure, her pussy got wetter when her pockets got dry, and she knew how to make a few bucks with Li'l Mama.

"Damn, let me get up and make some moves," she mumbled to herself. It was 12:00 p.m., and if she didn't make shit pop off, it would be her last day there.

After getting dressed, Keisha was ready to hit the streets. Being downtown, she paid more for a room, but there were a lot of businessmen with money, which meant her type of men. Keisha stepped into the elevator, wearing her oversized sunglasses, hoping not to be spotted by the wrong people.

"Keisha?" Sunshine questioned.

Raising her head, Keisha saw Sunshine standing there. She always thought that if they ever were to bump into each other, a fight would take place. But seeing Sunshine just staring at her and not knocking her head off, she wasn't sure what would happen.

"Hey," Keisha said, trying to rush off the elevator as soon as the door opened.

Sunshine wasn't even on a fighting tip, especially after getting her ass beat by Kyrah not too long ago. She really just wanted to see how she'd been doing after all this time.

"Keisha, wait," she said, grabbing the back of Keisha's dress.

"Look, Sunshine, I don't want to fight. I'm sorry for everything, and I'm paying for it now. Yeah, that's right. Karma is fucking me up as we speak," Keisha said, damn near in tears.

Sunshine could tell her ex-best friend was going through a lot by her appearance. Although she was pregnant, she hadn't gained any weight for real, and she was so stressed out that her edges were gone. Those sneaky links with Monsta weren't even worth it in the end.

"Hey, I'm about to go get some breakfast. Join me."

Keisha gave her a strange look.

"My treat," Sunshine said, closing the deal.

Keisha smiled. "All right, sounds like a plan."

As the two ex-best friends sat across from each other, Sunshine couldn't help but wonder what Keisha had been up to. The last time she heard anything about her was when Monsta beat her ass real badly, and she called the police on him. It's crazy how she never had the balls to do that herself.

"You really wanted to be Monsta's baby mama so badly that you would say fuck me and my feelings just to fuck him?"

Keisha knew this conversation had to happen one day, and she was all for it. She shocked Sunshine with her story. "First of all, let me tell you that I was fucking Monsta years before you were even in the picture. When he hooked up with you, I damn near begged you not to fall for his shit, but you didn't listen to me."

"What? Bitch, are you serious?" Sunshine yelled, damn near choking on her food.

"Yeah, dead ass. It wasn't no love type shit like what y'all had. I was more of the bitch that fucked the crew when they needed to bust a quick nut and didn't feel like going home to their main bitch."

Sunshine shook her head. She knew her friend was a ho, but damn . . . It was crazy how Monsta had been telling her about Keisha for the longest, but she never wanted to believe the stories. Hearing all of this coming out of her mouth was a different type of hurt.

"You saying y'all were just fucking, right? When did you decide to carry his child? I mean, he was so happy about me being pregnant, I would have never guessed he would get someone else pregnant too."

"I gotta be completely honest with you because we were once best friends. Monsta wanted to call shit off for good with me. At first, I was cool with that, but over time, I realized I didn't wanna keep fucking his friends. I wanted him for myself."

Sunshine put down her head. She thought she could handle the truth about everything, but hearing the betrayal was slowly killing her inside.

"We were best friends. I told you everything about us, from the abuse to him getting caught up with other bitches. I even told you about him forcing himself on me whenever I was mad and didn't want to fuck him. What in your mind made you think he would be perfect for you? What would make you cross me for him?"

At the time everything went down, Keisha allowed jealousy to take over and actually thought she was getting one up on Sunshine by still fucking with Monsta. Soon, no longer giving a fuck about their friendship, Keisha put her plan into motion. Now she wanted to cry for hurting her friend, but the damage was already done.

"I'm so sorry for everything I've done to hurt you, Sunshine. I know I was wrong, and I just want you to know that the bitch Karma is kicking my ass right now."

"As she should," Sunshine simply said, sipping on her orange juice.

Keisha wanted to tell her the whole truth about how she was so desperate for Monsta to be hers that she stole his sperm. But after giving it some thought, she didn't want to fuck up any chance of them becoming friends again.

"So, I heard about Monsta and what he did to you and the baby. I'm sorry you had to go through that."

Keisha knew she was on that bullshit with him, but she didn't think she deserved to be damn near beaten to death with her unborn child. "Thanks. You know the police were called on him, and now everything is so fucked up for me."

Sunshine could tell by the tears forming in her eyes and the way her body shook that she had a painful story to tell, and she was all ears. "What's going on, Keisha?"

Keisha hesitated to respond at first, not sure if she could tell Sunshine everything. Then she thought about how she was the one who betrayed their friendship, not her.

"After checking out of the hospital, some detectives came to talk to me. They want me to snitch on everyone."

Keisha started to cry, and Sunshine couldn't help but hug her ex-best friend. "It's gonna be all right, Keisha."

"It's not, and I'm scared shitless."

"What are you gonna do, girl?" Sunshine questioned.

Keisha wiped her eyes. "Girl, they talking about locking me up if I don't bring them whatever it is they're asking for. I don't wanna help them with this shit. I just wanna move on with my life."

"They can't lock you up. We both know you ain't have shit to do with Monsta's bullshit."

Tears still rolled down Keisha's face. "I moved out of my apartment so that they wouldn't be able to find me. Honestly, after today, I don't know what my next move will be. I'm fucked either way. If I tell on him, then I'm dead, and if he gets out, I'm dead. I grew up too fast, not really doing shit with my life, and now, I finally realize I wanna live a long life with my baby and probably won't have a chance now."

"Damn, Keisha, I'm so sorry you got caught up in this bullshit. Shit got rocky between us, but I wanna help you and the baby. We were once good friends. I can't just walk away from you."

Keisha could tell from her tone that she was genuine and still cared about her. She wasn't sure how she could help her out, but she was grateful.

"I'm gonna go pay for breakfast, then we can go back to the room. I have an idea how I can help you."

Once back in the room, Sunshine set up an Uber to go back to her house.

"What the hell are you doing here, Sunshine?" Jonas asked, still cleaning up.

"I forgot something," she simply responded as she ran up the stairs to her bedroom.

Poppa watched Sunshine go upstairs. He liked her for the most part and thought that she was good for his brother, but he could tell she was up to something.

"What's that all about, bro?"

Jonas played it off. "Shit, I don't know. That girl's attitude be having me confused as hell sometimes."

They both laughed.

"That's probably why I haven't found the right one to settle down with. I can't deal with all that bipolar shit."

Jonas laughed. "She's not bipolar; she's just learning how to love again," he tried to explain.

Poppa took a seat on the couch. He had helped out downstairs all morning and was dead tired.

"I'll order some food or something, bro. I really appreciate your help."

Poppa nodded his head in agreement. Eating some good, unhealthy food sounded great at that moment.

Sunshine returned downstairs with a bag. "What's that, baby?"

She rushed over to place a kiss on his lips. "The end of all my problems."

Not really understanding what she was talking about, Jonas nodded his head in agreement.

"All right, if you say so."

Sunshine then turned her attention to Poppa. "Thanks once again for saving my home. I really appreciate it."

"No problem, sis. You know I got y'all back. Oh yeah, congratulations on the wedding. I would have brought a gift, but I didn't find out until I got here."

Sunshine giggled. "It's all right. We planned on celebrating with everyone, but came home to this bullshit."

"All right, I understand that. By the way shit going, we'll be partying in no time."

"Hell yeah," Jonas added in.

Sunshine gave him another kiss. "I'll call you later, baby."

Trying to help her friend, Sunshine rushed back to Keisha, but this time, in her own car. She planned to give Keisha the bag full of Monsta's money so she could skip town and get the fuck away from Detroit and those crooked cops who were trying to pin her for Monsta's bullshit.

Sunshine knocked on Keisha's door. "Keisha, it's Sunshine."

Keisha looked through the peephole to confirm it was her friend and just her alone. She could never be too careful.

"Dang, girl, that was quick. Now, how are you gonna help solve my problem?"

Sunshine handed over the bag. It was way less than what she took, but anything would help Keisha out in her situation. Keisha's mouth dropped open when she saw the money in the bag. She never expected Sunshine to come through the way she did.

"Oh my God, are you serious? This is for me?"

Keisha pulled Sunshine into a tight hug to show her appreciation. "Thank you so much, Sunshine. You just don't know how much this really means to me. I love you, girl," she cried.

"It's all good, Keisha. I just want you to get the fuck on and never look back. Go to a whole new state and take care of that baby. Staying here will only get you hurt."

Tears rolled down their faces as they hugged. They were grown enough to realize Monsta played them both. They needed to have each other's backs, especially when it came to him.

Later that night while Keisha was in her room planning her escape from Detroit, Sunshine sat in her room thinking about all the bullshit Keisha shared about Monsta. Although she let Keisha's fucked-up story get the best of her and couldn't beat her ass like she always thought she would, she wanted to go off on Monsta's ass. Then she thought about how she did have a way to contact his ass. As she read over his letter and saw how he had tried to be nice, the more she hated him. Once again, he tried to play on her feelings. Not only did she hate him for her, but now, she also hated Keisha. Sunshine slowly dialed his number on the room phone.

"Who dis'?" Monsta calmly said into the phone, sending chills through Sunshine's body.

She hated him, but his voice still did something to her.

"Why did you want me to call you?" she questioned, getting straight to the point.

Monsta smiled. "You sound sexy as hell. I miss you, love."

"I'm not trying to hear that shit, boy."

Monsta laughed at her. "Yeah, right, muthafucka. You wouldn't have called if you didn't. FaceTime me so I can see you, baby."

Sunshine shook her head, knowing he was trying to play on her. "Nah, you good."

Monsta knew Sunshine always loved his voice and was easily turned on by it. "Why you playin' with me, baby? I know for a fact those panties wet as fuck by now."

Sunshine knew she had to take control of the situation, or he'd have her ass completely turned on and playing with her pussy over the phone.

"Stop talking to me like that or I'm gonna hang up," she demanded.

Monsta kept laughing at her. "Yo' nigga must be around 'cause you actin' funny as fuck."

"I don't have a nigga. I have a *real* boss who loved me enough to put a ring on my hand."

"What?"

Sunshine loved that she could now hurt him and get him in his feelings. "Yeah, that's right. I'm married now."

Monsta's smile was long gone. "Fuck that bitch-ass nigga. Do that nigga know you a fuckin' ran-through, bipolar-ass bitch?"

Now, Sunshine was laughing at him. "Bipolar? *Really?* Bipolar? Monsta, that's all you. And I have never been run-through, bitch."

Monsta held the phone, thinking of how he should handle this. He wanted to go the fuck off, but at the same time, he didn't want her to hang up and never call him again.

"I heard that nigga of yours playing house with you and my baby."

"And? He's doing a great job at it too," she snapped.

Monsta wished she were in front of him so he could choke the life out of her. He also knew there was one of two reasons she was popping off at the mouth like that. One, Jonas was right there listening. Or two, because she knew he couldn't lay hands on her at the moment.

"Bitch, he can have you, but I'm coming back to get my baby," Monsta calmly said.

"Your name isn't on a fucking birth certificate or anything. Mya knows who her daddy is." Sunshine finally knew what could hurt Monsta and played on his emotions. "Mya loves her daddy so much, I don't think she'll ever love anyone as much as him. Even in my stomach, she kicked and played with him every time he touched or talked to my belly. She never did that with you because she knew you wouldn't be a good daddy to her."

"You a stupid bitch actin' like I can't get you touched from in here. I'll kill you *and* that nigga. I don't mind leaving her an orphan. Shid, I'll leave Mya an orphan before I let y'all be happy with her."

"Touched like how you had somebody fuck my house up and leave that note. You right. Your goons really trashed my house. Stop making these fake threats and worry about not dropping the soap and becoming somebody's bitch," Sunshine sarcastically said.

"Fuck you, bitch. I swear when I get out, I'ma make you my bitch again."

"You know what? I wish Keisha would go ahead and give those detectives the info on you so you can spend the rest of your fuckin' life locked up. Crazy, bitch-ass nigga," Sunshine said, laughing.

"All right, bitch, you think shit funny. Jonas Antwon Bentley. 19728 W. 7 Mile. *Boom. Boom.*" With that being said, Monsta hung up.

As Sunshine ripped the letter and flushed it down the toilet, she realized the address he recited was Jonas's shop, *Bentley Cuts*. Panicking, she quickly tried to call Monsta back, but he didn't answer. Desperate, Sunshine tried calling a few more times and even left messages begging him not to do anything crazy. Since he wouldn't pick up or respond, she felt like it was too late.

Sunshine packed her bags so she could go home. At that point, she didn't care if the house was fucked up or not. She wanted and needed to be under Jonas. Going back to Keisha's room, Sunshine told her she was leaving and that since her room was paid for, she could stay there until she left Detroit. Keisha was all for it and happy that she hadn't paid for her room yet. Sunshine rushed home to be with her husband, wishing she had just left shit alone.

Walking into the house, she saw Jonas knocked out on the couch. Knowing she had once again fucked up, tears rolled down her cheeks. The thought of something bad happening to him because of her scared her. She even considered leaving him to keep him safe, but she knew he loved her and Mya enough to search for her, regardless of the consequences. After dropping her bags, Sunshine climbed onto the couch and lay beside him.

"What are you doing back here? I told you I just needed another day or so," he said, still half-asleep.

He waited a minute to hear her respond, but when she didn't, he looked at her to see her crying. "What's wrong, baby?"

"I just love you so much, Jonas."

"I love you too, but you ain't got to cry about it." Jonas kissed his wife. "You know you can talk to me if you need to get something off your chest."

"I'm good, Jonas. Can you just hold me so I can get some rest?"

Jonas hugged her a little tighter like she asked. He knew when something was bothering her and hated how she never felt comfortable talking about it. He hoped that in due time, she would get over that.

The next morning, Jonas snuck off the couch to shower. He had been on some bullshit and needed to get to the shop. Although Meka had been holding shit down and getting paid to cover his ass, he needed to get back to being the boss.

Jonas placed a kiss on Sunshine's lips just before he tried to walk out the door.

"Where are you going?" Sunshine asked as she jumped up.

"Work. I've missed more than a few days and need to go in."

Sunshine wasn't trying to hear that. She jumped off the couch, fearing the worst. "You can't go in today, Jonas." She started to cry.

"What the hell is wrong with you, Sunshine? You've been on some crybaby shit since you got back yesterday. What the fuck happened in the room?"

"Nothing, I just . . ."

"You just what, Sunshine?"

Sunshine stood there crying. How was she going to tell him she called Monsta, talking shit, and now he had her scared?

Jonas didn't like the way she was acting, and her not saying shit worried him. "Talk to me, baby, please."

"Just don't leave me."

Jonas had plans to go back to work, but the way Sunshine held on to him and begged him to stay, he knew he couldn't leave her like that.

Keisha spent the whole morning going over her plans. Thanks to Sunshine, she had enough funds to finally make it out of Detroit and far away from Monsta and his bullshit. She knew without her testimony, he'd be able to walk free in no time.

Standing in the shower, Keisha thought she heard a strange noise. Not knowing for sure, she stood there for a second trying to see if she would hear it again. After a short pause and not hearing anything, she finished letting the water rinse the soap off her body. She turned the water off, then pulled the shower curtain open.

"Aye, bitch, Monsta said, 'What up?'"

The masked man in all black let off two shots before she could even let out a scream. Before leaving, he grabbed the bag of money on the table in the front room. Monsta didn't mention any money, so he wasn't either. Keisha and her unborn baby never had a chance after being shot once in the head and once in the chest.

"No, Jonas."

Jonas slid out of bed. It was 6:00 a.m., and he wanted to get to the shop before Meka.

"Come on, baby, don't do this shit every fucking morning. I've been home with you for two days now. I gotta go to the shop," he tried to explain, then took a seat next to Sunshine on the bed. "What's up, baby? What the hell is going on that got you like this? Why are you acting like you don't want me to leave the house?"

"I just want you to stay here with me."

Jonas still felt like there was more to the story, and she was on some bullshit. "How about you get dressed and come to the shop with me today? I missed too many days. I'm sure you can help with some paperwork or something."

Sunshine thought about what he was saying before agreeing to spend the day with him. Even though she didn't really want to leave the house, she didn't want to be by herself.

Just as he wanted, Jonas beat Meka to the shop and was ready to work. He knew a few people were waiting for him to show his face again, and he didn't want to let anyone down.

"Look what the cat done dragged in. Congratulations on the wedding that I wasn't invited to," Meka said as she gave Sunshine and Jonas a hug.

"Yeah, I had to come back. I think people forgot who the real boss is."

Meka laughed. "Oh, don't get cocky like I wasn't holding it down for a little over a month, but who's counting?"

Hearing Meka say a little over a month caught Sunshine's attention. She thought he'd only missed that week they were out of town and the last few days. Jonas stared at the floor, trying not to look at Sunshine. A part of him wished he had been man enough to come clean, but getting married sounded better at the time.

"Let's go make sure everything is set up," he said to Meka to get her out of the office. He then turned to Sunshine. "You gon' be all right in here?"

"Yeah, baby. I'm actually about to call my mom and check on Mya."

After placing a kiss on her lips, Jonas stepped out, making sure to shut the door behind him.

"Meka, she doesn't know about my problem. Try not to bring that up in front of her."

Meka shook her head. "You snuck off and got married. Don't you think your wife should know about your problem?"

"I dealt with it. It's not a problem of mine anymore."

"Yeah, all right, Jonas, but what if it happens again?" she questioned.

Jonas took a seat in his work area. "I got her. It ain't coming back."

Meka decided to drop the subject. Jonas is the type of guy who, once he made up his mind, that was it.

Jonas greeted Poppa. "What's up, bro bro?"

"What's up, bro? Glad to see you back in this bitch. Can you line me up right quick before everyone gets here?"

"Sit your ass down. I got you."

In no time, Jonas was done, and people had started to walk in. Most heard Jonas was coming back and were ready for him to bless them with a cut. Sunshine sat at the desk answering the phone and making appointments. That's when something hit her. After graduating from high school, she attended beauty school to become a hairstylist, but she never pursued her license. Her mom used to talk major shit to her about not doing anything but following Monsta around, but now, this could be her chance to do something with her life.

As she thought about life, she couldn't help but think about Keisha and everything she was going through. She decided to give her a call and see if she had left safely. After not getting an answer, she decided to call again. Once again, still no answer. Sunshine didn't like that and got a strange feeling in the pit of her stomach. She decided to call the front desk. After talking to the lady at the front desk, she was told she hadn't checked out yet. Sunshine asked someone to check on Keisha in her room. She had to ask using her own name because she had given Keisha her room. Sunshine felt sick to her stomach every second she waited for the hotel to call her back with any details about Keisha.

Chapter 14

"Aye, man, I've been trying to reach you for the last few days. Everything was handled."

Monsta sat up in his bunk. "All right, good looking. After everything is confirmed, I'll hit up that account."

Darryl hung up the phone, worried. He wanted Monsta just to send him the money so that he could get the fuck on. What he didn't tell Monsta is that he didn't realize it was Keisha and not Sunshine in the room that morning until after he shot her. So, not only did he kill the wrong person, but he was also gon' try to play it off, hoping Monsta would send him the money without checking shit out.

That night, while they all sat in the rec room watching TV, the 6:00 p.m. news came on. Monsta smiled at the breaking news. Just hearing about a young lady getting murdered at the hotel did something to his soul. Then it hit him that a muthafucka really killed his baby mama. He started to feel bad and realized he wanted to kill Darryl now.

He continued to listen to the news reporter, but shit wasn't adding up. The reporter mentioned the victim being pregnant, and he knew for sure that was wrong. He knew Sunshine wasn't carrying that nigga's baby already. That's when Keisha's picture popped up on the screen. A part of him was happy that Darryl fucked up—but he still needed to die.

Returning to his cell, Monsta lay back, plotting on how he was gonna get that nigga back.

"What's on your mind, cuz?"

"Shit, just trying to make it home to my baby," Monsta calmly said.

After a while, he learned to keep his mouth shut around that nigga Roc because he ran his mouth, and he didn't like that. Monsta was really waiting for the right moment to take him out, even though they were cousins.

Waiting for Roc to fall asleep, Monsta couldn't wait to talk to Darryl.

Sunshine screamed, then burst into tears. She was lying in bed, watching the news announcer, when she heard that Keisha had been murdered.

Jonas ran up the stairs. "What's wrong, baby?"

Sunshine couldn't even answer him. All she could do was point at the TV and cry. Jonas held her in his arms as he listened to the report of Keisha and her unborn child's murder.

"Damn, baby, I'm so sorry about your friend."

Sunshine continued to cry hard. "It's all my fault. It's all my fault, Jonas."

"Stop blaming yourself for this shit. It's not your fault, baby," he said, rubbing her back, trying to calm her down.

"She would still be alive if it weren't for me."

Jonas knew she'd been different since coming home from the hotel early, and he prayed he could finally get some answers.

"Baby, come sit and talk to me. I need to know everything, so that I can protect you. Trust me, baby, I got your back no matter what."

It took Sunshine awhile to calm down, even after Jonas brought her a nice cup of hot tea.

"Jonas, I swear I thought I was doing the right thing and only fucked up even more."

"Tell me what happened, baby. I need to know everything."

Sunshine sipped on her tea. "I did something I shouldn't have, and now my friend is dead when it should've been me."

"Does this have anything to do with Monsta?" he questioned.

Sunshine knew it was time to tell him the truth about everything. "Baby, it has *everything* to do with him."

Not coming completely out with the story, Jonas felt like she was about to be on some bullshit. "What the fuck is going on?"

"Monsta had someone trash the house, and I found a letter from him. He left his number and asked me to call, but I didn't the first night I was there."

"So, you did call that nigga?" Jonas asked, jumping up from the bed.

Feeling like he was about to flip out, Sunshine tried to calm him down. "Jonas, please, I swear it wasn't like that," she yelled, following him out of the room.

"Then how the fuck was it, Sunshine? Every time I bring that nigga's name up, you catch an attitude. Now, you hittin' this nigga up while he locked up. Do you still want that nigga?"

"Baby, my best friend was just killed, and you worried about *that?*"

Jonas was furious. "You know what? I really do see why that nigga was going upside your fuckin' head. You say and do fucked-up shit, like you live and love this toxic shit."

Sunshine was pissed. "All this time I thought I was with a real boss and married a good guy, and now I find out the truth. You sound real happy that a nigga used to abuse me. You know what? Fuck you, Jonas. Get the fuck outta my house!"

"Fuck me?"

Sunshine jumped in his face. "Yeah, fuck you, nigga!"

Jonas snatched Sunshine up by her shirt. "You too fucking stupid to realize when a muthafucka really love your crazy ass."

For a moment, Sunshine thought he was going to hit her, and they would be in that bitch fighting, but he was a real man. Seeing she was uncomfortable, he released her.

"I'm sorry for that, but you do some fucked-up shit."

"I fucked up, Jonas, and I'm sorry. What more do you want me to say?"

Jonas had so much love for Sunshine, but it couldn't stop him from wanting to walk away from her. She admitted to calling the one who broke her down, and that shit hurt him. Feeling once again that Monsta still had some type of control over his wife, Jonas started walking down the stairs.

"Where are you going, Jonas?"

"I think it'll be best to give you some space so you can decide if this is really what you want. I love you, but if you still want him, you need to say that."

"I *don't* want him. I want the man that I married," she cried.

Jonas stopped at the front door with her right behind him. "Why the fuck did you call him? What did y'all need to talk about?"

Sunshine was crying, but that wasn't making Jonas ease up.

"You called that nigga 'cause you wanted something. What the fuck is it? What am I *not* doing to make you happy?" he yelled, making her cry harder.

"You're doing everything right, Jonas. I told you he sent that note. I just called to tell him I was happily married and all that talk about us getting back together and him seeing Mya was over. I called, thinking I was ending shit for good, but ended up getting my friend and her unborn baby killed."

Jonas could tell it tore her up and didn't hesitate to pull her into a hug. "You can't keep blaming yourself for the fucked-up shit he does."

"This time, I have to take the blame."

Jonas led her over to the couch and listened to her tell him about Keisha dealing with the crooked detectives and giving her the money to leave town.

"Baby, you meant well by trying to help her," he said, trying to calm her down.

"I called Monsta from the hotel phone so that he couldn't call me back. I wasn't thinking when I let Keisha have the room for the rest of the week after talking shit to him. I didn't think he would send someone after me. He wanted me dead for real this time."

Jonas knew, when it came down to it, Monsta had to die. He wasn't into all that street shit anymore, but when it came to his family, he'd do whatever to keep them safe.

"I got you, baby. You know I'm not gonna let anything happen to you or Mya. Do you trust me to keep my word?"

"Yes, Jonas, I do. Can you forgive me for creating this mess?"

Jonas planted a kiss on her lips. "Yes, baby. I just need you to talk to me *before* you make any decisions from now on."

He held Sunshine in his arms until she fell asleep.

Although he was trying to be a business owner and family man, Monsta was getting ready to have to deal with the Bentley Boys.

Darryl sat outside the house so no one could hear his phone conversation with Monsta. It'd been two weeks since he did that job for Monsta, and he still hadn't gotten paid yet. He figured Monsta must've gotten in trouble, and that's why he hadn't heard from him. He was surprised he finally got that call.

"What's up, Monsta? I was reaching out for my bread."

Monsta laughed. "You really are trying to play in my face? Bitch, I saw the news."

Darryl shook his head, knowing he fucked up. Now he felt like he should've just taken the bag of money he got from the hotel and gotten the fuck on. Trying to be greedy wasn't getting him anywhere.

"Shit moved so fast. I didn't realize who that bitch was until I shot her," Darryl stuttered to get out.

Monsta knew he was speaking straight bullshit, but decided he needed to use him for one more thing.

"I got another job for you," Monsta whispered as he checked to make sure Roc was still asleep.

Darryl knew this shit with Monsta was gonna be a long-term thing. He just wished he could see some money now. "I'm gonna need some funds in my account, Monsta."

"Your funky ass ain't did shit I asked you to do yet. Bitch, *you* owe *me*."

Darryl shook his head. "Look, I got something for you now that's worth some bread. If I send it to you, you gotta cash me out."

"What the fuck you got, nigga?" Monsta asked.

Darryl quickly sent over a picture that he was able to sneak of Mya, right along with Sunshine's phone number.

"What the fuck is this?" Monsta mumbled as he checked his messages.

Darryl waited to be blessed. "How much for that?"

Monsta didn't answer. It was his first time seeing his daughter, and that had his full, undivided attention at the time.

"Aye, man, you gon' cash me out or what?"

"I'll call your bitch ass back." Monsta hung up the phone.

Looking at his baby girl caused his brain not to think of all the evil thoughts in his head. He couldn't help but smile hard at the beautiful baby he helped bring into this world. She definitely had his eyes, but she was as beautiful as her mother.

"My baby girl, Mya. You so fuckin' beautiful. Daddy can't wait to see you in person. I promise, baby girl, Daddy will be out soon, and you best believe I'm coming to get you."

Monsta was so busy looking at Mya that he didn't even notice Darryl giving him Sunshine's number at first. It wasn't until later that night, after the count, that he pulled out his phone again and saw her number.

"Hello," Sunshine said into the phone, still half-asleep.

"You know if he had killed you, I was gon' kill him. To be honest, I'm still gonna kill him," Monsta explained.

Hearing his voice talking about killing someone woke Sunshine all the way up. "How the fuck you get my number?"

Jonas jumped up, snatching the phone from his wife. "You know, whenever I see you, I'm gon' beat yo' bitch ass, right?"

Monsta laughed. "You know how many niggas say that shit, and when they see me, they be on their best behavior? Look, bitch, neither you nor any other nigga put fear in my heart."

"Stay the fuck away from my family, dog."

It pissed Jonas off that every time he said something, Monsta would laugh like a fucking dumb ass.

"I busted in that bitch and made that baby, nigga. That's *my* fucking family," Monsta said, still laughing.

Before hanging up, Jonas yelled into the phone, "Fuck you, bitch!"

Now, Jonas turned his attention to Sunshine.

"How the fuck that nigga get your number? Didn't you tell me you called him from the hotel phone?"

"I swear I did, baby. I don't know how he got my number this time or any other time," she tried to explain.

"I'm not going to the shop today. We need to go get Mya."

"I agree. I miss my baby anyway. With all this shit going on, she doesn't need to be out of our sight."

Sunshine climbed out of bed, but noticed Jonas didn't get up with her. "What's wrong, baby?"

"I'm tired of this nigga and this crazy bullshit."

Sunshine felt bad because she knew everything was her fault, and she brought all this drama into his life.

"I'm so sorry, Jonas. Please don't hate me," she begged.

Jonas stood up to hug her and show her some love. There was so much shit going on, but he wanted her to know that no matter what, he had her back. At this point, if he had to kill to bring peace to their life, that's just what he had to do.

Before Jonas joined Sunshine in the shower, he called Meka to let her know about everything going on. She hadn't heard the old Jonas speak up in a while, and by that, she knew he wasn't playing behind his wife and child. At the shop, Meka let the family know Jonas was going through some shit, and later, on cousin night, they all needed to talk and get on board about going to war.

Jonas and Sunshine both played in Mya's face, praying for nothing but her safety.

"Ma, can I ask you a question?"

"What, child?" Ms. Mathews asked, still watching TV.

Sunshine didn't know how to ask, so she got straight to the point. "Did you give anyone my number?"

"Now, why would you ask me something so stupid like that? If I'm not at work, I'm here all damn day. Who would I possibly give your number to?"

"My bad, Ma. I know it wasn't you. This whole Monsta bullshit got me scared, and I don't know who's behind all this shit."

Ms. Mathews shook her head. "I tried to tell you about that nigga. I knew from jump he wasn't shit."

Sunshine rolled her eyes. "Yeah, Ma, I know. I've heard this story over a thousand times before."

"And you best believe every time I hear that muthafucka's name, I'ma bring that shit up."

Jonas didn't pay them any mind. He was just happy to see Mya smiling in his face. That nigga Monsta sat up on the phone talking about how this is his family and Mya is his, but the way her face lit up seeing Jonas, there wasn't shit anybody could say. Mya was *his* baby, and that's all there was to it.

"Where's Zoey?"

"She's in her room. Nasty ass been up all night busting it open for Darryl's junky ass."

"What? I hope my baby wasn't around that shit."

"Hell nah. I don't trust that nigga for real. He be lookin' all crazy like he high or something. That nigga up to no good."

That caught Jonas's attention. "What do you mean by that? What the hell is he up to?"

Ms. Mathews laughed, trying to play it off. "I'm just talking."

Sunshine and Jonas gave her a strange look.

"Ma, that ain't shit to play about, but let me go talk to your daughter."

Jonas didn't care what she said now because he knew she said that shit for a reason. He made a mental note to watch his ass from now on.

Sunshine opened her sister's bedroom door. "Wake up, Zoey."

Zoey didn't move. Sunshine didn't call out for her again. Instead, she took this moment to look around her room. Her first stop was her drawers.

"OK, bitch, you better not be hiding shit," she mumbled.

Not finding shit, she searched through the closet. Then Sunshine noticed something that looked really familiar. "Oh, hell nah."

Picking up the bag that held the money she gave to Keisha, Sunshine slapped Zoey in the face with it. "Bitch, what the fuck did you do?"

Zoey jumped up. "What the fuck you hit me for?"

Sunshine wasn't in the mood to talk. Instead, she swung on Zoey again. "You supposed to be my fucking sister."

Zoey wasn't sure why they were fighting, but she tried her best to fight back.

"I didn't do shit, stupid bitch!" she yelled.

Ms. Mathews jumped up to separate her daughters. She too had grown tired of their bullshit. Jonas sat Mya down in her car seat and was right behind his mother-in-law.

"I'll be back, Mya. Let me go get your crazy-ass mama and auntie."

Jonas went straight to the room to break them up. Walking in, he could see that although their mother called herself breaking up the fight, she really was trying to hold Sunshine's hands, seeing as she was getting the best of the fight.

"Break this shit up!" Jonas yelled, stepping in between everyone.

Once they calmed down, he was able to pull Sunshine to one side of the bed while Ms. Mathews pulled Zoey to the other side.

"What the fuck is going on? I told y'all I'm sick and tired of all this fighting shit."

Zoey spoke out first. "I was asleep. This little stupid bitch came in here fighting me. I was just defending myself."

"What the fuck is going on, Sunshine?" Jonas asked.

At this point, Sunshine was crying. "Look, Jonas, look at this bag."

Ms. Mathews was just as confused as Zoey. "What the fuck that bag got to do with you fighting your sister?"

Sunshine no longer trusted the people who lived in that house, so she gave Jonas all of her attention. "Jonas, this is the bag that I had Monsta's money in. I gave this to Keisha," she cried out.

"Sunshine, that's *not* my bag," Zoey yelled out, defending herself.

"Monsta sent somebody to kill me. Whoever it was took this bag and killed Keisha."

"Oh my God, Sunshine, you should know better than to think your sister would have anything to do with this shit," Ms. Mathews said.

There was a quick pause before everything started to make sense.

"Darryl—that was Darryl's bag," Zoey screamed out.

Jonas was the first to run out of the room. He was ready to find and kill Darryl for every time he saw Sunshine scared or even crying. Everyone else was right behind him, on his ass.

"Where the fuck is Mya?"

Chapter 15

Monsta had been trying to keep a low profile, and so far, everything was going well. After learning the detectives had Keisha helping to bring him down and his organization, Monsta was happy Darryl had fucked up and killed her ass. He laughed, knowing that without Keisha and him being on his best behavior and staying out of the hole, he'd be out in no time. With his fucked-up way of thinking, he knew Sunshine still wanted him and wouldn't dare tell all the bullshit he'd been on lately.

"Damn, I got to cut all loose ends before a muthafucka has me jammed up," he mumbled just as Roc walked into the cell.

"What's up, cuz?"

Monsta stared at him for a minute. He could tell he was up to no good. It was all in his face. Monsta never really fucked with niggas whose loyalty he had to question. Lately, he could tell Roc had either turned snake or had been one all along, and he didn't know it.

"Fuck outta my face, nigga."

Roc grimed him. "Fuck you too, nigga. I guess you hot shit 'cause they about to close your case. No face, no case, right?"

Monsta stood up from his bunk. "Bitch, get outta my business."

"Damn, now you know we better than that. Let's calm down and talk blood to blood. What you gon' do if they let you go? You thinkin' about gettin' your spot back on the streets or what?"

Monsta shook his head as he tried not to snap that nigga's neck right then and there. That bullshit conversation let him know the detectives not only tried to get to Keisha, but also his blood cousin as well.

"My spot? What you talkin' 'bout, Roc? When I get out, I'm going home to my baby and be the father she needs me to be. That's the spot I'm taking over. Matter of fact, I've been thinking about taking some cooking classes and maybe one day owning a food truck or something. Maybe when you get out, you can come work with me since we blood."

The look in Monsta's eyes and the tone of his voice told Roc his cover was blown. He damn near shitted on himself knowing he was next to die at the hands of Monsta. He shook his head, wanting to beg for forgiveness. Monsta wanted to kill him for turning snitch, but knowing everyone was waiting to get him jammed up, he walked out of the cell with a smirk on his face. He had a few homies who wouldn't give a fuck about murking a muthafucka for him because they were already doing life.

Walking into one of his homies' cells, Monsta didn't say anything. He slipped him the cell phone he'd been using to handle his business.

"For sure, bro," Tony said as Monsta walked out. Tony wasted no time hiding the phone right along with his.

Monsta returned to his cell and waited for a guard to escort him to his appointment with the therapist. He had a story to tell. During their hour session, Monsta expressed how he felt like he was being followed around the jail. He made that move so that if anything happened, he could have it in writing that others were out to get him all along.

"I've been working hard to get you out of this shithole. To tell you the truth, everyone was against my decision at first, but I think I'm winning them over. They see that you're taking your medication, staying out of the hole, and staying out of trouble, but I have a little more fighting to do."

"A little more fighting to do? Fuck that mean?" She gave him a crazy look, and Monsta immediately corrected himself. "I'm sorry. I meant to ask what that meant."

"That's better. Anyway, that means you might be going home soon."

Monsta smiled. "Are you serious?"

"Yes. I told you I was fighting for you. You might have to go home with meds, but you'll be at home with your daughter."

Monsta was escorted back to his cell with a big Kool-Aid smile on his face. It only left when he reached his cell and saw a few guards searching his room.

"What y'all doing? Y'all tearing up my house," he yelled.

One guard stepped to his face. "Where's the phone, boy?"

"The phones are downstairs, but we can't use them until tomorrow afternoon."

"Stop playing with me, boy. We were told you had a phone and were using it to do dirt on the outside."

"Sorry, sir, but I don't know what you talkin' 'bout," Monsta said with an evil smirk on his face.

They tore up his room even more than what needed to be done, hoping to find something since Roc and Keisha fucked up. They were pissed that they couldn't find a phone, and their little inside man gave them nothing against him, which meant wasn't shit stopping him from leaving now. Knowing Roc had been on some rat shit, Monsta was happy he was smart enough to hide the phone elsewhere. He couldn't wait to laugh in Roc's face whenever he did come back into the room.

Monsta did make it his business to sneak back to Tony's room later that night to handle the last of his business before getting rid of the phone for good. Or so he thought. When he returned to his room before the count, Monsta learned Roc had been moved out of the cell they shared, which only served as more proof that he was a snake. They must've known he would be killed for being a rat. Monsta was gonna get him killed, but first, he wanted some time to pass so that he wouldn't be the first person they looked at. Tony was already on the job.

Turning his phone back on, Monsta watched as his screen reminded him he had ten messages and twenty missed calls. As he looked into it, he saw they were all from Darryl.

"I hope this muthafucka ain't calling about that bread he thinks I owe him," Monsta mumbled as he tried to call him back.

"What the fuck you callin' me for?"

"You played me on my money, so I decided to play you, nigga."

Monsta laughed. "I don't talk crack language. Talk so I can understand yo' bitch ass."

"I'm glad you think everything fucking funny. I got a joke for you, nigga."

"What's that?" Monsta questioned.

"I got your daughter over here with me."

"Bitch, I'll kill you. Don't fuckin' play with your life like that," Monsta warned.

Darryl really didn't think things through. Now, he was starting to realize he had made a huge mistake by taking Mya.

"I just want my money, that's it. I'm not gonna hurt her," Darryl explained.

Monsta held the phone, trying to think of how he could get his daughter and kill Darryl, all while still locked up.

"All right, take her to my mama's house. I need you to have my mama call me to verify my baby is with her and unharmed. Soon after, I'll make sure your account is nice and full."

Darryl liked that plan. "All right, I can do that. I just want you to know this shit is all business."

"Oh yeah, nigga, I know how the game go."

Monsta wanted to get rid of the phone that night, but he needed to make sure his mama could reach him once Mya arrived.

Sunshine sat on the couch, crying her eyes out, rocking back and forth. Her baby was missing, and nothing anyone said could calm her down. Jonas was pissed off too, but instead of sitting there comforting her, he was pacing the floor and constantly repeating, "I can't believe this shit."

"I'm so sorry, y'all. I had no clue what Darryl was up to."

Sunshine snapped. "Shut up, bitch. It ain't no telling. You probably were in on it with him."

Usually, Jonas would try to keep the peace between the sisters, but this time, he stayed out of it. He agreed with Sunshine. Maybe they did work together, considering how Zoey always acted like she was jealous of her sister.

Sunshine stood up. "I need to be out there looking for my baby."

"I called my cousins over. Wait for Meka to come get you."

"I don't want to wait on anybody. I wanna go *now*," she yelled.

"Calm down, Sunshine, and call the police," Ms. Mathews ordered.

Neither Jonas nor Sunshine wanted to get the police involved. They felt like they would only accuse them of foul play and probably get locked up. Before Sunshine could say anything, Jonas's family was knocking on the door. Zoey let them all in. After speaking, Meka rushed over to Sunshine and pulled her into a hug.

"I'm so sorry, baby, but we got your back."

"Just get me out of this house and help me find my baby. I need my baby," she cried.

Sunshine followed Meka out the door, not saying shit to her mama or sister. Ain't no way they live in the same house as Darryl and didn't know shit about him working with Monsta all this time.

Once they gathered outside, Jonas held Sunshine as he told his cousins how Darryl was behind everything and had been working with Monsta all along.

"Let's go find this nigga then, cuz. You know we down for whatever," Mason said, lifting his shirt to show him his gun.

Everyone jumped into their cars, ready to hit the streets to find baby Mya. Sunshine got in the car with Meka.

"Aye, Meka," Jonas called out.

Meka jumped out of the car, wondering what he wanted. "What's up, cuz?"

Jonas and Meka had always been close cousins and counted on each other, so there was no surprise when Jonas damn near broke down to her.

"I need you to look out for my baby, man. She hurt, not knowing where Mya at right now. Don't let her do anything stupid."

"Sunshine's my girl too. I got you, cuz. You didn't even have to say shit."

Jonas hugged her. "I'll sit down for them and all y'all, you know that, right?"

"We'll do the same. Now, go find Mya."

Everyone drove off in different directions searching for Darryl's car. They had promised to call one another if they saw him first. Jonas didn't want anyone to kill him because he needed to be the one to lay hands on his bitch ass.

Sunshine's legs shook as Meka drove around. She never imagined her baby would be kidnapped. Monsta did a lot of things, but kidnapping was a new low.

"This is all my fault. My baby is missing because I told Monsta Mya would never know him, and she had a daddy."

"Stop that shit, Sunshine. This shit is not your fault, and that nigga gon' pay for this shit."

Sunshine cried harder. "I just want my baby back. She didn't do shit to nobody. She's just a baby."

"I know, girl. We're gonna find her," Meka assured her.

Mason cut down the music as he answered his sister's call.

"Where everyone at? I'm at Meka's house, ready for cousin night."

"Damn, Nakia, we've been trying to reach your ass all night," Mason said into the phone.

Nakia smacked her lips. "I had a few shots and was knocked out. Anyway, why y'all not at Meka's house for cousin night?"

Mason shook his head. It hurt him to repeat the news to her, but he had to. "Somebody kidnapped Mya, and we all out here looking for her now."

"So, cousin night canceled?"

Mason wanted to hang up on his sister, but tried to explain shit to her just in case she was still drunk. "I just told you somebody kidnapped Mya, and we looking for her. What the fuck you think?"

"I was just asking. I don't see why y'all canceled our family night for somebody that's not family."

Mason shook his head at how ignorant his sister could be. He couldn't even respond to her stupid ass. Hanging up was the only way to handle that situation.

"What she talkin' about?" Poppa asked.

"A bunch of bullshit," he responded.

"I love my cousin, but she be on that bullshit."

Mason nodded his head in agreement. "Yeah, I know."

That night, everyone rode around searching high and low for Mya. But at the end of the night, they all went home without her.

"Baby, go get in bed and get you some rest."

"Jonas, we don't know where our baby is. I can't get no fuckin' rest until my baby comes home. Maybe we should get the police involved."

Jonas stopped pacing the floor long enough to wrap his arms around his wife. "I'm sorry, baby. I'm sorry I couldn't figure this shit out about Darryl earlier. I'm supposed to protect you and her from everything."

"Is my baby gon' come home and be all right?" she cried.

Jonas didn't want to make any promises to her. At the same time, he couldn't disappoint her or hurt her any more than she had already been. "We're gonna find her and kill everyone behind this shit."

"I love you, Jonas."

"Love you too, baby."

He saw she wasn't trying to lie down, so he went into the kitchen to make her a hot tea, which usually worked. He still wasn't sure about the police and tried his best to avoid the question.

Chapter 16

"Wake your lucky ass up," the guard yelled, poking him with his baton.

Monsta slowly sat up. "Fuck you bothering me for?"

The guard smiled. "You lucky son of a bitch. How the fuck did you get so lucky?"

Monsta gave the guard, Timothy Brown, a strange look. "What the fuck your faggot ass talkin' about?"

"Word around here is you gettin' out later today."

Monsta was still half-asleep and not really in the mood for his bullshit. "Wake me up when it's time, then, bitch."

Tim walked away. He couldn't care less about the shit Monsta was talking. Monsta was known for running his mouth all the time because he was a little "off." As soon as Tim was far away from his cell, Monsta got up to hang up his sheet. Most people thought that meant he was taking a shit, but for real, he needed to handle his business.

He turned on his phone again. He saw he had one missed call. Calling the number back, he realized it was his mama's number when she spoke on the phone.

"What the fuck are you getting me mixed up in?" Ms. Caldwell yelled into the phone.

"Hey, Ma," Monsta calmly said into the phone.

"Hi, Monsta, what's going on? This ugly, black-ass nigga has been here since last night, talking about him not leaving until we get in touch with you. Why is Mya here?"

"This shit really not my fault, Ma. Tell that nigga I'm about to send that cash now so he can get the fuck on."

"You on speakerphone, so he hears you," she replied.

Darryl was scared but tried to act hard. In his head, he repeatedly prayed that he made it out of the house alive so he could get the fuck out of Detroit. The money he got from Keisha really wasn't enough for him to disappear, all while having an addiction he couldn't kick, so he needed this bread. Monsta wasn't in the mood to even argue with him. As far as he was concerned, Darryl would be dead before the night was over.

Darryl looked down at his account. "Hey, Monsta, like I said before, this shit was all business. Thanks for the nice payment."

"Bitch, get the fuck outta my mama's house."

Darryl went ahead and left, hoping he never had to see or hear from Monsta again.

"Tell me what the fuck is going on. I haven't heard from you in months, then this nigga drop this baby off because you owed him some money. I wanted to see my grandbaby, but you didn't have to get somebody to kidnap her and bring her here."

"Ma, I didn't do this shit. Can you just make sure my baby good, and I'll handle everything else?"

"Yeah, you know I got you, Monsta," she said, not knowing just how much trouble he was putting her in.

Monsta texted one of his boys on the outside for a quick favor. He hated leaving loose ends around, and Darryl was a major problem.

Monsta: Need you, my boy.

Jerome: Got you. What's up?

Monsta: Darryl

Jerome: Say no more.

After getting off the phone, Jerome got dressed, knowing Darryl's dope fiend ass was probably at the spot somewhere trying to cop. He knew his job would be easy. Jerome ended up driving to three different spots Monsta ran looking for Darryl. He wasn't sure what he did and really didn't give two fucks. If Monsta needed him gone, that's what the fuck was gonna happen.

"Where the fuck this bitch-ass nigga at?" he mumbled to himself as he turned the corner.

Darryl had just pulled up to the house after arguing with Zoey about some Sunshine bullshit. She also accused him of kidnapping Mya, which he denied, of course. He thought that if he showed his face, everyone would see she wasn't with him, and he wasn't responsible for her being missing. After a good forty-five minutes, Zoey finally agreed to come out and talk to him.

"Make this shit quick," she said with attitude.

Darryl tried to hug her, but she pushed him away.

"Damn, it's like that? OK, then," he said, acting like he really gave a fuck.

The other reason he was trying to act nice was to get into the house to get the money he had stolen from Keisha. The day before he came to the house, Mya was sitting in her chair in front of the TV when everyone was in Zoey's bedroom fighting and yelling. The idea of snatching Mya was only to make Monsta pay the money he owed him so he could get the fuck on.

"I see you still have a funky-ass attitude."

"Where the fuck my niece at, muthafucka?" she snapped.

"I told you I don't have her. I hope y'all muthafuckas ain't go to the police with this bullshit. What the fuck I'ma do with a baby, and I don't even fuck with my own kids? And I'm not dropping any other babies off to my mama."

Zoey shook her head. "You a triflin-ass nigga, and this is why I'm done with you."

Just as Darryl was about to go off and tell Zoey how he really felt, Ms. Mathews ran outside with a bat. Asking no questions, she swung, hitting Darryl in the shoulder with the bat.

"Where the fuck my granddaughter at, muthafucka?"

Not giving him a chance to answer, Ms. Mathews kept swinging. Darryl tried to run to his car to avoid the hits, and that's when the gunshots rang out.

"Get down!" Ms. Mathews yelled.

Jerome lucked up pulling up to the house where he knew Darryl rested his head. When he pulled up, he was getting his ass beat with a bat by some older lady. Not giving a fuck, Jerome let them shots fire out before speeding off. Zoey sat up, looking around. Her first instinct told her to check on her mama.

"Ma, Ma, you OK?" she yelled.

Slowly sitting up, she responded. "Yeah, I'm all right, just a little shook up."

"Darryl, Darryl," Zoey called out while walking his way.

As Zoey got a little closer, she saw Darryl lying on his stomach with a growing puddle of blood under him.

"Oh my God, Darryl, get up. Get up now, baby," she screamed as she hurried to hold on to him.

Ms. Mathews rushed into the house to call the ambulance, hoping they could save him. Zoey cried and begged him not to leave her, but by the time the ambulance and police arrived, it was too late. Darryl was pronounced dead at the scene. Ms. Mathews felt bad for how her daughter acted out over his death, but her tears were for Mya. With Darryl being dead and gone, the chances of finding Mya were very slim.

"What's your plan, nigga?" Jerome asked, passing Monsta a blunt.

Monsta smiled, then hit his blunt. "A nigga finally free, and to be honest, all I wanna do is go home and see my mama. Being on bullshit, I fucked up with her badly. I need to fix that shit for real, man."

"You know I've been going to that shop and checking ol' boy out. He ain't even been there like that for real."

"It don't even matter. I might need you for something later. Can you handle another job?"

"You askin' too many questions, my boy. Drop that paper and whatever needs to be done, I got you."

Monsta stared at his mom's house for another second before climbing out of the car. He wasn't a bitch in no type of way, but this moment was very special to him. Walking into the house and seeing Mya sitting on his mama's lap, playing and laughing, almost made a real gangsta cry.

"Ma."

Ms. Caldwell jumped a little. "Damn, boy, you scared me. I'm telling you now, if you had somebody take her from her mama and then escaped, I'ma kill your crazy ass."

Monsta laughed while sitting beside her and Mya on the couch. "I got released."

Ms. Caldwell noticed how Mya had stopped playing so that she could stare at Monsta. She'd never seen him before, but for some reason, she wanted him. It's as if she knew who he was to her.

"Go ahead, boy, take her. I know you ain't even trying to be scared now."

Monsta slowly grabbed Mya. Ms. Caldwell got up to let him have some privacy. She could see he was emotional about finally meeting his baby girl.

"Hey, Mya, I'm yo' daddy."

Mya rested her head on his chest, and Monsta was grateful for that. Holding his baby girl, he realized just how crazy he had acted toward Sunshine. She had carried, then pushed out his first and only child, and he needed to appreciate her for doing a great job while he was acting like an ass.

As he rubbed Mya's back to help her fall asleep, he came up with a plan. He knew Sunshine was going crazy without her, and he didn't want her to suffer. He figured that maybe if he let her come get her, they could probably work out a schedule where he could get her from time to time. He didn't even care about sharing her with Jonas since he knew Sunshine wouldn't make any moves without that nigga's say-so. Monsta gave Mya a few kisses on her cheek as she slowly dozed off, staring into his eyes.

"I love you so much. I promise I'ma act right so I can be in your life."

Ms. Caldwell listened from the kitchen and knew deep down her son was telling his baby the truth. Although he had just come home, his attitude was so different, as if he really had matured.

"She is so beautiful, isn't she?" Ms. Caldwell asked as she walked back into the living room.

Monsta had a huge smile on his face. "Yeah, man. She looks just like Sunshine, but got my eyes for sure."

"That baby looks like you. She's just yellow like her mama."

Monsta questioned her opinion. "You think so?"

"Hell yeah, boy," she replied.

Monsta sat there for a few minutes in complete silence. He needed to talk to Sunshine, but didn't want to scare her or anything. He just wanted to apologize and go from there.

"Ma, can you call Sunshine for me?"

"Fuck no. Besides, that girl never gave me her number when I saw her in the market a few months ago."

Monsta reached into his pocket and pulled out the phone he had been locked up with. "I got her number."

"You call her then."

"Nah, you call her on your phone and get her over here. I don't want her to know I'm out yet. I got an idea. I just need you to help me."

Ms. Caldwell reluctantly nodded. "All right, let me go get my phone."

Before giving her the number, Ms. Caldwell and Monsta went over the plan. From what she heard, it was a good plan. All they needed was for Sunshine to come over without an attitude.

"Hello."

They had her on speakerphone and could tell she'd been crying, but only stopped long enough to answer the phone.

"Hey, Sunshine, this is Wendy. How are you?"

Sunshine's mind was everywhere, and because of that, she never gave any thought to how she got her number.

"Hey."

"Look, can you come over? I want to talk to you."

Sunshine didn't want to go over, knowing the first thing she'd ask was where Mya was. On top of that, Jonas left with his brother and cousins to search for Mya and asked her not to leave the house.

"I don't think that's a good idea."

"Please, I really need to speak with you. It's about Mya."

Sunshine jumped up. "What about her?" she asked, damn near yelling.

"Just get here," she demanded.

"I'll be over there in a few."

Sunshine noticed her mom and sister were blowing up her phone while she was on the line with Monsta's mom.

"Fuck y'all, and y'all bitches better find my baby," she yelled. She needed to hold her baby and make sure

she was all right. She then started to think that maybe
Ms. Caldwell knew where Mya was.

"She just pulled up, Monsta."

Monsta picked up Mya and her car seat, then disappeared in another room while his mama unlocked the
door for Sunshine.

"Hey, come in, baby."

Sunshine slowly walked in and sat on the couch. "Hey,
what did we need to talk about? What you got to say
about my baby?"

Ms. Mathews didn't have to answer the question
because Monsta walked into the room holding Mya.

"Damn, you still so fucking beautiful."

Sunshine jumped up, hearing his voice. "Monsta, give
me my fucking baby," she yelled.

Monsta walked toward her. "Chill out. I just wanna
talk to you. I swear I'm not on no bullshit."

"You kidnapped my fuckin' baby. That's all bullshit.
Now, hand her over."

"I'm not trying to be on that shit. I really wanna work
out our problems and make a schedule so I can visit her.
I'm willing to share her with your husband. I just wanna
be in my daughter's life."

Sunshine wasn't trying to hear that shit. "You not her
fuckin' daddy, now, give me my baby."

Ms. Caldwell shook her head, knowing her saying that
shit would push him overboard.

"Why the fuck you keep saying that bullshit? Look at
her. Go ahead and look at her. That's *my* fuckin' baby."

All the screaming made Mya cry.

"Please, Monsta, give me my baby. You got her crying,
and she's scared. She needs her mama."

Ms. Caldwell finally got up. "Sunshine, my son is really
trying to be in his child's life. By law, you can't just push

him out of her life like that. He called you over so y'all can work shit out. He isn't even trying to fight with you."

"He kidnapped my fuckin' baby, so let's go ahead and get the law involved," Sunshine snapped.

"See, bitch, I tried to be nice to you, and now you wanna bring the police in this? You need to be thanking me for getting her back. That nigga Darryl did this shit to blackmail me for some money, if you really wanna know the fuckin' truth."

"I just want my baby back."

"Can I at least get her every weekend?"

Sunshine couldn't believe he was serious about Mya spending time with his crazy ass. There's no way he was going to be in her life.

"Fuck *no*."

"See, bitch, I tried to be nice, but you wanna talk shit to me and deny me my rights to be a father. You beggin' the bad guy to come out. You must miss me fuckin' you up, huh?"

Sunshine started digging in her purse for her phone, which only made Monsta nervous. He quickly snatched her purse from her.

"You not about to call nobody over here," he yelled.

Ms. Caldwell saw this whole thing going left. It was clear that there was only so much Monsta could take before he went off. "Just give her the baby and let them leave."

"No, fuck that shit."

With Mya still in his arms, Monsta stormed to his bedroom.

"Just leave, girl. You pissed him off. Leave now," Ms. Caldwell warned her.

"Are you fuckin' serious? I'm not leaving without my fuckin' baby."

Sunshine headed to his room to get Mya, but he met her at the door, holding Mya in one hand and his gun in the other.

"No, Monsta, please don't hurt me," she said, backing up.

Monsta had an evil smirk on his face. "You wanna talk about my visitation rights now?"

Sunshine was scared and couldn't stop crying. All she could think about was him killing her and not being able to see her baby growing up.

"Boy, put that gun up!"

Monsta faced his mama. "Ma, take Mya upstairs with you. Me and her mama got some business to handle."

As she reached for Mya, Sunshine kept crying and begging Monsta not to hurt her.

"Monsta, you ain't got to do this. Please don't hurt me," she cried.

"I tried to be nice, but you like for a muthafucka to dog yo' ass."

Sunshine looked at Ms. Caldwell. "Please help me."

"Ma, I said, take my baby upstairs, and don't be on no bullshit. I'd hate to have to hurt y'all in this muthafucka."

As she headed for the steps, Sunshine cried out, "Please don't leave me with him!"

Ms. Caldwell didn't want to leave her, but she didn't want any problems with her son. She ignored Sunshine's cry for help and took the baby upstairs.

"Get your ass in the room, *now*," he demanded.

Sunshine stood there shaking and crying. She was scared he was gonna kill her. She didn't move until he placed the gun back to her head.

"I don't wanna die, Monsta," she cried as she slowly entered the bedroom.

Monsta had her scared, in the corner. He started kissing her, making her very uncomfortable.

"Monsta, please."

"I was gonna let that nigga have you, but you had to fuck shit up. I only ever loved your ass, and you talk to me like I'm a bum nigga on the streets."

"I'm sorry, just please, let me go home with my baby."

At this point, Monsta's free hand was roaming up her dress. Her tears couldn't stop the way his dick was growing and craving her at that moment.

"Take that shit off," he ordered.

"No, Monsta, please. You don't have to do this."

Monsta was no longer in the mood to talk. All he could think about was fucking her like he used to.

"You have been fuckin' that other nigga. Now you wanna act like you too good for a nigga like me? Take that dress off and get your ass in bed."

Not moving quickly enough, Monsta slapped Sunshine down to the floor, then snatched her up by her hair and tossed her on the bed. She tried to kick him away from her, but that only made it easier for him to position himself between her legs.

Ms. Caldwell sat on the steps crying as she heard Sunshine scream out for help. She knew better than to stop what he was doing and figured Sunshine would be all right since this wasn't his first time doing this to her.

The whole time Monsta violated Sunshine, he whispered in her ear. "I'm so sorry, baby. I really wanted us to work shit out."

The more she cried, the more he told her everything was her fault because she wouldn't hear him out about being in Mya's life.

Chapter 17

Jonas stopped by the house with Poppa to drop off food for Sunshine. He knew that while Mya was still missing, she wasn't cooking. She barely wanted to eat.

"This girl is so fucking hardheaded. Before I left, I told her not to go anywhere."

Poppa shook his head. "Her baby missing, bro. She wasn't about to stay here while we were out searching. If anything, she's out looking too."

"You right, bro."

Jonas looked at his phone again as it went off. He quickly sent whoever to voicemail.

"Who was that?"

"My mother-in-law. I'm so pissed at them, I don't even wanna talk to them right now."

"Yeah, that was some foul shit going on over there."

Jonas's phone went off again. Thinking it was them calling again, he yelled into the phone without checking the caller ID. "What?"

"Jonas, it's me, Meka."

"My bad, cuz, what's wrong?" he questioned, hearing what he thought was crying.

Meka tried to calm down so she could explain to him what was going on.

"Meka, talk to me. Is it Mya?"

For some reason, those words rolled out first, although he prayed her crying had nothing to do with his baby.

"No, Jonas, it's the shop. Somebody set it on fire and—"

"I'm on my way down there now."

Jonas didn't say anything, but Poppa knew to follow him out the door.

Pulling up to the strip, Jonas broke down, seeing what he had worked so hard for go up in smoke.

"Damn, bro, what the fuck," Poppa yelled, jumping out of the car.

Jonas was so hurt that he couldn't even get out of the car. His mind was all fucked up. First, he couldn't find Mya, which made him feel like a failure as a father, and now his shop was gone.

Being numb, Jonas could barely talk to the investigators and the fire department. Lucky for him, Meka was there to save the day again and tell them whatever they needed to know. The family stood around deep in their feelings as the firefighters fought to put the fire out completely. Afterward, only bricks remained on the outside. The inside was completely destroyed.

"What now?" Mason asked.

"Fuck this shit, man. I need to go find my baby," Jonas coldly said.

The family watched as he jumped back into his car and drove off.

"That nigga hurt, man."

"Hell yeah. Do y'all think we need to follow him home?" Meka asked.

Everyone looked at her. She was the one everyone followed for guidance, and now they were stuck because she didn't have any answers.

Mason tossed Poppa his car keys. "Cuz, go check on your brother. Make sure that nigga ain't going home to end it all. I'm gonna ride with Meka."

Poppa jumped into his car to get to his brother.

***

Monsta sat up in bed, waiting for Jerome to call him back. After Sunshine cried herself to sleep, he went ahead and texted Jerome to fuck up the shop. At this point, Mr. Nice Guy was gone, and all that therapy bullshit didn't mean shit to him. Sunshine really did bring out the worst in him just as he was told.

"Aye, bitch, wake yo' ass up before I fuck you again."

Sunshine opened her eyes, looking around, not really remembering where she was.

"Wake yo' ass up and get the fuck outta my fuckin' house," he yelled.

This time, Sunshine jumped up. "Where's my baby, Monsta?"

"You know I loved the fuck out of you for real, and it's gonna take some time to get over you, but I can't fuck with you no more. I came home on some positive-type shit. All I wanted was to come home and be a good daddy, but you wanna be on bullshit talkin' about Mya's not mine."

His words had Sunshine scared. She'd seen shows where the daddy killed the baby because of the mother. She started to cry again, praying this wasn't the case here. She now regretted telling him he would never be Mya's father, even though that's how she felt.

"Where's Mya?" she asked again.

Monsta laughed, knowing she was scared. "You gon' get her back, bitch."

After Sunshine put on her dress, Monsta grabbed her by the hair and dragged her out of his room.

"Monsta, that's enough. You had your fun for the day, now let her go home," Ms. Caldwell said, holding Mya.

Sunshine was crying, begging for Mya, but Ms. Caldwell wouldn't hand her over until Monsta said it was all right for her to do so.

"Monsta, if you want her to leave, you gotta let her have her baby back."

With tears in his eyes, he took Mya out of his mother's arms. "Mya, my baby girl, Daddy loves you so fuckin' much, man. I'm sorry things didn't work out the way I wanted them to."

Monsta then placed a kiss on the baby's cheek before handing her over to Sunshine.

"Now, hurry up and get outta my house before I tie your ass up in the fucking basement."

Sunshine ran out of the house so fast that she almost tripped while holding Mya. She was so scared he would change his mind that Mya was still in her lap in the car when she took off. She made it seven blocks away before she pulled over to cry and thank God for setting her free. She sat there crying her eyes out, trying to get her thoughts together and process exactly what the hell happened. After sitting there for what seemed like forever, Sunshine finally drove home. She wasn't sure what she was gonna tell Jonas, but Monsta had crossed the line and needed to pay.

Jonas was on the couch with a bottle. Poppa tried to get him to calm down when he got there, but he wasn't trying to hear shit.

"Bro, I can't sit here and watch you kill yourself. You gotta be stronger than that."

Jonas took another swig from the bottle. "I didn't ask you to come here. Look, just let me do me."

Poppa stood up, making Jonas feel like he was about to leave. To Jonas's surprise, he slapped the bottle out of his hand, causing it to fly across the room.

"You *not* about to do this shit to me, bro. We already lost pops from this shit. Are you trying to go out like him?"

Jonas could see the hurt in his eyes, but that didn't stop him from going after the bottle that was on the floor.

"Fuck that shit, bro," Poppa yelled this time, trying to tackle Jonas down.

Jonas tried to fight back, but soon gave up. His mind went back to how his father's death affected everyone.

"All right, man, let me go."

Sunshine rushed in the door holding Mya, causing the brothers to pause and stare at her. Jonas used whatever energy he had left to rush to them. Sunshine damn near fell into his arms.

"Jonas!" she cried.

She was crying so hard he could barely make out what she was trying to tell him.

"Calm down, Sunshine. Baby, I can't understand shit you're saying."

Sunshine felt sick just thinking about retelling her story. Jonas noticed she was looking sick, like she wanted to vomit. He grabbed Mya, handing her to Poppa. Racing upstairs, Sunshine made it to the toilet just in time with Jonas right behind her. With her in a better light, Jonas was able to see that her face was swollen. That shit alone killed his buzz completely.

"What the fuck happened to you?"

Sunshine kept crying as she ran the water for a shower. "Can you please bathe Mya, then put her in our bed?"

"What the fuck happened, and where the fuck did you find her?"

Sunshine snapped. "Jonas, please, just give me a minute."

"You know I don't like this shit, right?"

"Just a minute, *please*," she repeated.

Jonas went downstairs with Poppa. Mya was playing with her uncle, but it was clear she was tired. After a bath, he knew she would be knocked out.

"What's up with her?"

"I don't know, but I'm about to find out. Her face is all fucked up and shit, but she acts like she doesn't wanna talk about it right now."

Poppa didn't like that. "Man, she trippin'. Did she even tell you where Mya was?"

"Nah, she talkin' 'bout give her a minute."

Poppa shook his head. "Bro, your daughter was missing, and she came home fucked up with Mya in her arms. You gotta make her ass talk."

"Yeah, you right. I'll holla at you tomorrow. Let me deal with my family."

"Nah, I'll be on the couch. I got a feeling you might need me."

Jonas's mind was clear now. "Fuck you talking about, bro?"

"Go talk to your wife," Poppa said, lying on the couch.

Poppa knew something was about to jump off, and Jonas would need him. Jonas was the family's businessman and would help anyone out, but he was also the muscle, never afraid to pull the trigger, especially to protect the family.

After putting Mya in their bed, Jonas went to check on Sunshine. Hearing the shower water still going, he rushed into the bathroom.

"What the fuck, Sunshine?" he yelled.

He saw his wife sitting in the shower with her legs pushed against her chest and her head down on her knees, crying her heart out. Her body trembled because the water had turned cold. Jonas cut off the water, then wrapped her up in a towel.

"Come on, baby," he mumbled as he carried her back into the room.

As Sunshine lay in bed, Jonas rubbed her back, hoping to calm her down and get her to talk to him. She wanted to tell him everything, but she was scared. It wasn't that she thought he couldn't deal with Monsta. It's because she knew he could and would do that shit. She knew Jonas would kill anyone who brought harm to her or Mya, and *that's* what scared her. She loved him and couldn't imagine him getting hurt or locked up behind her.

"Talk to me, baby. You gotta tell me what happened, please."

"Wendy called, saying she needed to talk about Mya. When I got there, Monsta was there playing with Mya," Sunshine cried.

"What? That nigga had my baby?" Jonas barked.

"I just wanted my baby back. I fought hard, and I'm just so sorry."

Jonas hugged Sunshine. "It's all good, baby. I'ma handle this shit."

Not wanting to hear anything else, Jonas grabbed his gun from the closet before taking off downstairs.

"Aye, bro, we need to roll out."

Poppa sat up, grabbing his gun off the table. He knew shit was about to go down, and for that very reason, he didn't bother to take his shoes off or close his eyes before lying down. "Let's go."

Previously, when they were out and about, Sunshine had pointed out where Monsta and his mother stayed. While Jonas was telling him where they were going, Poppa was on his phone texting Mason. They were family and lived to ride for one another.

"I'm proud of you, Monsta. I'm surprised you let her go."

Monsta shook his head. "Man, shut the fuck up. I'm sick of her ass, and you too. Instead of sitting in my face, you need to be getting the fuck outta this house."

"Why am I leaving?"

"Why the fuck you think? I need you to leave just in case shit gets hot."

Ms. Caldwell disagreed with her son. "Boy, bye. As much shit y'all been through, that girl ain't bringing no drama this way. Shit, she never did before."

Before walking away, Monsta mumbled, "This time might be different."

Monsta had never been the type to bitch up, so leaving his own shit wasn't an option. His mind was racing. Maybe Sunshine would pop up, or perhaps he was just being paranoid as hell. After gathering his thoughts, he took out his phone to line up his shit just in case he needed the backup. Not many knew he was out, and he wanted to keep it that way. With that being said, he texted Jerome.

Monsta: It might be something on the floor.

Jerome: Let me know.

While Monsta was in his bedroom trying to figure out if he had to kill somebody that night, his mother was on the phone telling her brother Dwayne to come get her.

"Do you know what time it is?" Dwayne yelled into the phone.

"Fuck all that. Some shit might pop off, and I don't wanna be in the middle of all this bullshit," she tried to explain.

Dwayne sat up in his bed. "What the fuck you done got yourself into?"

"It wasn't me, Dwayne. Now, are you coming?"

"Oh, hell nah, that boy back home? Don't tell me he's causing problems already, Wendy."

Shaking her head, she hung up. She didn't have time to play with his ass.

Monsta got up to see her coming back downstairs. "Unc coming to get you?"

"Nah, he's on some bullshit. That muthafucka don't give a fuck about nobody but his own fuckin' self."

"Fuck him. You should've let me fuck him up years ago, and he would've learned how to act right."

Ms. Caldwell stared at her son. He saw no wrong in the shit he said or did. "I really did pray they would get you some help while you were locked up. I don't see how they just let your crazy ass out."

"Bitch, I'm like this because of you. You got me all fucked up in the head and never wanted to get me help."

"Fuck you."

"Fuck you too, bitch," he yelled back.

Not in the mood to hear any more, she stormed outside. It was dark out, and she had nowhere to go, so she stood on the porch smoking her cigarette.

"Whew, God, that little muthafucka in there gets on my fucking nerves so bad. Why did you give him to me?"

While his mother was outside smoking away her problems, Monsta went to lie down. With all the shit that was going on, all he could think about was how good Sunshine felt when he slid into her. He couldn't help but laugh to himself, knowing he was fresh out of jail and nutted in a bad bitch three times.

"That's still my baby," he mumbled.

Ms. Caldwell tossed her cigarette in the grass before turning around to go back into the house.

"Don't move, bitch. Move and I'll blow your fuckin' head off."

"Please, I swear it wasn't me," she cried.

Jonas slapped her in the head with his gun. "Shut the fuck up and open the door."

As she opened the door, Poppa gave her a warning. "Don't scream or try anything stupid."

Ms. Caldwell was so scared, but for some reason, she did the complete opposite. As soon as they entered the house and shut the door, she screamed.

"Monsta, help me!"

Monsta jumped up, gun in hand. He didn't give a fuck how he treated his mama, but ain't no other nigga gonna hurt her as long as he was alive. He rushed out of the room, busting off two shots before ducking back inside. Ms. Caldwell was smart enough to get down, but that didn't stop her from screaming out in fear. Monsta popped out again, shooting. Poppa and Jonas shot back, praying to hit his ass before he got them.

Monsta dipped off into the bedroom. He went straight to the closet to grab his other gun. Somebody was gonna die that night, and he'd be damned if it was him.

"Y'all muthafuckas better get the fuck outta my house before the coroners be carrying y'all out," he yelled.

"Come the fuck out, bitch-ass nigga," Jonas yelled.

Monsta started laughing. "Is that Jonas? The nigga that tried to take my boo boo from me."

Jonas couldn't believe how they were in the middle of trying to kill each other, and this clown-ass nigga was reciting movies and shit. Poppa was sick of the bullshit and knew if it came down to it, his brother would bitch up. He'd spent too much time trying to live right. But unlike Jonas, he loved that gunplay shit. Without hesitation, Poppa put one shot in Ms. Caldwell's head.

"Bitch, come out now."

Monsta ran out of the room, shooting wildly at Jonas and Poppa, but never expected Mason to catch him, slipping in from the back. While they snuck in the front door with Ms. Caldwell, Mason snuck in the back just in case a muthafucka tried to escape. Everything worked. Seeing they had murked Monsta, they ran out of the house, untouched.

***

Jonas peeked into the bedroom and saw Sunshine and Mya cuddled up in bed. He was forever grateful that he made it home to them. After a long, hot shower, he climbed into bed with his family. Sunshine felt his warm body on hers, then turned around to face him.

"I'm so sorry, baby. I didn't know all this was gonna happen."

Jonas placed a kiss on her swollen lips. "Shh . . . Baby, don't worry about that shit. It wasn't your fault. Matter of fact, don't ever bring that nigga up again."

"Jonas, I can't continue keeping secrets from you. I have to tell you something."

Hearing her cry alerted him. "Talk to me, baby. You don't ever have to be scared to tell me anything."

Sunshine hesitated to tell him about the rape at first, but the thought of not telling him and hurting him later made her open her mouth. "Jonas, Monsta raped me," she cried.

Jonas held her in his arms a little tighter as she cried. He felt bad as a husband for allowing that shit to happen.

"I'm so sorry, baby. I'm so sorry I wasn't there to protect you, but I promise that shit will never happen again."

Chapter 18

The next morning, Jonas and Sunshine cuddled in bed watching the news. Although he needed to handle shit about the shop, he didn't want to leave her side. They listened as the reporter stated how the day before was only the first day of summer, and already, so many crimes had been committed. That was how they both learned about Darryl.

"Damn, that's probably why they were calling all day."

"Yeah, they were calling me too, Jonas. I'm not sure if I'm ready to talk to them yet," Sunshine admitted.

"I'm on whatever tip you on, baby."

During that news segment, Sunshine also learned that the shop had burned down.

"Oh my God, baby, I'm so sorry. Did you know about this?"

"I found out last night when the shit went down. I'm not as pissed as I was last night. I'm gonna use the insurance money to get me a new shop. With your and my family's support, I know this one will be bigger and better."

Sunshine kissed him. "Can I work at the new shop?"

"Woman, are you crazy? No wife of mine is gonna be working," he said, laughing.

She also laughed. "Jonas."

Her beautiful smile is all he wanted to see after all she'd been through over the past few days.

"I was just playing. When you feel comfortable enough to have Mya in a day care or something, it's whatever you want. I was waiting for you to bring that up."

Sunshine wanted to do something with her life, but the mention of day care suddenly made her wonder if this was what she wanted.

"We'll see, baby."

After talking about the other latest news, they reported on a house shooting on the East Side, where the mother was found dead with one bullet to the head, with her son still fighting for his life after suffering several gunshot wounds. Jonas cut off the TV, pissed that Monsta wasn't dead. Sunshine had a bad feeling; she knew who the report was about, and the change in Jonas's attitude told her he was also pissed.

"I still love you, baby, no matter what."

"I love you too."

Sunshine laughed as Mya climbed over her, squeezing between her mama and daddy.

"What's up, Mya Pie?"

Mya laughed, grabbing her daddy's beard. "Dada."

Jonas's face lit up. That was his first time hearing her call him that. Sunshine didn't say anything, but she heard Mya say it the day before when playing with Monsta. She couldn't crush him like that. That was a secret she would have to take to the grave.

The night of the shooting, Dwayne had a change of heart and went to pick up his sister. He hated getting out of his bed so late, but she sounded terrified. Besides, there's no telling anything with crazy-ass Monsta running around. He knew there was a problem instantly when he pulled up to the front door, which was wide open. He quickly called the police before walking through the door against the police's orders.

"Oh God, no!" he screamed, seeing his sister lying on the floor in a puddle of blood.

Dropping to his knees to hold and cry over his sister, he noticed Monsta's body laid out in the dining room.

"Monsta, Monsta!" he called out. Dwayne got up and raced over to his nephew.

"Monsta!"

To his surprise, he was about to find a small, faint pulse. Truth be told, he was pissed his sister was dead, and the devil himself was still breathing.

Monsta put up a long, hard fight in the hospital, but he won the battle. After being hit by eight bullets, he was alive, pissed, and hurt about his mama, but still alive. Once his few weeks of hospitalization were up, Monsta thought he was gonna get discharged, then pop up at Sunshine's house for revenge, but the state had other plans for him. Detective Marshall was on the case and made sure to put him where he belonged. In prison. Finding his phone was all she needed; seeing everything he did was on that very phone.

Once he was locked back up, Monsta tried that "he needed help" shit again, but they weren't having it. They were gonna make sure he served all of his time this go-round. He thought that was bullshit. This time, he *was* traumatized because he'd witnessed the death of both of his parents and couldn't get revenge.

Monsta lay in his bed thinking about his mama. He was sad about the way shit went down with her, but he tried to warn her. He begged her to leave the house that night. For a while, he blamed himself, but then it became clear that his uncle was at fault for not picking her up earlier when she had asked. It was easier for him to find a way to blame everyone except himself. He still saw no wrong in his actions.

"At least I got a chance to hold my baby. No matter what, that's *my* fuckin' baby," he mumbled to himself.

Monsta was so caught up in talking to himself about Mya that he didn't see his new enemy sneaking up on him.

"What's up, nephew? I heard you were back," Big Roc coldly said.

Before Monsta could sit up or even speak, Big Roc stabbed him in the neck with his shank.

"That's for Roc, bitch."

Big Roc was already doing life and didn't give a fuck about nothing after losing his son not too long ago. Word got around that he was helping the state bring Monsta down, but everything went downhill, and Monsta was set free. After they found Roc in the shower stabbed up, Big Roc knew he had to kill his own nephew.

Three Months Later . . .

Sunshine stepped out of the shower, still feeling sick to her stomach. "This shit can't be happening again."

Just an hour ago, she pulled out the brown bag she got from the pharmacy the day before. She knew deep down inside what the test was gonna say, but that was the least of her worries. Looking over her calendar for the last few weeks, Sunshine knew if she really was pregnant, then she got pregnant around the time Monsta attacked her, which was right after their vacation. Although she wasn't sure, she didn't feel right knowing the baby could be Monsta's. Just the thought of it made her sick again.

It took her forever to return to the bathroom to check her test, but it had to be done. She sat on the bed with her towel wrapped around her, holding a positive pregnancy test with tears in her eyes. At this point, she wasn't sure if she even wanted to tell Jonas about the baby. She then thought about how they were working on being completely honest with each other. She couldn't just abort the baby without him knowing.

Jonas had just walked in from checking on his new building. Everything was falling into place, and within a month or so, the new shop would be up and running. He raced upstairs to tell his wife the good news.

"Hey, baby, what's up?"

Sunshine lifted her head, looking sad.

"I dropped Mya off with Meka so that you can get some extra rest. What's wrong? Why are you looking like that?" he questioned.

Sunshine sat there shaking, trying not to cry.

"Come on, baby, I told you to start talking to me. Good communication is the only way we can work out any problem."

"Jonas, I'm scared. I try to talk to you about everything, but I'm scared."

"Of what, baby?" he questioned.

Sunshine passed him the test.

Jonas's face lit up. "You serious? This for real, Sunshine?" he asked, pulling her into a tight hug.

Sunshine loved how excited he was about them having a baby, but she knew the news was gonna crush him.

"Why are you crying? This is great news, right?"

Sunshine pulled away from Jonas, crying. "Jonas, I'm so sorry."

"Fuck you sorry for? Talk to me now, Sunshine," he yelled.

Sunshine kept crying, but it got Jonas thinking. "Aww, hell nah. Are you fuckin' serious?"

"Sorry. I'm so sorry, baby."

Although Jonas knew the backstory and what went down, just the thought of her carrying a baby for Monsta broke his heart. He wasn't ready to face reality. He took off downstairs. He needed to get away from Sunshine before he said some shit he didn't mean.

Sunshine ran behind him, but he was long gone by the time she put on her clothes. Standing on the porch, she felt stupid for even telling him.

"So, you back on this shit, bro?"

Jonas lay across his couch, drunk with an empty bottle on his chest. It had been three weeks since he spoke to Sunshine, and loneliness was getting the best of him. He knew the rape wasn't her fault, but just the thought of the baby not being his made him hate Sunshine in a way. They had been fucking without a condom and nothing. But the first time Monsta got free and had his way with her—*boom*. A baby . . . maybe.

Poppa got the bottle from him and tossed it into the trash. Jonas was getting on his nerves. Here he was about to open up the new Bentley's Cuts in a few days, and he could barely get off the couch.

"I should beat his ass. What do you think, Poppa?" Mason asked.

"Nah, bro gon' be good."

"Poppa, you my nigga and all, but I need to be honest with you. He's *not* gonna get better like this. When he gets in his feelings and shit not right with Sunshine, he drinks like this. Then they get back together, and he stops or whatever. I think we need to check him into rehab so he can get clean for real. That's the only way, cuz. I love y'all and wouldn't tell you anything wrong."

Poppa sat there, thinking about what Mason said, and he knew he was right.

"Can you help me look into this shit?"

"Hell yeah. Besides, I'm trying to get Nakia some help too. She is getting out of control."

Poppa called Sunshine over so they all could talk. Since she was his wife, they wanted to run the idea by her.

"Hey, y'all, what's up?" Sunshine said, walking in and greeting Poppa and Mason.

"We called you over here to talk to you about something important."

Sunshine was confused as she looked around for Jonas. It had been weeks, and she missed him. This meeting worried her.

"Where's Jonas?"

Poppa and Mason led her to the living room, where Jonas was knocked out on the couch.

"Jonas, get up," she yelled, shaking him a little.

"He's not gonna get up."

Sunshine turned to Poppa. "What are you talking about?" she asked, touching his chest to make sure he was still breathing.

Mason tried to jump straight to the point. "Have a seat. We wanna talk to you about saving Jonas."

"What's wrong with him?"

Poppa shook his head. He had forgotten that Jonas had never told her about his secret all this time. Once Sunshine was comfortable on the couch, they told her about his past with abusing alcohol and how he had relapsed again and had been on and off for the last few months.

Sunshine was speechless. She had no idea that on top of *her* bullshit, *he* was battling his own demons. She stopped crying long enough for them to tell her about a rehab he could enter so he could get the proper help he needed. Although she was all for it, something in her still wanted to talk to him first.

After Mason and Poppa left, Sunshine stayed at his apartment and cleaned up for him. She couldn't believe how he was really living. It was crazy how most of the bottles were in the living room as if he never made it to any other room in the apartment.

"Where my shit at?" Jonas mumbled in a grouchy, drunk voice.

Sunshine walked into the living room. "All that shit is gone, Jonas."

"What you doin' here? Who let you in?"

She took a seat on the couch beside him. "Your family told me what was going on with you, and they want me to have you sign some papers so you can get into rehab. What do you think about that?"

"Fuck I need rehab for? I don't have a fuckin' problem, and I'm not going nowhere."

"Jonas, we have a baby on the way. You gotta be sober to help raise it."

Jonas didn't say anything. The last thing he wanted to do was think about Sunshine carrying Monsta's baby. He stood up, barely making it to the kitchen. Sunshine followed him as he searched for another bottle.

"You are too much of a man to go out like this, baby. Listen, I know you're upset about there being a chance this is Monsta's baby, but Mya is his for sure, and you love the fuck out of her."

"That's not it, Sunshine."

"What is it then, Jonas? If it's not about me being pregnant with this baby, what is the problem?" she questioned.

"I love you and Mya, and I know I will love the baby you're carrying. When you first told me you were pregnant, and I figured out what you were scared to tell me, to be honest, my feelings were hurt. What had me fucked up was how I handled the situation. I ran out on you like

I wasn't a man, and yet, here you go, making sure I'm all right."

Sunshine grabbed his hand. "We both have some issues we need to work on, but as long as we have each other and support and love each other, everything will be all right."

Jonas leaned over to kiss her. "I love you so much, baby."

Sunshine smiled as he rubbed her tiny stomach. "I love you too, and we're gonna get through whatever."

Jonas and Sunshine chilled and talked about their future with another baby. They decided to keep the rape and the possibility of Monsta being the father a secret. Not that it was anyone else's business.

"Hold up, baby," Jonas said, getting up from the couch so he could answer the door.

Meka, Poppa, Mason, and Nakia walked in, carrying Mya and food.

"What are y'all doing here?"

"Surprise, cousin night," Meka said, handing Mya over to Jonas.

Jonas placed a kiss on Mya's cheek. "What's up, baby girl? Daddy missed you so much."

Mya was all smiles as she pulled on his beard. That was her way of showing him love.

Everyone was eating, talking, and having a good time but Nakia.

"It's boring. Where the drinks at?"

"Chill out, sis. We ain't on that shit tonight," Mason told her.

Nakia rolled her eyes. "So, I can't drink 'cause Jonas has a problem? That's really fucked up."

Sunshine started to say something, but Meka beat her to it.

"Shut up, girl. You have a problem too, and the sooner *you* accept it, the sooner we can get you help."

"I don't have a fuckin' problem," Nakia said, getting up.

Poppa was getting irritated. "Tonight, we wanted to come together as a family so we could help one another. Me and Jonas lost our father due to his abusing alcohol, and I think if we stick together and support one another, we can make sure no one ends up like my daddy."

Jonas stared at the ground. He felt like all eyes were on him, but he understood where his brother was coming from. "I've been hiding what I was from my beautiful wife up until today. Still buzzed a little, I promised her I would get all the help I could. We are expecting another baby in a few months, so I need to be here and in the right state of mind to help raise my family."

"Aww, congratulations to you two," Meka said with a huge smile on her face.

It seemed as if everyone was happy but Nakia.

"That ain't got shit to do with me. I don't have a fuckin' problem like Jonas."

"We both have a problem. The only difference is that I know and wanna get help, while you're still in denial. Let them help you too."

"Fuck all y'all. This bitch done came in this family acting like she Miss Goody Two-shoes, and now, y'all wanna point out people's flaws. Fuck her too. She not even in our family for real."

Sunshine jumped up. "What's the problem?"

"Bitch, *you* the problem. It was *always* you, bitch. Jonas didn't relapse until he got with your toxic ass."

Jonas tried to stand in the middle of them to prevent a fight, but when Nakia tried to swing, Sunshine went crazy. For the simple fact that she got her ass beat by Kyrah, she made sure to fuck up Nakia, showing her she wasn't the one to play with. Everyone tried pulling

Sunshine off Nakia, but her little ass had turned into The Hulk and had so much strength that it was difficult to do so.

After finally getting them apart, Nakia started yelling. "Y'all supposed to be *my* fuckin' family, and y'all stay takin' this bitch's side. Did y'all forget her *real* baby daddy killed my fuckin' brother?"

"Nakia, we ain't forgotten shit, but that nigga got what he deserved," Mason replied.

"Fuck that. Monsta only got dealt with when it came to that bitch and *her* baby," she yelled.

Meka set Mya back down since she was no longer crying. "Nakia, all that shit is in the fuckin' past. We are all family now and need to move forward."

"Fuck y'all," Nakia yelled, storming out the door, making sure to slam it behind her.

The apartment was quiet for a while. Everyone was in their own thoughts.

"Sunshine, I don't care how Nakia feels about you. You my fucking sister, and I think you good for my brother," Poppa admitted.

After that, everyone else spoke out on how much they loved Sunshine and Mya. Come to find out, only Nakia had a problem with her.

Soon, everyone headed out, leaving Sunshine there with Jonas and Mya. It was late, and she decided to stay there with Jonas.

"If you check yourself in, what are you gonna do about the opening of the new shop?"

"Meka's gonna help out like she's been doing. I don't want to hold up the opening, but I know I need help. I have to be strong for everyone."

"We're all gonna be strong for you too, baby."

Jonas kissed his wife before they both dozed off. Everything was looking up for them.

Let's Chat . . .

Email me your answers at Messiah.nf@gmail.com.

Do you think things would have been different if Monsta had gotten the help that he needed at a young age?

Do you think Sunshine played mind games with Monsta?

What were your thoughts on Ms. Caldwell?

Did you think Ms. Caldwell was a major problem in Monsta's life?

What were your thoughts regarding Ms. Mathews?

Do you think she was to blame for her daughters not getting along?

Do you think Sunshine was moving too fast in her relationship with Jonas, or do you think she was trying to prove that she could move on from Monsta?

Who do you think was behind keeping Monsta updated with Sunshine's information?

After the police handled Monsta, do you think he would have been done with the bullshit or gone harder to do his dirt?

What about Keisha? Do you think she would have helped the police or gone ghost?

Was Sunshine wrong for giving Mya Jonas's last name?

About the Author

T. Friday was born and raised in Detroit, Michigan. At the age of 36, she is the mother of five children. Three handsome boys, ages 19, 14, and 13, and two beautiful girls, ages 9 and 8.

At a very early age, T. Friday fell in love with reading books such as Baby-sitter's Club, Sweet Valley High, and Goosebumps books by R. L. Stine. It wasn't until she was in her early teens that she was introduced to Urban Fiction books. That's when she knew that she wanted a career in the book industry. In January 2016, T. Friday had her left leg amputated and that was when she realized that she had been taking her life for granted, and it was time to make her dreams come true. She picked up a pen and paper and started writing. In May 2017, T. Friday signed her first contract with Racquel Williams, who is the owner of RWP. Now, in 2021, she is the author of twenty-four books. She has plans to continue writing until the day all of her books are turned into movies.